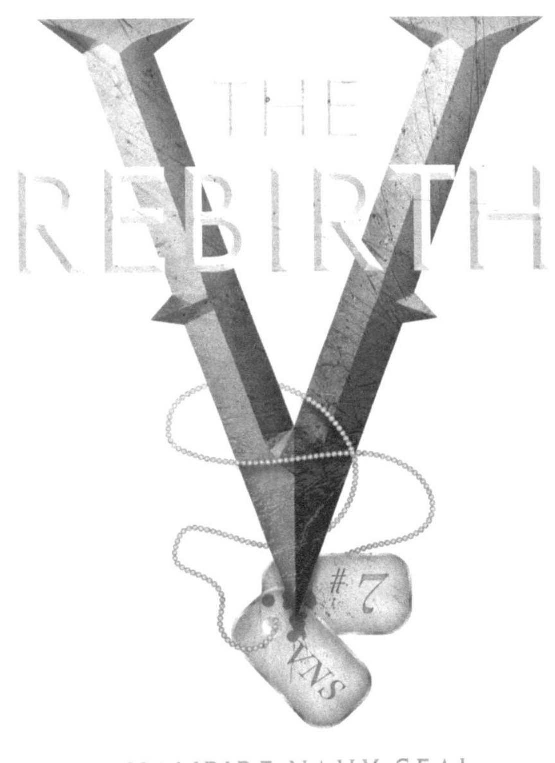


# VAMPIRE NAVY SEAL

# S.B. ALEXANDER

# COPYRIGHT




Cover designed by Hang Le
Cover copyright © 2023 by S.B. Alexander
Visit: https://sbalexander.com

First Edition: August 2023.
The Rebirth
Book seven: Vampire Navy SEAL – Sam and Layla Series

E-book ISBN — 13: 978-1-954888-44-9
Paperback Print ISBN — 13: 978-1-954888-45-6
Large Print ISBN — 13: 978-1-954888-46-3
Audiobook ISBN — 13: 978-1-954888-48-7

# BOOKS IN THIS SERIES

Books in this series should be read in order for a better reading experience.

1. The Hunted
2. The Predator
3. The Union
4. The Dawning
5. The Prodigies
6. The Prophecy
7. The Rebirth

# ALSO BY S.B. ALEXANDER

## THE MAXWELL SERIES

*Upper Young Adult/New Adult Contemporary Romance*

Dare to Kiss

Dare to Dream

Dare to Love

Dare to Dance

Dare to Live

Dare to Breathe

Dare to Embrace

The Maxwell Collection Boxset

The Kade & Lacey Collection Boxset

## THE VAMPIRE NAVY SEAL: SAM & LAYLA

*Paranormal Romance*

The Hunted

The Predator

The Union

The Dawning

The Prodigies

The Prophecy

The Rebirth

Sam & Layla Box Set 1-3

**THE MAXWELL FAMILY SAGA SERIES**

*Young Adult Sweet Contemporary Romance*

My Heart to Touch

My Heart to Hold

My Heart to Give

My Heart to Keep

Maiken & Quinn Collection

**STANDALONES**

*New Adult Contemporary Romance*

Crazy For You

Unforgettable

Breaking Rules

Rescuing Riley

Holding On To Forever

**THE HART SERIES**

*Romantic Suspense*

Hart of Darkness

Hart of Vengeance

Hart of Redemption*

**THE VAMPIRE SEAL SERIES: Jo & Webb**

*Young Adult Paranormal Romance*

On the Edge of Humanity

On the Edge of Eternity

On the Edge of Destiny

On the Edge of Misery

On the Edge of Infinity

The Vampire Navy SEAL Collection

*Coming 2024

Visit https://sbalexander.com/all-books/ to learn more about S.B. Alexander books and future releases. Please note release dates are subject to change based on reader demand and the author's schedule. Subscribing to the author's newsletter or following her on Facebook is the best way to stay updated with planned new releases.

# THE FINAL CHAPTER BEGINS...

*The Rebirth* unveils the extraordinary journey of love, loss, and redemption in the final chapter of this paranormal romance featuring Sam & Layla. Their story started in *The Hunted* with a spark that ignited a love that has grown from enemies to lovers, defying all odds between a vampire and a vampire hunter. This seven-book series is filled with suspense, snarky banter, a slow-burn romance, twists and turns, jaw-dropping moments, and an ending that will have you swooning and cheering.

# 1

## SAM

"Layla!" I shouted over the idling engine of the SUV that had just plowed through the barn and skidded to a stop. Only moments prior, Layla and I had grabbed Orion and Luna from the cribs in the North Dakota farmhouse where their kidnappers were keeping them and fled.

We'd just approached the opening of the barn when the SUV sped toward us. We had no choice but to separate. She'd gone right, and I'd darted left.

Fuuuuck! Why couldn't we catch a break? We were so damn close to freedom with our children.

"Tripp, come in!" I shouted into my comm as I fished out earplugs from my pants pocket and inserted them into Orion's ears. Layla and I hadn't had enough time to protect Orion and Luna before we ran out of the farmhouse.

Then I pulled out my gun from the holster on my leg as I ran around the backside of the barn with my son Orion strapped to me in a padded baby carrier. Thank fuck we had the fortitude to think ahead about a baby carrier so our hands were free to use weapons.

"Layla!" I called out as loudly as I could despite the howls, growls, and gunfire splitting the thick night air all around me.

The barn was still collapsing, the wood splintering and creaking like a thousand cries for help. I prayed like a mother-fucker that Layla had made her escape with Luna to our rendezvous point north of the farm where Olivia should be waiting in a getaway vehicle.

I tried Tripp again, then Olivia. Nothing from either of my Vampire Navy SEAL comrades.

"Sam." Layla's tight voice was high and loud and carried over the rampant noise. "Get Orion to safety."

Orion squirmed in my arms as if he was reacting to his mother's voice.

"Yep, that's your mom," I said. "And we're not leaving without her or your sister." I slowed to a walk at the corner of the barn and peered around to find a black SUV idling, taillight on and the back door open. "Where are you, Layla?"

"I'm dealing with an issue," she responded, sounding closer now. "Just go."

"Who's with you?" I shouted.

I could barely see the driver's head, but there wasn't anyone else in the vehicle.

"Sam Mason, why don't you join us?" a very familiar voice said in a snarky tone.

"Roman Brown, is that you?" I asked through clenched teeth.

That motherfucker was like a cockroach that wouldn't die. Those fuckers could live through the depths of hell and come out unscathed.

"It seems we meet again." He had too much excitement in his voice for my liking. "Now show yourself and hand over your son. You and Layla are not leaving this farm with your children."

"Wanna bet, asshole?" I fired back.

I was fed up with fuckers like him wanting my DNA to further their own twisted schemes for power, money, and control. Now my wife and children were the target, not only of Roman but also of Maeve Monroe—Layla's great aunt and a powerful witch who I hadn't had the displeasure of meeting yet. She wanted my wife dead and all four of my children for a blood ritual so she could fulfill a prophecy of becoming a Mystic witch with ultimate power.

Not fucking happening.

*Think, man.* The vehicle that had driven through the barn had to at least have a driver in it. But if I knew Roman, he had an army with him, which was evident by the multitude of growls, howls, and gunfire.

"I am going to have some fun with Layla!" Roman yelled over the distant battle sounds. "I might not have your niece, Abbey, yet, but I can do wonders with your wife. I understand she's a Monroe witch. That means she has supercharged abilities. There are many of my colleagues who will pay top dollar for a witch."

I gritted my teeth so hard I believed one cracked. Roman Brown, head of one of the largest blood cartels among our kind, had to die.

"Touch Layla or my daughter, and I'll rip off your balls and stuff them in your mouth until you choke to death." My voice was caustic and brittle. "Layla, hang tight."

*Stick to the plan, dude. Get Orion out of there. You've come too far to fail now.*

It had been a grueling fourteen days since Orion and Luna had been snatched from their cribs at my sister Jo's house in Maine. Two solid weeks of anguish and close calls with death. Not to mention Layla taking the life of her paternal grandmother Harriet Aberdeen. In a short span of time, my wife had been subjected to more bad shit than anyone I knew. To say she was resilient—one of the many qualities that had drawn me to her—was an understatement.

Nevertheless, Layla didn't stand a chance against Roman—not unless the blood she'd drunk from her maternal grandmother several minutes ago unlocked her witchcraft. Even then, Layla had no idea how to wield magic. So I wasn't abandoning my wife to deal with Roman or even Maeve by herself.

"Tripp, come in," I said into my comm. "Anyone."

I needed someone to take Orion so I could fight freely without hurting him or throwing him in harm's way.

"Go," Tripp said, breathing heavily.

"Finally. Thank fuck. Where are you?" I rubbed Orion's back to keep him calm and hopefully to slow my racing pulse.

"Near the road on the backside of the farm. I just severed the head of a brute of a vampire," he replied. "Get the fuck out of there. Kendra just called. Maeve is on her way from the gala. I would rather not deal with that powerful witch."

*Me either.* "Roman has Layla and Luna."

"Fuuuck!" he shouted in my ear. "I'm on my way. Don't do anything until I get there. Where's Ben and Kraft?"

*Oh fuck.*

"I don't know. Ben was in the loft, but the barn is on its last leg. And Kraft followed me around to the front of the house earlier. That was the last time I saw him."

Maeve had cast a spell on the entrances to the doorways of the house to ward off vampires, so I hadn't been able to enter. Layla had fixed that problem with her banshee scream—a weapon of sorts that had broken down the magical barriers Maeve had erected.

"Ben should be fine," I replied. My SEAL brother was half vampire and half human. If he was under the rubble, he would survive, as would Kraft.

"Do you have Orion?" Tripp asked into my comm.

"Yes. I need to get him somewhere safe so I can fight."

Someone swore and growled nearby.

I jerked to my left and stepped out from the shadows with my gun trained on the rubble.

A tall familiar figure emerged covered in dirt and dust. "Motherfucker," Ben said, throwing wood planks off himself. He raised his arms, the whites of his reddish-brown eyes standing out in the dark of night. "It's me, Sam." He climbed over piles of splintered wood planks, blood dribbling down from his temple only to coagulate as it stopped, thanks in part to his half-vampire side.

"I found Ben," I said to Tripp in my earpiece.

A beam of orange light lit up the darkness behind Ben.

Suddenly, he was grabbing his head, wincing and swearing once again. "What's happening to me?" He stumbled, spun around, and whipped out his gun, pointing it at the young, brown-haired woman. "She's doing something to my head. It feels like she's crushing my skull."

Her palms pointed toward the star-laden sky, and her orange eyes were twin spotlights shining in our direction.

I, too, trained my weapon on her. But she didn't seem fazed at all about the fact that she was about to die.

"Is this what a witch looks like when using their powers?" Ben asked in a pained voice. "Eyes filled with fire?"

The woman stood about ten feet from us, her arms stretched out as she mumbled foreign words I couldn't understand.

Orion started crying.

I realized whatever she was doing was probably hurting Orion. He was wrapped in a bulletproof blanket, but that wouldn't protect him from witchcraft. On the other hand, I wasn't affected, since I was wearing an infinity protection bracelet to ward off any spells cast by a witch.

"Sam, go," Ben said. "Get Orion out of here. I got this."

We had no clue how to fight a witch, and while I would normally have his back, I needed to reach Layla before Roman and his men hauled her away. I was about to take off when the witch extended her arm in my direction.

With an accompanying flick of her wrist, she said, "You're not going anywhere, Sam Mason."

"Wanna bet?" I growled as I lifted my foot to move—but couldn't. It seemed my boots were stuck in the dirt.

*Motherfucker.*

Ben fired his weapon at her. The bullet stopped in midair inches from her face before dropping to the ground.

She guffawed. "You vampires don't stand a chance against witches like me. And once my mother arrives, all of you, including the werewolves with you, will be dead. Then we'll have your son and daughter in our arms once again. We already have people heading to retrieve your two daughters."

Fury blazed through me as a knot twisted in my gut. I would like to believe no one could penetrate the shifter compound in the Catskills, but anything was possible.

"You must be Patricia." When Layla had been inside the house, she'd demanded through her comm that someone find Patricia, Maeve's daughter.

"You're correct," she returned in a distinct mousy tone that rattled my nerves. "I'm as powerful as my mother."

For a second, I wondered if she was the woman who'd been with Norman Collier in the nursery that night my kids had been kidnapped. Layla's sister Jordyn had heard a woman's voice.

My answer came swiftly when a summer breeze whipped up the dust from the pile of wood from the barn and mingled with the scent of eucalyptus. Sure, the plant could be growing nearby. But it wasn't a coincidence that the vampires guarding the Maine house that night had smelled eucalyptus right before they'd passed out. Plus, one of the guests at the Dewsbury Inn had checked in under the name of Patty Smith. Patty *was* short for Patricia.

"You kidnapped my babies from the nursery," I said rather than asked. "You were with the vampire guardian, Norman Collier."

"Guilty as charged," she boasted, reminding me of Roman. "You vampires didn't even see us coming. Our cloaking spell wins every time."

Movement to my right made Patricia whip her head toward whoever was approaching.

I took that time to holster my gun, rip off my bracelet, and place it in Orion's carrier, hoping it would keep him safe from witchcraft. Besides, it was time to show this witch what I was capable of.

I lifted one foot, then the other. She must've broken the spell when whoever was approaching drew her attention away from me.

Tripp eased out of the shadows, wasting no time in firing at Patricia. She blocked every bullet as if she had a shield of armor, chanting a series of mumbo jumbo words.

Ben joined in but also failed to hit her.

*Let's see what the bitch can do against my elemental powers.*

I dug deep for the prickly heat that came right before my fire element kicked in. Rage flooded my veins as that tingling sensation zipped down to the tips of my fingers. I swung my arms back, then forward, launching one fireball, then another.

A ring of fire circled her but quickly died as she jerked her head in my direction and laughed. "Come on, vampires. Show me what else you got." She raised her hands into fists, keeping an eye on Tripp, Ben, and me.

I threw another fireball.

As a Vampire Navy SEAL, Tripp could wield two elements, not four like me. He was known more for manipulating water than fire. But with no water in sight, he bowed his head, bared his fangs, and rubbed his palms together. Flames spat through his fingers before he opened his hands and flung softball-size spheres of fire at Patricia.

One was on a trajectory to hit her head. At the last second, she flicked her wrists at Tripp, and the fireballs dissipated. Then a crisp snapping sound cracked through the air. Suddenly, Tripp was flying backward.

Ben was reloading his gun when she turned on him.

"Bullets won't hit me, asshole," she said to him right before she swung her arms out from her sides, then in a flash, clapped her hands together.

Ben froze, turned the gun on himself, and pulled the trigger several times until he fell to the ground.

"Your turn, Mason." She stomped toward me, her orange eyes deepening in color as she waved a hand toward me.

"I don't think so." I kept throwing fire at her unsuccessfully.

She flicked her wrists, and my body stiffened.

I tried to move my legs but couldn't.

She cackled loudly. "My mom will be so proud of me."

Orion started bawling.

"I will end you, bitch," I sneered.

She trudged toward me. "No, you won't. You can't win a fight with a Monroe witch."

I *wanted* to say, "My wife will gut you," but until Layla had her witchcraft, she couldn't best Patricia, no matter how good Layla was with daggers—or any weapons, for that matter.

The closer Patricia got, the less clearly I could think. My brain suddenly felt fuzzy.

She chanted some gibberish lines followed by "You're not a powerful vampire anymore, Sam Mason." She unhooked Orion from me.

I couldn't move my arms or legs or do a damn thing. I stood

there like a fucking lump on a log while she hauled my son into her arms.

"Come here, little one," she cooed.

I growled, baring my fangs at her, itching to tear out her carotid artery. But even my head wouldn't move.

With the snap of her fingers, I heard the bones in my neck crack before darkness consumed me.

**2**

---

# LAYLA

For the last few minutes, I'd been nervously standing between two SUVs with Luna snuggled against me in her carrier as I stared at the blond vampire I hated. I didn't expect to see Roman Brown on a farm in North Dakota.

His sinister grin was both maddening and frightening as he lingered in front of me, next to the vehicle he'd climbed out of.

My heart was in my throat, my mind a ball of knots, and I was weaponless. Not a fucking thing to defend myself with. Not even any magical powers, which I was hoping would shoot out of me. After all, only seconds after I grabbed Luna out of the crib, Agnes, my maternal grandmother, had given me a few drops of her blood—the key to unlocking my Monroe witch powers.

Then again, with Roman's two vampire goons behind me and Roman ogling me, I couldn't escape even if I still had my daggers. His men had swiftly taken my weapons when they poured out of their vehicle like flying saucers from the mothership.

Roman sauntered up to me, wearing an award-winning smirk that I wanted to smack off his face.

"Sam!" I shouted. "Are you still there?"

Part of me prayed he'd heeded my advice and had fled with Orion. The other part of me needed his elemental powers.

Luna was quiet as I held her tightly to me, stroking her not only to calm her but to soothe my frayed nerves.

I listened intently, and after two long beats, no response. My pulse pounded in my ears, sounding like a drum solo at a rock concert, muting the gunfire around us.

The blue-eyed vampire sized me up as though he'd won a gazillion-dollar prize. "Sam can't help you, darling."

I stuck out my middle finger at Roman. "Don't call me that, and where's your pinstriped suit?"

The last time we'd met, many months ago on the battlefield at the naval base in Massachusetts, he'd worn a suit to a fight and wielded a sword as his weapon of choice. Tonight, he was garbed in all black with a gun holstered to his hip.

He knitted his eyebrows. "What?"

"Never mind," I said. "So, how is this going down? Did Maeve give you orders to kill me?"

A chill skated down my spine as my insides twisted and turned. I was fucked. She wanted me dead so she could break the connection I had with my four children. In doing so, she could use them in her blood ritual to rise as the Mystic of witches.

*Where are those witch powers I should have? Agnes said it would take time. Time I don't have.*

Roman snapped his fingers. "Did you hear me, Layla?"

I flinched, blinking rapidly and found him standing so close to me that a putrid scent wafted off him as if he'd been buried in decayed earth. I wrinkled my nose and darted to the side.

He was quicker than I was and blocked my path to freedom. "You're not going anywhere." He glanced past me. "Take her to the basement in the main house and throw her in a cage."

I spat in his face. "Touch me, and I'll rip off your arms."

He threw his head back and laughed just as the spotlight on the house came on. "Humans are so stupid."

"Who said I was human?"

He wiped my saliva off him, then stuck his fingers in his mouth. "I've always wanted to taste you. I'm sure your blood is much better than this."

I wrinkled my nose. "You're disgusting."

"Vampires can feel a witch's magic. You don't have any." He sniffed my neck and moaned. "But your sweet smell of fear is driving me mad."

I attempted to push him. He didn't budge.

Instead, he started to remove my baby carrier. "She belongs to me."

My pulse shot from a hundred to two hundred in a matter of seconds as rage barreled through me faster than the speed of light. Before I could think, I headbutted Roman.

The crack of my skull on his stymied me. Instantly, pain gripped my entire head, but I brushed it aside. I didn't have time to whine or worry or cry.

Roman faltered, narrowing his eyes, fangs dripping with hunger and revenge.

I stomped in his direction as Luna began to cry. She was probably sensing my fear.

"Touch me or my daughter and—"

Roman's face reddened. "When will fucking humans learn that they're low on the food chain?"

Before I could track him, he grabbed me and sank his fangs into my neck.

I screamed as loud as I could, but I couldn't dig deep enough to unleash my inner banshee. It wouldn't matter if I could. Vampires were immune to my Hollywood scream.

I should've never told Sam to flee.

*Sam would never leave you. He will save you.*

Wolves howled around us.

I took comfort in the realization that the shifters weren't dead. But where the hell were the Vampire Navy SEALs—Olivia, Kraft, Ben, and Tripp? Or even Conrad, who was a vampire scout and my bodyguard. Had the witches gotten to them? Where was Agnes? Although she was of no help since Maeve had taken her powers.

*Where are you, Sam? Luna and I need you.*

Roman yanked on my hair with one hand and clutched my throat with the other while he continued to suck my life essence as if he was bloodthirsty. A laugh zipped around in my head. He probably was starving.

I kicked and squirmed, but that only made things worse. The more I fought, the deeper his fangs tore at my skin.

*Be still,* my inner voice supplied.

*Fuck my subconscious voice.*

A woman shouted, "Get off her, vampire!"

Agnes? That sounded like my grandmother. But I couldn't be sure. I was fading, watching the SUV in front of me spin like I was on a merry-go-round. Nausea churned in my stomach like a violent storm at sea.

"Stop," I said weakly. "You're draining me."

He squeezed my throat harder, not releasing his fangs.

The dizziness multiplied—or rather, the spinzies, as my mom had liked to call them anytime my sisters and I were dizzy.

A white-haired woman came into view with anger steeped in her brown eyes.

"Agnes, is that you?" My voice was barely audible.

She grabbed Roman's hair. "I told you to get off her, vampire. You'll kill her."

Roman released me and swung at Agnes. As she disappeared from sight, all I heard was a screech followed by a thud.

My pulse slowed to a crawl.

I couldn't scream or speak, and I was fading fast.

*Sam, I love you with all my heart. Take care of our children.*

This was how I would die. This was how Maeve planned to kill me—by using Roman to do her dirty work.

My muscles weakened, my eyes rolled back in my head, and my knees buckled.

Oh my God. I was about to fall with Luna attached to me.

*Please don't let me hurt her.*

The last thing I heard before darkness consumed me was Roman's voice. "You'll never see your daughter again."

**3**

——————

## SAM

My eyes flew open as a pungent odor of mildew filled my nostrils and entered my lungs, cloying and thick. I pushed my hands into the dirt floor, swearing like the sailor I was as I stood to my full height. I wiped away the rocks and debris that were embedded in my face and spat out the crud that was in my mouth.

A quick scan of my surroundings revealed I was in a cage in a basement. Agnes Monroe, the nice witch who was Layla's grand-mother, was in a second cage beside mine. There were round fluorescent lights hanging from wooden beams, a camera in the far-right corner, a curtained wall to my right, and a solid metal door directly ahead of me. The space reminded me of an isolated dungeon deep in the caverns carved into a mountain in the middle of nowhere.

Hell, I could very well be in the mountains for all I knew. Yet my watch said otherwise. According to the date and time, only two hours and forty-five minutes had passed since Layla and I had entered the farm.

Where the hell were my wife and babies? I prayed—like I had

15

as a boy in the confessional as I told my weekly sins to a priest—that Layla had fled with Luna. My gut was screaming that she hadn't.

I banged on the bars of my cage and quickly removed my hand. The damn thing was cobalt. Smart move on my captor's part.

I kicked the cage this time, hoping to wake Layla's grandmother. "Agnes." The white-haired woman, wearing pajamas, a robe, and slippers, didn't move.

I sharpened my hearing, and aside from Agnes's pulse, I could faintly hear another sound coming from somewhere behind the curtained wall.

I sniffed for a scent but was met only with putrid mildew odors that seemed to be stuck to my nose hairs.

"Agnes." My voice boomed.

Layla's maternal grandmother looked like she'd seen better days. Her face was wrinkled, and her nails were yellow. Despite the volume of my voice, the woman wasn't moving. I detected a heartbeat—slow and steady. So she must've been tranquilized.

The only way to free myself was to melt the steel bars of the cage. I inhaled deeply, calling forth my fire element. But that prickly, throbbing sensation before heat traveled down my arms to the tips of my fingers never came. I tried again and nothing. Absolutely, fucking nothing.

I took a trip down memory fucking lane, recalling what had happened right before I passed out. *Oh fuck. Was Tripp okay? Ben?*

I checked the room one more time for either of them. Maybe they were behind the curtain. Still, I growled and tried to kick-start my earth element by making the ground shake or the walls crumble. Epic failure.

Then Patricia's words seared my brain. *"You're not a powerful vampire anymore, Sam Mason."*

The witch must've zapped my powers from me.

I was so fucked and furious but didn't have a chance to think before the metal door creaked open.

Roman Brown strutted in, clapping and laughing. "It's a gas to watch you through the camera." He feigned a pout. "What's wrong, Mason? Did you lose your elemental powers?" He tapped his lips with his forefinger. "Oh, wait. Patricia stole them. You'll never get them back."

I clutched the bars, not giving a fuck that my skin was melting.

On Roman's heels was Adam fucking Emery carrying a large square box. The man hadn't lost the arrogance in his brown eyes since the last I'd seen him on national television. At his early morning news conference last month, he'd announced to the nation that he was building prototype vampires by using humans as guinea pigs. He'd even gone as far as to show the public a true vampire.

Roman pulled a dagger from a sheath on his leg and twirled it in his hand. "You've got to love a witch, Mason."

My wife was supposedly a witch, as was my daughter Rorie. So I couldn't say I hated all witches—just certain ones.

Roman cleaned a fingernail with the tip of his blade. "Seeing you in a cage calls for a celebration." He flicked his blue eyes at Adam. "Don't you think?"

Adam set the box on the dusty, dirt-ridden floor at his feet. "This should be fun." He swiped a hand through his coiffed brown hair, smug and proud.

"Are you trying to impersonate a soldier in those fatigues that look hideous on you?" I asked Adam. The fucker probably didn't know what it meant to serve his country.

Ignoring me, Adam said, "I always knew I would capture you again."

I pried my fried skin from the bars, my burning flesh masking the stench in the room. "Don't be so pompous. The day isn't over yet. And at some point, I will follow through on my threat to hang you from a fifty-story building by your toes. In fact, I'll even make sure it's one of your skyscrapers in Chicago."

He tucked his hands into the pockets of his fatigues without a care in the world. "I should cut out your tongue."

"What are you waiting for?" I was surprised I wasn't already dead. "Why haven't you killed me?" I doubted he needed my DNA, since he had probably taken Orion's and Luna's already.

He puffed out his chest. "Because you're my leverage. I want my brother Fred, as well as Carly Aberdeen released from your prison."

I let out a derisive laugh. "I want my wife, son, and daughter. Until then, fuck off."

"Your father will agree to my demands," Adam said confidently.

I snorted. "That will never happen."

My old man, Steven Mason, didn't bargain with the enemy. Although he now had grandchildren whose lives were on the line. I wanted to believe Adam had a heart when it came to babies, but desperation had a way of overshadowing a person's morals.

"Why do you want Carly? Do you even know what happened to your precious scientist?" I asked.

Adam rubbed his chin. "I'm well aware that Rianne injected her with the serum."

My eyebrows drew down. "You want a monster working for you?"

If Carly followed the same route as her brother-in-law, Noah Aberdeen, she would eventually be unable to string words together, let alone conduct a science experiment. The end result of her genetic-altering trials was either immediate death for those who were not healthy or a creature who became barbaric, with no sense of who he was, just like Noah. Adam knew all this.

"She has information you need for your experiments." That had to be it.

The last I knew, the trials were failing, and that update had come from Matthew Costner, an inside source.

He flinched slightly. "Your father will release Carly and Fred. I'm sure he doesn't want his daughter-in-law to die either. You see, I'm the one keeping Maeve Monroe from killing Layla." He stabbed a thumb at Roman beside him, who was still picking his fingernails with the dagger as if he was bored. "And him from killing you. So you should be thanking me, Mason."

Roman sheathed his dagger, went over to the freestanding curtained wall, and slowly moved it.

My vision blurred, my heart fell to my feet, and acid punctured holes in my lungs.

Roman cackled. "This is your first surprise. Isn't she beautiful?"

Layla's wrists were shackled to a stainless steel table with an IV bag of blood flowing into her veins. Her face was pale, her heart rate scarily slow, and she had a bandage around her neck.

Roman was licking his lips as he continued to stare at her.

Rage so strong had me embedding my fangs into my lower lip. "What the fuck happened that she needs blood?" My voice boomed and cracked at the same time.

I knew the answer to my question, but I wanted to hear the fucker say it.

Roman grinned and shrugged. "She left me no choice but to drain her to within an inch of her life. She was quite delicious, Mason."

My stomach was writhing as if a nest of vipers had come out to play inside it. The command to kill roared through my mind like a firestorm. How the fuck could I murder him? I was trapped in an impenetrable prison with no elemental powers. But that didn't stop me from becoming the vicious bloodsucking creature that I was. I grabbed the cobalt bars, summoning all my inner vampire strength, and pulled them with such force that my skin blistered and peeled as it was roasted by my kryptonite.

The nauseating reek of scorched skin infiltrated the space, triggering a deadly stillness in the grungy basement.

Adam watched with amusement that contrasted with his fear that wafted into my nostrils.

Roman, on the other hand, stood over Layla, watching me with a calculating grin as if he knew something I didn't. "Maybe this time I'll taste her here." He pressed his fingers into her thigh, boosting my ferocity to free myself from the prison.

Images of torturing the asshole brightened before me like the blazing sun in the middle of summer.

In record speed I mangled the bars, creating just enough of an opening for me to shove my big body through. Once on the other side, I charged Adam first. My body hit an invisible wall, and I flew backward and hit the cage.

*Motherfucker.*

Roman cackled. "I'm enjoying seeing you sweat, Mason. It sucks that Layla is only fifteen feet from you, and you can't reach her. Again, you have to love a witch and her ability to erect a magical barricade to prevent you from helping your wife. It's the ultimate torture."

I had to agree with Roman on the last thing. He was crucifying me. I felt the emotional pain as if he'd nailed me to a wall.

Adam sighed as he laughed with Roman.

"Roman, you should've killed me before I woke up," I bit out. "Because when I get my hands on you, I will chop off every limb on your body while you watch. Then before I whack off your head, I'll pluck your eyes out and feed them to the wolves."

Roman's blue eyes spun to black, lightless pools of glass, as if someone had jammed them into his sockets, dead and deadly.

"You're in no position to make threats." His fangs protruded from his upper gums, almost dripping in hunger.

If I were human, the sight of him might've made me piss my pants. But instead, I couldn't help but laugh.

"You see, Mason, we have the upper hand." Adam lifted his chin, defiant yet confident. "Your father will do as I ask. Otherwise, I'll be shipping not only your head and Layla's, but the heads of each of the SEALs we have in custody." He briefly looked at the box on the floor.

"I call bullshit." I snarled the words. "If you have anyone from my team, where are they? I don't see them here. You have an empty cage beside me."

Maybe he wasn't blowing smoke up my ass. I would be gutted if he had the head of Tripp, Ben, Olivia, Kraft, or Conrad in that box. I was tempted to ask him about the shifters, but I had a more important question.

I flashed my fangs at Adam. "Where are my children?"

"As I told Layla," Roman answered instead. "You'll never see them again."

Red stars floated in my vision. I desperately wanted to slice and dice these fuckers.

My fury and trepidation multiplied when Adam bent down and tossed the lid off the box.

"This is proof that I mean what I say." He dangled Matthew's bloody head. "If your father doesn't comply with my request, I'll be sending him one head at a time."

Roman tucked his fangs away, and he rejoined Adam. "Who will be next?"

Mere feet separated us, yet I couldn't do a fucking thing. "You think my father cares about Matthew?" My dad would be gutted that Matthew was dead. Matthew's mother, Alia Costner, even more so. "And he was working for you. Wasn't he?"

I'd been confused by Matthew's actions ever since I'd seen

him speak at Adam's news conference. I'd gotten the impression that Matthew was working with Adam of his own accord until I'd learned that Matthew had sent messages to a secure server on his grandfather Victor's estate. According to Wyman, Victor's computer expert, Matthew had detailed three things—he was fine, we shouldn't think he was working for Adam, and the genetic experiments were failing. Not to mention, there were two shifters helping Matthew free others. We suspected Matthew was referring to Dane Gray's brother, Ross and Sergeant Rebekah Whyte's brother, Tucker.

I walked by Agnes's cage, feeling for an opening in the invisible wall as I eyed my wife in the distance.

Adam dropped Matthew's head into the box. "Whatever would give you the idea that Matthew was working for me? Ah, the news conference. He did brilliantly that day, afraid that if he didn't, his family would die. But that ship sailed when we caught him sending messages to his grandfather."

I returned to stand before Adam and Roman. My brain was fuzzy, and my gut felt as though sharp claws were gouging out my insides.

I really wasn't in the mood to listen to Adam's monotonous tone. However, I was curious about something. "Why did you even kidnap Matthew?"

Adam scratched his jaw. "I guess it doesn't matter if you know. We went through your uncle Patrick's notes with a fine-tooth comb. He'd outlined Matthew's genetic-mapping sequence and how it was a success. We realized Matthew was the one for us to study."

He confirmed what I had originally thought. "If he was your prisoner, how did he get computer access?"

"We had someone in our ranks who believed Matthew would pay him a hefty sum in exchange for help," Adam said.

"That person's head is no longer attached to his body," Roman bragged.

One thing I could count on with Roman was he liked to play games, but he also liked to gloat.

"Where are Ross and Tucker?" I asked.

Adam and Roman exchanged satisfied looks before Roman said, "You should be worried about yourself and your family, including my beloved Abbey. I didn't know she could be the first female vampire to procreate. Color me shocked when Matthew told me that. I've always wanted kids, Mason. And now Abbey is my number one target."

He was goading me into reacting in some way. But my hands were tied, and I needed to reserve my energy to think of a way out before Adam chopped off more heads, especially my wife's or those of my team.

"No response?" Roman asked.

I stared at him with a blank look. "Do you want one?"

"I like your threats," he said. "They don't mean anything to me. But I do like to rile you up."

I laughed, and only because he was right. He knew how to light my anger on fire. "You know very well that Abbey is out of your reach, and it's not me you have to contend with but my sister and brother-in-law."

I considered myself to be a great fighter, but Abbey's dad, Webb London, could be much more lethal than me. Jo could as well.

Roman studied me intently. "Who says I don't have her already?"

A cold chill clawed its way down my spine, giving me the feeling that he wasn't lying. "Bullshit." Although he could be telling the truth. I hadn't had time to think about Abbey. After all, my children were my number one priority, especially in light of Patricia's threat—*"We already have people heading to retrieve your two daughters."*

A phone ringing broke the iceberg-thick tension.

Adam dug in his pants pocket and removed his cell. "Maybe this is your father now. Hello," he said, answering the call.

I sharpened my vamp hearing and listened. The man on the other end wasn't my dad, and I didn't recognize his voice either.

Adam walked away, shoulders hunched upward as he gripped the phone tightly.

Roman came closer until he was an inch from me. "Odd that I can stand here without anything between us except an invisible wall. I want to rip out your fangs."

"That's all?" I volleyed back. "Take down the wall and give it your best shot."

"Roman," Adam said firmly. "We've got company."

Roman pressed his nose against the invisible wall.

I threw a punch that did nothing to hurt him.

His laughter was maddening. "By the time I return, Layla should be awake and ready for round two. And I can't wait for you to watch." He pivoted on his heel.

"You're a dead man," I called out.

He held his middle finger high in the air as he and Adam left.

Once I was alone, I punched the cage until my bones broke.

# 4

## SAM

It was approaching the witching hour. That time of night when supernatural beings were at their most powerful. I had to laugh because I certainly didn't have any of my abilities. I was dead in the water—imprisoned behind a fucking invisible barricade that separated Layla and me.

For the past fifteen excruciating minutes, I'd been pulling out my hair, walking around the cages, checking for weak spots in the magical prison wall. I'd even climbed up on top of the cages, thinking there might be an opening. No such luck.

In between, I tried to wake Agnes and Layla. I had my doubts if either of them could help. I would bet that Agnes didn't have her powers either. I didn't think Maeve or even Roman was stupid enough to throw a witch into a cage knowing she could cast a spell or wave a hand to free herself.

Layla might become our savior if her powers were unlocked. I was reaching for a miracle. Even if Layla whipped up her magic, the only exit out of here was through the same door Adam and Roman had used, which would lead us right into their hands. On top of that, we were being watched. As soon as our enemies saw us trying to escape, they would converge down here in seconds. I couldn't worry about that now though.

Agnes stirred, blinking several times and holding her head.

"Finally." I stood in front of her cage, keeping my burnt hands away from the bars even though my skin was growing back. "Where are we? How do we get out of here?" My pulse was off the charts, and my patience was running on thin ice.

She rose, wobbling as she cinched her dirty pink robe closed. "Slow down." She grabbed on to the bars with confusion in her brown eyes. Then she glanced at Layla. "Is she alive? I gave her my blood when they threw us in the car." Horror was etched in her tone. "But then they knocked me out."

"Her heart is beating. We need to focus and work together. Your evil sister, Maeve, or your niece, Patricia, put a spell around us." I slapped my hand in the air where the wall was. "Can you take it down?"

She clutched the back of her neck, wincing. "Maeve stole my powers."

"Patricia took mine. And let me guess. The only one who can return them is the witch who zapped us?"

Her nod mimicked a bobblehead.

Fucked didn't even begin to describe the situation we were in. Not to mention, I had no earthly idea where Orion and Luna were.

"How do we get out of here?"

"There are two escape routes, but both require magic. There's a tunnel through the cement wall behind the cage." She flicked a thumb behind her. "It leads to the house where Orion and Luna had been. The other exit is through the wall behind Layla. That one leads to the outside."

A maniacal laugh bellowed out of me. There wasn't a witch around to help us. Panic wasn't something I succumbed to, but it rose from the depths of hell, consuming me as I began to pace once again, frantically pounding my booted feet on the ground in an agitated rhythm.

Agnes released an exasperated sigh. "I'm exhausted from all this. I hate my sister and niece. I can't stand Roman and Adam."

"Join the club. But why are you with your sister, and why did you even leave your husband?"

Frankly, I didn't give shit why or what her reasoning was. I just needed noise. It helped me think.

"That's a story for another day." She had a faraway look in her brown eyes.

I cracked my knuckles, still pacing like a nutjob on steroids. "Then tell me why Adam is in charge and Maeve hasn't killed Layla yet. I mean, that's your sister's goal, right?"

Her jaw hardened. "Last week Maeve made a deal with Adam. She would leave Layla alone until Adam gets his brother Fred and his scientist, Carly."

Maybe that was why Maeve hadn't tried to murder Layla in her dreams a second time.

I stopped and folded my arms over my chest. "How does Maeve know Adam or even Roman?"

Agnes hugged herself. "Fred paid us a visit about two years ago. He was looking for my great-granddaughter Abbey. He claimed she had special abilities, and he and his brother, Adam, wanted to help the child."

Help my ass. The Emerys were out to use Abbey for her unique genetic makeup.

"Did you know about Abbey before Fred showed up?" I asked. I was getting the impression she had.

"In a roundabout way, yes," she said. "I knew my granddaughter, Rachel, was pregnant by a vampire. After she graduated from boarding school, Rachel took off to explore the world. That was when she met a vampire. But Rachel's mom, Vanessa, and I didn't know much more than that. At the time, we only knew of the prophecy that a Monroe witch would give birth to quadruplets, and the seer had seen one of these children turn the entire Monroe coven into vampires. We were afraid for Rachel. We thought it was best for her to disappear. If Maeve had learned that Rachel was pregnant by a vampire, regardless of whether she gave birth to one baby or four, Maeve would've killed Rachel. And any witch in our community would've helped Maeve since they thought that if the Monroe coven could turn, then maybe their covens could as well. Keep in mind that the Mystic prophecy hadn't surfaced yet." She took a breath. "We even advised Rachel to consider terminating her pregnancy."

I silently cursed that a two-hundred-year-old prediction had severe consequences that affected Abbey, as well as my wife and children.

I clutched my neck. "Abbey's father, Edmund Rain, ended up killing Rachel—and not because of some prophecy either. He was livid that Rachel had hidden Abbey from him. That's how sick in the head he was."

Tears welled up in her brown eyes. "Fred Emery had told us Rachel died but never said how. I should've protected Rachel. But my hands were full when Vanessa found out she had ovarian cancer."

In my book, Agnes was a lost soul looking for redemption and hoping to correct the wrongs of her past. Yet, I understood her desire to protect Rachel.

My father had kept Jo and me hidden in foster care from the likes of Edmund Rain for years because Edmund wanted to use my sister and me as lab rats for our DNA in his attempts to build his own personal army of vampires. I'd hated my father for so long, thinking that he abandoned us. But over the years, I'd come to understand his motives. Hell, I was in the thick of things with my own children. Their lives were at stake for the same reasons Jo and I had been hunted.

"You knew Edmund Rain?" she asked.

I stretched my neck. "Enemy number one. Five years ago, he teamed up with my uncle Patrick and tried to develop a serum for genetic altering, much like Adam wants to do. My uncle was a renowned genetic scientist with his own thirst for immortality that he failed to capitalize on before his vampire father died. Anyway, he used my sister and me as his test subjects. As a result, he was successful in transforming two people out of hundreds."

Silence dangled for a beat.

"There's one thing I'm confused about," I said. "Why would Maeve agree to help Adam when she has her own agenda?"

Agnes sighed. "She needs a coven and their collective magic to perform the blood ritual for the Mystic ceremony. We don't have many Monroes left, and Maeve has pissed off the witch community. Adam—or rather, Roman—thinks he can find powerful witches for Maeve." She lifted a shoulder. "For now, Maeve has agreed to stop her quest against Layla. Once Adam has his brother and the scientist, then he and Roman will give Maeve her coven."

Roman certainly had a large network of contacts in his blood cartel business. I would imagine that if Roman didn't know many witches, he had clients who did.

"Do you think the Mystic prophecy will give a witch the ultimate power or even come to fruition? And what does it mean by ultimate power?"

My questions went by the wayside at the sound of Layla moaning, which kick-started my damn black heart.

"Baby doll. Thank fuck."

Layla rose up on her elbows, looking in my direction. "Sam? Where am I? Where is Luna? Orion?" She glanced at her arm. "Why is there an IV of blood in my arm?" Her eyes widened. "Roman. I will kill him." She tugged on her restraints, her blue eyes flashing to a sunburst yellow.

My jaw came unhinged. "What's the significance of yellow eyes? Aren't they supposed to be orange?"

"Not sure, but I would go out on a limb and say it's related to the Mystic," Agnes said in a rush. "Layla, listen to me. You can free yourself, but I need you to believe that you're a Monroe witch. We don't have much time. First, you'll need to place a drop of your blood onto one of the cuffs around your wrist."

Layla's pulse was creeping upward. "It's kind of hard to do without the use of my hands."

"Baby doll, bite your lip and drip it onto the metal cuff."

"Help me, Sam," she said.

"I can't. Either Maeve or her daughter Patricia put a spell around the cages. The same one that was on the entrances in the house to ward off vampires. I can't get to you. You can do this, baby doll."

Wincing, Layla bit her lip. Once the blood dribbled out and down her chin, she struggled to sit up as she lifted her arm just enough that her mouth was barely over the cuff.

"Do the same to other restraint." Agnes's tone brooked no argument.

Layla obeyed. "Now what?"

Agnes began talking with her hands. "In order for this spell to work, you have to believe, Layla. See the process—the cuffs falling from you. Repeat after me. My blood is pure. My blood is strong. I unlock these chains, so let it be done. See it, believe it, and repeat it until you're free."

Layla followed orders as I watched in quiet fascination. If anyone had told me I would fall in love with a beautiful witch, I would've thought they were crazy. But as I fixated on Layla, her auburn hair shaping her gorgeous face, her full lips chanting the spell over and over again, and her magic filling the grungy room, I felt as though I was in heaven rather than hell. I swore I could actually see a soft glow of yellow around her.

One of the cuffs clicked open, then the other.

Layla hurriedly yanked out her IV, climbed off the table, and fell on the floor. "I'm fine." She swore as she rose. "My legs are weak." She came over to us slowly, her yellow eyes glistening. "How do we get out of here?"

I reached up and flattened my hands on the invisible barrier separating us. "You need your banshee scream to shatter the spellbound barrier between us. Then we'll figure out the next step."

She mimicked my move, our hands mirroring each other's as if our palms were touching. "This is weird. I don't see anything between us, yet I can't feel your hand." She knocked on the air—or rather, the invisible wall—on both sides of me. Then she tried to walk into it only to stumble backward. "This spell is different from the one Maeve put on the doors to the house to prevent vampires from entering."

"It is," Agnes said. "The spell around the cages is the same one Maeve cast on the door to the bedroom Orion and Luna had been in. Remember, Layla? You couldn't get into that room until you shattered the barriers with your banshee scream."

Layla stepped away. "All right. Here goes." She inhaled and exhaled a few times and was about to rock this place with her Hollywood lungs when the metal door groaned.

Patricia glided in with an older woman wearing an evening gown who resembled Patricia. That had to be Maeve Monroe.

I didn't know if I should be afraid for Layla's life or not. Maeve was an older witch with years of practice under her belt. I growled my hatred of and annoyance at the fact that I was dead in the water and couldn't do squat to help my wife. But I had trust and faith that Layla could give Maeve a run for her money.

**5**

---

# LAYLA

I was giddy that I'd actually freed myself. But my excitement was short-lived as a surge of anger had me stomping along the invisible wall to my right and into the open aisle that led to the metal door in the distance to my left.

"Layla, be careful. Maeve's and Patty's powers are explosive when they're together." My grandmother sounded frightened.

I had no clue how to cast a spell and no business confronting two witches who had more experience combined than I was prepared for. But I was leaving this godforsaken place with my children and my husband.

I balled my hands into fists, stuck out my chin, and took my stance in the aisle as the two angry women marched in my direction.

My grandmother's warning fell on deaf ears despite the icy horror drenching my veins. I swallowed the nerves scratching my throat—or maybe it was bloodthirst or both. During my pregnancy, I'd developed a hunger for blood, and even after giving birth, the cravings persisted. Dr. Vieira had warned me that weaning myself off it would take time. Whatever the reason for

32

that ticklish burn, I shoved it aside. I had bigger things to deal with.

"She can handle herself," Sam added as he came closer to me, though he couldn't help. And I would bet that it was driving him insane that a magical wall separated us, making it so he had no way to protect me or fight with me.

A shot of confidence seeped into my soul, knowing that my husband had trust in me. I might be a novice with magic, but I was a quick learner, especially when my life was on the line. Back when I'd hunted and killed vampires, I'd never had time to think, just act—fight, protect, and do everything to save myself and those in harm's way.

*You can handle these witches.* It was good to know my subconscious also had faith in me, because doubt could be my own worst enemy.

It was uncanny how mother and daughter looked alike—brown eyes, high forehead, round face, and thin lips. The only difference was that Patricia was shorter than her mother, and Maeve had streaks of gray running through her brown hair.

Maeve wiped her hands on her blue evening gown. She must've just arrived from the charity event where she and her husband had been the honored guests for their efforts in raising money for the new children's hospital in Bismarck. How ironic that she supported a children's hospital given that she was instrumental in kidnapping our babies.

"Why are her eyes yellow, Mom?" Patricia asked.

If I'd heard Agnes correctly, she thought it was the Mystic. Interesting.

"It means I drank Agnes's blood, and now I'm a full-blooded Monroe witch and the rightful owner of the Mystic title," I fired at Patricia and Maeve.

According to the Mystic prophecy, the Monroe witch who bore quadruplets would become the Mystic. Meaning the one true witch wouldn't need a coven to exercise her power. That scenario fit me like a snug winter glove.

Frankly, I couldn't care less about rising to the supreme being of witches. I just wanted my children home and safe. I wanted to be the best mom I could be, to see Orion, Luna, Ellie, and Rorie grow up and thrive. To be a great mother, wife, and partner. And I wanted to help my sister Jordyn find her happiness.

Maeve stopped near a medium-sized open box that had red stains around its bottom edges. "Your yellow eyes mean nothing more than that you're a witch." Maeve didn't sound like she believed her own words. Regardless, she swung out her arm to stop Patricia from advancing on me. "Wait."

Surely, Maeve wasn't frightened of *me*—unless she believed I was the Mystic. If the prophecy came to fruition, would I have to perform a blood ritual? Or maybe the ceremony was only for Maeve because she wasn't destined for the role. Or maybe my magic was stronger than hers.

Tripp and a couple of others in my camp had told me that they could feel my magic. Maybe I was selling myself short. After all, the spell I'd recited to free myself from that table was cool as shit and had worked. Of course, it had been because of Agnes. Without her, I might be dead.

Maeve's eyes flashed orange, a sign she was preparing to use her witchcraft. "Agnes, you disobeyed me. I told you what would happen if you gave Layla your blood."

"Luckily, I was able to when she showed up on the farm, since the vial of blood I had hidden at Sacred Flame Academy had been stolen. You stole it, Maeve. Didn't you?" Agnes asked.

Patricia's snicker was sardonic. "My mom did no such thing. I did—or rather, I had a friend who goes to school there help me."

"You're worse than your mother." Agnes's tone was abrasive. "I'm done taking orders from both of you. If you're going to send me to my grave, then stop threatening me and do it.

Because if I get out of here, I will do everything I can to make sure you never become the Mystic. You know that forcing or changing a prophecy has dire consequences on humanity."

I'd just met Agnes, and she hadn't exactly wowed me. My impression was that my maternal grandmother didn't have a backbone. Even when she visited me in my dreams or waking visions, she seemed timid and frightened of Maeve. It was good to hear her stand up for herself.

"You've been trying to stop me for years," Maeve said to her sister. "You think that because Layla's here, you can now?"

"I've been waiting for the right moment," Agnes replied. "And what better moment is there than this?"

"You can't kill Layla," Sam chimed in. "You made a deal with Adam to leave Layla alone until my father freed his brother and the scientist."

Interesting turn of events. But Steven didn't strike me as the type to bargain with enemies. Still, maybe I should thank Adam for my window of reprieve and for the chance to end Maeve once and for all.

"Adam can find another way to free his brother," Maeve said. "The game has changed. Layla dies tonight along with the two of you." She pinned a glare on Sam and Agnes.

"Then you'll never get the coven of witches you need for the ritual." Agnes's voice dripped with venom.

Lowering her arm, Maeve glowered at Agnes, pursing her lips as her nostrils flared.

It seemed Maeve was between a rock and a hard place.

"What's it going to be, Maeve? Me or you? Are you that desperate to risk *your* life to rise to power?" I asked.

"You think you can hurt me?" Maeve's tone was incredulous.

"You're not invincible." I opened and closed my fists as that familiar tingle radiated in my legs, and warmth rumbled from my feet to my arms.

Her daughter bowed her head, mumbling foreign words.

"Hold up, Patty," Maeve said. "Let's see what she can do." Maeve opened her arms. "Give me your best shot."

A laugh zipped around in my head as I quickly looked to Agnes for help.

"Agnes can't help you." Maeve's voice was grating on my nerves.

"Where are our children?" Sam asked. He was probably trying to stall while I figured something out.

Patricia tucked her elbows into her waist, her forearms parallel to the ground, and her palms facing each other. "Which ones? The two we have here or your two daughters in the Catskills?"

Fear and fury coursed through me as I jerked my head at Sam. The game had certainly changed on my part as well. Holy fucknation. Ellie and Rorie were in danger. So was Jordyn. I would like to believe Patricia was bluffing, but she'd nailed their general location.

He fixated on Patricia, fangs out, green eyes flashing to silver.

Patricia laughed, the sound reminding me of Roman. He had that same cocksure laugh when he dropped a bomb on us. "Bloodsucker, you know you can't do shit. Even if that invisible wall wasn't there, I took your powers away."

News to me, but that wasn't important right now. I had to figure out how to knock both Maeve and Patricia on their asses.

Maeve held her arms at her sides and slightly behind herself while her palms were aimed in my direction. "Your children are mine."

Rage enveloped me like a thick black fog, clouding my vision and distorting my perspective. "I'm so fucking over you and others thinking that my children belong to you." I bowed my head, blinking several times, and when I did, my vision sharpened.

"You don't stand a chance against me or my daughter."

I snarled at Maeve. "I'm the true Mystic."

Just because I fit the definition of the prophecy didn't mean anything at the moment, but it was fun to trade barbs with Maeve.

Maeve's face turned red. "That will never happen."

Patricia kept her elbows secured to her waist and her forearms in that same position, as if she were squeezing a ball. "I'll handle her." She mumbled something I couldn't make out.

Sam sucked in a breath, sounding as if he knew what Patricia was about to do.

Narrowing my gaze, I envisioned Patricia bleeding from her eyes. *See it and believe it.*

I'd used mind control once before when my sister Rianne had been ready to drive a dagger through my pregnant belly. Then I'd imagined her stabbing herself. As if I'd willed it so, Rianne had turned the blade on herself, ready to drive it into her chest when Harriet had intervened.

No one would stop me today. *See it and believe it*, I repeated to myself.

Patricia continued to mutter foreign words, and suddenly, I was thrown against the invisible wall. My body felt like it was burning, as if she'd lit me on fire.

Fury ignited inside me, causing an electrical charge to race down my arms and legs. Once again, I pictured Patricia's eyes pouring out blood.

Patricia screamed, touching her face with her hands before she glanced at them. "I can't see. What's happening, Mom?" She stumbled into the sinister box, and a head rolled out. "Mom!"

I didn't want to see who the head belonged to. Otherwise, it would break my concentration. As I focused on Patricia, I could see Maeve coming toward me.

"The blood that runs through your veins is mud," Maeve chanted.

"No!" Agnes blurted.

Freezing, I zeroed in on Maeve. Her orange eyes glowed brightly, almost blinding me.

I should use mind control on Maeve or tackle her to the ground, but my legs seemed glued to the floor, and my brain had shut down.

"Mom, make it stop," Patricia cried.

Maeve grabbed my chin and squeezed, repeating the phrase she'd just said.

"Maeve!" Agnes shouted. "I'll do whatever you want. But don't use that spell on her."

Sam grunted, trying to plow through the invisible wall and failing.

Maeve captured my gaze in hers. "The blood that runs through your veins is mud," she repeated.

"Don't look at her," Agnes warned.

It was hard not to. The light in Maeve's eyes was drawing me in, making me dizzy and a little nauseous.

"The blood that keeps you alive is poison," Maeve chanted.

As if that last word was a trigger, I felt as though my veins were ready to explode.

"Layla, repeat after me!" Agnes yelled. "Fire boils your blood. Ice freezes your soul. From here to the end, you'll die a slow death. Say it!"

Maeve traded my chin for my neck and dug her nails into my skin.

I yanked on her wrists, trying to breathe. My lungs were on fire, and dizziness was making me even more nauseous.

"Baby doll, do as Agnes says." Sam's voice cracked with panic.

I growled, but it sounded pathetic. This bitch wasn't about to win.

I dug deep for strength as I closed my eyes and pictured Maeve gripping her own throat and silently chanted, *See it, believe it, repeat it.*

Suddenly, she released me, swaying as she clutched her neck with both hands.

I gulped in air, coughing.

Her face deepened to dark red as she inched backward.

"Layla," Agnes pleaded. "The spell. Say it. Fire boils your blood."

I stared at Maeve, painting an imaginary picture of her lying on her deathbed. "This ends tonight." I marched toward her. "Fire boils your blood. Ice freezes your soul," I intoned. "From here to the end, you'll die a slow death." Just to make sure I drove home the spell, I said it one more time.

Maeve tripped over the head.

The dead blue eyes and blond hair were eerily familiar. I'd seen him before.

"It's Matthew Costner," Sam said.

Patricia tried to rush over to her mother. "I will end you, Layla. Then I will burn your children and vampire lover at the stake."

Maeve fell to the floor, and Patricia listed to one side before she joined her mother.

Despite my shock that Alia's son Matthew's head had been chopped off, I had to deal with Patricia.

I yanked Patricia by the hair until she was standing. "What you *will* do is return my husband's powers, or I will make sure you're buried alive in this dungeon."

She spat in my face. "Go to hell."

I shoved her toward her mother. "Suit yourself."

She faltered but stayed upright.

"The invisible wall," Sam rushed out.

I regarded Agnes and Sam. "Both of you cover your ears."

"No," Sam said. "They'll hear you upstairs."

"He's right," Agnes said. "Patricia needs to take the spell off."

I stomped over to Patricia, who was on her knees and shaking her mother. "Wake up, Mom."

I grabbed her by the hair once again. "Drop the wall, or I'll make blood come out of your mouth—or better yet, crush your brain."

She snarled. "Fuck you."

"Suit yourself," I said.

Within seconds, she had blood spurting from her mouth.

"Okay," she choked out. "With the shield surround, remove the wall that has you bound." Then she resumed trying to wake her mother.

Sam took a tentative step toward me, then another until he was wrapping his arms around me. "I'm more in love with you than I've ever been. You were fucking amazing."

Butterflies took flight as I inhaled his woodsy scent. I beamed up at him as I eased away. I was once again giddy inside that I'd been able to do all that. But there was no room for celebration.

We needed to get the fuck out of there and find Orion and Luna. I pitied anyone who got in my way.

**6**

---

# SAM

Sweat soaked my body from the overwhelming feeling of helplessness while I'd been watching Layla from behind that invisible wall. The fact that I couldn't do a fucking thing to help had driven me insane, particularly when Agnes panicked over the spell Maeve had been about to use on Layla. I had no idea what the outcome of that spell was, but I would bet my life that it was death.

My body was slightly trembling, and I was afraid to let go of my wife. Yet we were being watched, so we didn't have much time.

I had one problem though. I could punch my fist through concrete, but my hands weren't quite back to normal yet. I needed blood to heal them quicker. Or regaining my elemental powers would be even better.

I released Layla. "Help your grandmother. I'll deal with Patricia." The bitch was going to give me my powers back or else I would drain her to a drop of her blood.

Patricia was sitting on her haunches, tapping her mother's face. "Wake up, Mom."

Maeve was out cold, though her heart was beating. Too bad. Both of these witches belonged in a casket and buried twenty feet beneath the earth.

I yanked Patricia upright by the scruff of her neck. "You and I have unfinished business."

The bitch was covered in blood, which was driving me mad. I didn't even think. I struck, sinking my fangs into her. The second her bitter blood filled my mouth, I almost spat it out but didn't. The sounds in the room grew louder, and the myriad of odors grew stronger.

She whined, squirming and kicking to no avail.

I sucked with great pulls while Agnes schooled Layla on how to magically unlock the cell. It was a spell similar to the one Layla had used to free herself from the table.

A rat squeaked somewhere in the room. Footsteps clamored above before voices filtered into my ears. When I heard Roman's, vengeance made me suck harder.

"Ernie, take the babies' things to the car," Roman said. "We're leaving here shortly."

"Roman, what are you doing?" a man asked. "The babies stay with Maeve and me until you give us the witches we asked for. And why did you unplug the cameras?"

"Because, idiot, if the authorities or even the media get ahold of the footage, we're done. Not that I care, but Adam does. Now, I would suggest, Warrick, you get your wife and leave. The farm is compromised," Roman said.

"Where are you moving your operation?" Warrick asked. "It seems anywhere you and Adam go, either the Feds or the Vampire Navy SEALs are right on your asses."

"My contact from Europe is here. He's taking Adam to the new headquarters as we speak," Roman replied. "Right now, we need to clear this place out."

"Boss, the babies' things are in the SUV. I'll round up our prisoners."

"No, Ernie," Roman said. "I need you to help me with the babies. Warrick, get your wife and daughter. They can help load the prisoners in the van. It's parked in front of the SUV."

I retracted my fangs. "Layla, we have to go. We'll take Patricia with us." This witch would be glued to me until I got my elemental powers back. "Agnes, you need to show Layla how to break down the wall for the exit."

"I'm not going anywhere with you." Patricia ran and stumbled her way to the metal door.

With vampire speed, I blocked her. "Nice try."

When Agnes was finally free, she and Layla hurried in my direction. Agnes stopped to scrutinize her sister. "Layla, in order for that spell to work on Maeve, you need to give her your blood. Otherwise, all it will do is weaken her powers."

Layla didn't blink an eye as she looked to me for help. "I need a fang, vampire."

I dragged Patricia with me and punctured Layla's fingertip with a canine.

"Please don't do this, Aunt Agnes," Patricia whined.

"Why? So Maeve can hunt Layla and her children and kill them like she did my mother-in-law?" Agnes asked.

Layla and I exchanged knowing looks. Agnes's father-in-law, Everett, had believed Maeve was responsible for his wife's death.

Layla dripped her blood onto Maeve's tongue. "Anything else?" she asked Agnes.

"No. She'll die a slow death. Once she's gone, I'll have my powers again. I'm sorry, Maeve." Agnes stood over her sister, her tone mixed with sadness and anger. "You left me no choice."

"Wait," I said. "If Patricia dies, then I get my powers back. Is that right?"

"No," Agnes replied. "Since you're not a witch, Sam, Patricia has to return your powers."

Fuck. I wouldn't have any problem killing Patricia right now.

Layla placed a hand on Agnes's arm. "I know this wasn't an easy decision for you. But Maeve would've obliterated anyone who got in her way of becoming the Mystic." Sorrow etched Layla's tone.

"You'll regret this, Aunt Agnes." Patricia spat blood at Agnes.

Agnes glowered at her niece. "Sam, we're not taking her with us. She stays with her mother."

"Then do you have a way to return my powers?" I hauled Patricia with me as I wound around the crap in the basement and over to the wall behind the table where one of the exits was located.

I had no desire to use the one that led to the other farmhouse. Orion and Luna were right above us, and it was best to use the exit that led outside.

Patricia tried to pull away from me. "Without your powers, you won't get past my father. He's ex-military and knows how to kill."

Chuckling, I yanked on her arm and was about to say something sarcastic when her body jerked into me. I felt something hard in her back pocket. Before I realized it was her cell, she had it in her hand.

I was attempting to take it from her when she threw it across the room. "Ha. You didn't think I would make it easy for you, did you?"

It would've been nice to have a way to communicate with Tripp or any of my team. As it stood, I didn't have my comm or cell.

"Ladies, move," I commanded.

Layla and Agnes hurried over.

"Layla, you'll need to do the spell to make an opening here." Agnes nodded at the cement wall.

Patricia started to chant, but Layla smacked her in the face. "Do you want to choke on your own blood?"

Patricia threw Layla the finger while Agnes gave Layla instructions on what to do.

Holding up her palms, my wife drew an imaginary circle over the dirt wall, chanting words that I tuned out.

I was too busy listening for enemies coming our way. We had maybe five seconds.

Finally, the exit appeared.

We rushed through the hole just as the metal door groaned, and a man shrieked Maeve's name.

Once on the other side, I covered Patricia's mouth as Agnes gave Layla the commands to magically seal the entrance.

My vision quickly adjusted to the small room that had a set of stairs leading up to a cellar door.

"Hold Patricia," I said to Layla. "I want to check before we rush out."

Agnes caught my arm. "Wait." Her pulse was beating rapidly. "Before we leave here, I have an idea to return your powers. If we don't do it now, I'm afraid you'll never get them back."

I had to agree. All sorts of things could go wrong. If we lost Patricia, I was fucked.

"It has to be done quickly. I'm sure Roman will know we're missing in less than a minute," I said.

"First, Layla, I want you to say these two words as you look at Patricia."

Patricia shook her head. "Don't do it, Aunt Agnes."

After Agnes gave the command to Layla, then my wife glanced at Patricia and said, "Gravayire Nawturi."

Patricia opened her mouth to speak or shout, but nothing came out.

"Next, both of you join hands with Patricia," Agnes ordered. "Layla will be the conduit between Sam and Patty."

Patricia's mouth was moving, but I wasn't paying her any attention as I clutched her hand tightly.

Agnes gave Layla the spell.

My wife's sunburst-yellow eyes brightened as she chanted, "By the power of water, the cleansing of air, the flames of fire, and the grounding of earth, I bestow nature's elements once again to Sam Mason." Layla trembled as if she was freezing cold. Her eyes flashed from yellow to blue to dark orange.

Suddenly, an electrical charge careened up my arm, and I felt as though a million bolts of lightning had zapped me. I closed my eyes briefly, welcoming the familiar tingling, throbbing, and pulsing that usually came with my elemental powers.

Layla's hand slipped from mine as her body went limp.

I caught her before she fell.

Patricia dashed up to the door that led outside, but Agnes was quicker as she yanked her niece down the stairs and held her hostage.

I bit into my wrist. "Drink, baby doll." I didn't know if she needed blood, but considering all the spells she'd performed and the fact that Roman had almost drained her, she was probably weak.

My wife suctioned her lips to my wrist.

Someone was pounding on the other side of the wall.

I petted Layla as her heart rate increased. "We have to go, baby doll. We're almost home."

As if the last word triggered something inside her, she pulled away. "I'm good."

I wiped the sweat off her forehead. "Are you sure?" If she wasn't, I would carry her.

She nodded a couple of times in quick succession. "Time is running out."

I grasped her hand. "Are you ready to show these fuckers how powerful we can be together?"

Layla's face lit up like the Fourth of July. Her ball-squeezing blue eyes had returned. "Fuck yeah."

"Then let's get Orion and Luna and go home," I said.

Home sounded like a pipe dream. But as long as Layla, my kids, and I were together, I didn't give a fuck if we lived in a tent.

**7**

---

# LAYLA

Sam cracked open the cellar door and peered outside. "I don't see anyone, but I hear an engine idling."

"Best thing to do is head for the cornfields," Agnes suggested. "We can hide there until we figure out our next move."

Agnes seemed to have drunk a high-octane energy drink. I also got the feeling she had been in tense situations before where she needed to think on her feet and act fast. A far cry from the frightened façade she'd given me up to now.

I quickly regarded Patricia. "Are we taking Patricia with us?"

We couldn't risk her escaping. When we finally left here, I didn't ever want to deal with her again, and without a doubt, she would definitely seek vengeance. There was no question about that in my mind.

Before I could track my husband, Sam snapped Patricia's neck. "We have no room for what-ifs. We end this tonight." His tone was rough and husky with furious undertones.

The sounds of bones breaking wasn't pleasant, but I wasn't complaining about what Sam had done. He was so freaking right. *Eat or be eaten.* That was something my dead uncle Ray had said

48

many times when preparing to hunt for vampires. Yet I felt a sting of nausea at killing a human and another family member. *But she would've hunted you and your children.*

Agnes sucked in air.

"Where are the cornfields in relation to where we are?" Sam barked at Agnes.

My grandmother flinched. "We're on the back of the main house. So we'll make two rights once we're outside. Then you should see the cornfields ahead."

More pounding reverberated the wall as if someone was breaking it down with a sledgehammer.

The three of us made it outside with Sam in the lead. We stayed close to the house as we cautiously but quickly made the two right turns.

The air had a chill to it as an eerie feeling blanketed me. Before Roman had bitten me, gunfire and the howling of wolves had lit up the night. Now, it was as quiet as a mouse as if our enemies were lurking and watching.

Sam held up a fist, indicating for us to wait. He peeked around the front corner of the house.

I glanced behind us. Something felt off, like it was a trap.

Then I heard Roman's voice coming from inside the house. I looked up, and the window was cracked open.

"What? They escaped? We're all out of men. It's just you and Ernie. We had Maeve and Patty as our weapons. Motherfucker!" Roman was more pissed than I'd ever heard him. Even before he'd bitten me, he was angry but not like he was now. "Find them and pump a box of tranquilizers into them."

Sam looked over his shoulder, jabbing his finger to the window above us.

"Living room," Agnes mouthed.

The cornfields were a stone's throw from us. But there was a light shining from the house in that direction. If Roman was by the window, he would see us or even hear our hearts beating. Hell, mine was racing like a horse at the Kentucky Derby.

I lost any sense of caring about Roman finding us when a baby's cry had me darting around Sam.

He caught me and shook his head.

I gritted my teeth. Our children were so close yet so fucking far that I was about to be sick.

He pointed to the cornfields and opened a telepathic connection. *Regroup. We'll get in there, but we need to be smart. I don't want to put Orion and Luna in any more jeopardy.*

I responded telepathically as a panicked mother to the calm father and soldier. *If we don't act now, we could lose them.*

He ran across the front yard with me tethered to him. I had no recourse but to follow since he was moving at breakneck speeds.

Agnes, brave and courageous, followed us, only she was slower.

*Our children are in that house*, I complained.

*Baby doll, I know how you're feeling. Please, trust me.*

Sam and I ran down the path between two rows of corn, leaves brushing against us.

"Sam, this way," Agnes said in a low voice.

We backtracked and followed her.

I was becoming dizzy, angrier, bordering on hysterical.

"We'll have a direct view of the house over here," she said, not sounding alarmed.

The more I learned about my grandmother, the more I liked her.

A voice peppered the air nearby, causing the three of us to stop cold.

Sam walked backward to the juncture where two rows converged amid the stalks that were twice as tall as Sam.

In a blur, someone lunged out from the cornstalks and tackled

Sam. The two flew deeper into the vegetation in a cacophony of grunts and growls.

We were far enough away from the house that I doubted Roman could hear us. Though he *was* a vampire.

"Sam?" Tripp's voice carried on the breeze. "Thank fuck you're okay."

The two hugged before emerging from the corn.

"Man, did you not notice it was me?" Sam plucked leaves from his hair.

Tripp fixated on me with his eyebrows up near his hairline. "I'm still a little off-kilter from that witch throwing me earlier. My head hit a tree trunk."

"That witch was Patricia," Sam said. "The same woman who kidnapped Orion and Luna out of the nursery. She admitted as much. She also used a cloaking spell, which was why the guards outside the house that night didn't see anything."

The guards had mentioned there was a distinct odor in the air. "She was the one who smelled like eucalyptus?" I clarified.

Sam nodded. "That's how I knew it was her. Anyway, Patricia is dead, and her mother Maeve is out of the picture. So the witches shouldn't be a problem."

Tripp was still staring at me, and if he had any questions for me, he didn't ask them. Instead, he put on his military hat. "I managed to get a closer look through the window as I was heading into the cornfields. I saw Roman, two men, and your two children."

Sam folded his arms over his chest. "One is a vampire named Ernie. The other is Warrick, Maeve's husband. I believe he was in the basement when we escaped."

"That leaves Roman and his guy upstairs," Tripp said. "Perfect. Because Ernie is the only one alive among Roman's men. Also, the second home on the property is empty."

"What's the plan?" I chomped on a nail. "Because we don't

have much time. Roman has men heading to the Catskills. Our daughters are in danger." I would die if Ellie and Rorie were taken.

"Where's Dane?" Sam asked. "He can call Cooper."

Tripp's jaw came unhinged. "Fuck. Unfortunately, Dane is hurt. The shifters took him to a nearby vet."

I was ready to puke. I had two babies inside the farmhouse and two others in jeopardy, and we had no way to help Ellie and Rorie or even my sister, Jordyn.

Tripp whipped out his phone. "I'll see if I can reach Cooper. Better yet, I'll have Kendra do it while we get Orion and Luna, and then we leave this place as fast as we can." He typed out a quick text to the female vampire. "Kendra's waiting at the private jetport. She'll call Cooper and your father. He can have a team and a chopper in the Catskills quickly." He pressed on his ear. "Kraft, come in. We have two of the four packages." He listened a second then continued, "You and Ben head toward the main house and take up a position across from the back deck. Copy that."

I felt a smidge better knowing Steven would jump into action for his grandchildren.

Sam rubbed his lips together. "Where are Olivia and Conrad?"

"A car drove up, and Adam jumped in. So they're tailing him."

"I heard Roman say something about his contact from Europe being here and taking Adam to their new headquarters," Sam said.

"Let's hope they lead us right to it." Tripp swung his bronze gaze to Agnes. "Give us the layout of the house," he commanded in his lieutenant tone.

As she outlined the floor plan, I removed the bandage from around my neck. It felt like it was strangling me all of a sudden.

Once she finished, I said, "Here's what I suggest. Roman doesn't know that I have my witch powers. Which is why my eyes are yellow," I added for Tripp's benefit since he'd been staring at me earlier. "I'll handle him while you guys deal with Warrick and Ernie. Have Ben and Kraft come in and grab Luna and Orion. Agnes can stay with a car. Do we have one?" I was dishing out orders as if I were the lieutenant.

"Our vehicle is parked on the road behind the property, which is about a mile out," Tripp said.

"Then we use Roman's SUV," Sam said. "It's perfect anyway. He had his man pack the vehicle with baby things."

I didn't care which car we used as long as we got the fuck out of here with our children. That was all that mattered. Hell, I would sprint with both babies in my arms if I had to.

Agnes cleared her throat. "Layla, you won't have me in there to help you with spells. Your strongest ability right now is your mind control. Use that." She flattened her hands on my face. "It's important to know that emotions play a role in witchcraft. So, I caution you." Her tone reminded me of my mother's. "If you don't want your loved ones to get hurt, it's critical your focus is on your target only. All too often new witches lose control, and everyone in their path suffers. Think before you act."

She just put a kink in my confidence, but I understood her caution. The problem was when facing off with an enemy, there was no time to think. A second's hesitation would be detrimental to me and the task at hand.

I nodded at Agnes. "I'll do my best."

She lowered her hands. "One last thing. If everything works in our favor and the babies are out of the house, I want you to commit this spell to your memory. Fire purifies. Fire cleanses. It's by my hand that this house doesn't stand. This is my will. This is my way. When I walk out, wash it away. Got it?"

"You want to burn down the house?" Tripp asked. "If so, Sam and I can do that."

Agnes's expression was serious. "I don't care who does. But in the event you two can't, you need a backup."

"I'm beginning to like you, Agnes," Sam said with a grin.

I repeated Agnes's words, praying I could remember the spell, and if I did, that it worked.

# 8

## LAYLA

I just wanted this night to be over with. I felt like we were walking through the fires of hell with no way out.

The four of us made our way to the edge of the cornfield, the same way we'd entered. Sam, Tripp, and I were ready to dart up to the porch when a bald man dressed in black came out.

He sniffed the air, his fangs elongating as he searched the area with a mechanical precision.

"Follow my lead." I jumped into the fray before Sam and Tripp could protest.

It was time for the fireworks to begin.

I swayed my hips, putting on a flirty smile. "My car broke down on the main road, and my cell is dead. Can I use your phone?" The lie fell out easily.

He sized me up, and I could feel Sam's hard gaze piercing my back as I inched toward the average-height vampire. I'd dealt with bloodsuckers most of my life, so he wasn't anything new. Except I didn't have any cobalt daggers on me. This time I had a better weapon—my brand-spanking-new witchcraft.

Baldy's forehead wrinkled. "Nice try, witch. I know who you are." He had the gun out of its holster before I could blink.

Smiling, I pictured blood coming out of his eyes as he shot himself in the head.

In seconds that image took shape, and butterflies took flight inside me. I had never thought that I would ever get used to magic, but I was loving the hell out of it. As soon as Baldy pulled the trigger on himself, Sam and Tripp came running. In a blur, both disappeared into the house.

Our enemy wasn't dead, but it would buy us time to do what we needed to do.

A baby's cry had me flying up the porch and in through the open front door.

Tripp wasn't in sight, and Sam was stalking around the staircase to my right.

The crying baby was magnetically pulling me in that direction until I was side by side with Sam in the living room. It took me a second to gain my bearings, but when I did, fury blinded me, and my heart fell out of my chest at the sight of Roman holding a gun to Orion's head.

Standing between the island and the stove, he threatened, "I will shoot him."

The floors began to shake, and a picture on the wall next to me fell to the living room floor. I didn't know if I was the one making the house rock on its foundation or Sam was.

It had to be my husband. He had his hands fisted at his sides, his head was bowed, and the formidable vampire was breathing heavily. "I told you, fuckwad, that I would chop off your limbs if I got free. But I'll do more than that if you so much as put a scratch on my son."

I swallowed down the bile creeping into my throat. "Roman, put him in that car seat next to his sister. Then we can talk. You can take me." I said all of that surprisingly calmly. Inside, I was anything but.

Sam whipped his steely gaze at me. "The fuck?"

Ignoring my husband, I fixated on Roman. "I promise that I'll leave with you. Just give my children to Sam."

Roman did a double take. "How the fuck did you get yellow eyes?"

"That's not the question you should be asking." I inched along the back of the couch toward Roman.

Tripp came into view and set his two daggers on the island next to Luna. Then he raised his hands. "Put the gun down. We can make a deal."

Orion was bawling as if he knew he was in danger. I wouldn't doubt he could detect tension.

Sam slid up next to me, his hands in the air as well. "You can have all my DNA. Sell it on the open market. You know it's worth millions. Think about it. Now that humans know vampires are real, scientists will be drooling to test vampire DNA. Hell, the human government would pay you a hefty amount for mine alone. Didn't you tell me in the basement that you wanted kids? Surely, if you want to be a father, Roman, you wouldn't do this."

*Roman wants children? Huh?* He would make a terrible father. But I was digging where Sam was going with his ploy. Psychological warfare, especially with a guy with an ego whose actions were driven by money.

Every cry out of Orion was sending shards of pain through my chest. My little boy needed his mom and dad. It broke me in two that he and Luna had been with these horrible people, and there was no telling what they had done to them.

As Roman considered Sam's offer, I was thinking of a way to hurt Roman without affecting Orion. If I made Roman's eyes bleed, Orion's might as well.

Roman considered Tripp, Sam, and me. He was stalling for something or someone.

"You have no men here, Roman," Sam said. "I heard everything you said when I was in the basement. Maeve is on her deathbed. Warrick is probably trying to revive her. Patricia is dead. Your man, Ernie, is down for the count outside. That leaves just you. What's it going to be, Roman?"

I could feel the rage dripping off Sam. *Make him bleed, and I'll snag Orion, and Tripp will take Luna,* Sam said telepathically.

"I'll make a deal," Roman finally said, not lowering the gun. "I'll call off my men in the Catskills, and in return, I walk out with your boy."

Sam choked on a growl. "The fuck you will."

Tripp hadn't moved as he glared at Roman. He was the closest one to our son and daughter.

Roman's bravado was irritating and maddening and driving the rage within me to new heights.

I lowered my chin slightly, keeping my sights on Roman, picturing blood pouring out of his eyes as Agnes's warning blared in my head. Nothing was happening. Probably because I was afraid that I might hurt my little boy.

*Concentrate, girl.*

Roman grinned at me. "You're not a true witch. Your eyes should be orange, not yellow. Maybe you're a witch outcast. You know, one of the rejects."

Sam's voice pierced my brain. *Now would be a good time to unleash your mind control.*

*I'm afraid whatever I do will affect Orion since Roman is holding him. What if I fuck up and the gun goes off?* I replied telepathically. I couldn't take that chance—but then, an idea hit me. *Sam, I'm going to have Roman shove the gun to his own head. When he does that, it will be a good time to snag Orion and for Tripp to grab Luna. Once the babies are away from him, I'll have Roman shoot his brains out.*

The *boom, boom, boom* of my heart rammed against my ribs. *See it. Repeat it. Believe it.*

Inhaling, I fixated on Roman, concentrating on the image of him raising the gun to his temple.

Nothing was happening except Roman laughing as if he'd won. "Reject."

I squeezed my eyes shut for a quick beat, then tightened every muscle, and once again, I imagined Roman shooting himself.

Roman's arm lifted and quaked. "What's going on?" he asked in horror.

My gaze never wavered as Sam slowly moved forward, and when Roman had the gun kissing his temple and his mouth ajar, Sam and Tripp pounced.

Sam pried Orion from Roman. "Rot in hell, asshole."

Tripp took Luna, and both men ran through the kitchen and out the sliding glass door.

Sweat was gliding down my nape as I stayed the course. Then the next few seconds were a blur.

A door creaked before a hefty man stalked up to the island with Maeve in his arms. "What the fuck are you doing?" he asked Roman.

Roman slowly swung his gaze from the man with a military-style haircut, who had to be Warrick, toward me, the weapon never wavering.

Warrick stomped toward me. "I will end you for what you did to my wife."

I had Roman point the gun at Warrick while I made blood come out of Warrick's hazel eyes.

Warrick smirked like he wasn't fazed. "I'm used to witches. You don't stand a chance." He marched into the living room like a soldier going to war and set Maeve's limp body on the couch.

I inched backward, looking at Roman, willing him to pull the trigger.

"Man, I can't stop myself," Roman complained as he shot Warrick in the back.

The hefty guy lurched forward and fell on top of his wife.

Sam returned, sidled up to me, and threaded his fingers with mine. The second our skin touched, an electrical charge danced up my arm.

"Feel that, baby doll."

Oh, I did, and the sensation rivaled anything I'd ever felt. It was electric and energizing. My senses sharpened even more.

Roman pressed the gun to his chest. "You know I'll live."

Not if I had anything to do about it.

Sam raised his free hand, producing a fireball in his palm that vanished. He tried again, and the same thing happened.

Sam opened up a telepathic connection. *My fire element isn't working. Say that spell Agnes told you to do. I don't know if it will help, but we can say it together. I remember the words.*

Sam had a way of compelling others by chanting a series of numbers, which to me was witchcraft, in a way. Maybe it would have more impact with both of us reciting the spell.

Roman snorted. "Seems you're screwed."

"You should've taken my deal," Sam fired back.

"Deal? You would've never followed through," Roman replied.

Sam and I said in unison, "Fire purifies. Fire cleanses. It's by my hand that this house doesn't stand. This is my will. This is my way. When I walk out, wash it away."

Nothing was happening.

Roman dropped the gun and charged in our direction.

Sam blocked him from me and threw Roman across the living room. He hit the fireplace, laughing.

Warrick groaned.

Sam stomped his foot once, opened his arms out to the sides, and lowered his head. Suddenly, glasses on the counter next to the sink rattled, furniture slid around, and a picture fell from the wall.

Roman hurried to stand.

Sam grinned at Roman, smug but deadly. "You die tonight." He lowered one arm and closed his hand into a fist. The couch with Warrick and Maeve on it moved toward Roman until the vampire was locked between the fireplace and the couch.

"I'll live!" Roman shouted. "You know this, Mason. Fire will burn me to the bone, but I'll walk out of here a skeleton. I've done it before."

Even if he was telling the truth, we were burning down this house no matter what. At least when I left, I would feel like I'd done everything I could to murder the bastard.

In a loud and commanding voice, I started again. "Fire purifies." My body began to vibrate with electricity. I held up my arms as if an invisible being was programming me. "Fire cleanses." Flames shot out of the fireplace, setting Roman aflame.

He screeched like a hyena.

"It's by my hand that this house doesn't stand." Flames crept up the wall on both sides of the hearth.

"This is my will. This is my way. When I walk out, wash it away," I chanted.

Heat and smoke filled the room as more furniture caught fire.

Sam rushed up to me. "Time to go."

"I will kill you both!" Roman yelled.

I hoped that asshole did die, but right now, we had Orion and Luna, and that was all I cared about.

**9**

---

## SAM

I grabbed Layla's hand as we flew off the porch and to Roman's idling SUV. The windows blew out of the living room just as Layla dove into the back seat and I jumped into the front.

Tripp gunned the gas, and I jerked forward before I had a chance to close the door.

Breathing heavily, Layla said, "Wait. I want to see if anyone comes out."

"The human authorities will probably be here in no time." He touched his ear. "Kraft, Ben, check in." He tore away from the property, cutting the wheel hard as we turned onto the main road. "Get out of there now. Meet us at the jetport."

"I'm surprised the cops haven't shown up, given all the gunfire earlier," Layla said as the firm click of her seat belt resonated behind me.

"Maeve knows the couple in the farm a mile from here," Agnes chimed in from the third row. "If I'm not mistaken, they're out of town. Other than them, there's a feed business and a machine shop nearby. And Warrick is in tight with a handful of cops. They use Warrick's shooting range on the property."

"But a fire is a different story." I turned and regarded Layla. "Baby doll, are you okay?"

"A little shaken, but I'll be fine." She lit up when she glanced at Luna in the car seat beside her. "Hey, baby girl."

I flicked my attention to Agnes. "How's Orion?"

After Tripp and I ran out of the house with Orion and Luna, Agnes had helped to secure them in the SUV, which was set up with two car seats for the babies.

"He's fine. He's sucking on his pacifier," Agnes said.

I popped my head against the seat as I faced forward, holding my chest, willing my heart to calm the fuck down. Fear had dug its claws into my soul, and I'd never been more frightened in my life. I would like to believe Roman wouldn't hurt a child, especially one who was too valuable to the genetic-altering program. But the fucker would probably do just about anything to save himself.

Tripp sped down the darkened two-lane road toward the city of Bismarck. "Dude, are you okay?"

"Not yet, man. I don't think I'll ever be able to erase that image of a gun being held to Orion's head." Truth. I would probably have nightmares for eons. With every death-defying event of the past few months, I swore I wouldn't sleep for a hundred years.

"Momma's here, baby girl. We're going home," Layla cooed to Luna.

Just hearing Layla's soft, sweet voice was soothing my nerves. "Whatever you do, man, don't stop. Keep driving as far from this fucking city as possible."

A hand landed on my shoulder before Layla said, "I love you, vampire. We did it. We have our Orion and Luna. But I'm worried about Ellie and Rorie now."

I briefly closed my eyes and touched her hand as my muscles tightened. "Where's your phone, Tripp?"

He fished his cell out of his cargo pants pocket and tossed it to me. "Passcode is 9245. Call Kendra and see if she got a hold of your father."

"I will, but first I want to call Cooper. We need to talk to someone on the compound."

Tripp's knuckles were white on the steering wheel. "He's in my contacts."

I found Cooper's number and tapped on it. The line rang several times before his voice mail picked up. After I left him a detailed message, I noticed Tripp had a text. I opened up the app.

"Kendra texted. She spoke to my father and said to call her as soon as we see this," I said, finding her name in his contacts. Once the line rang, I hit the speaker button.

She answered on the first ring. "Tripp." She sounded worried.

"It's Sam," I said. "Layla, Orion, Luna, Tripp, and Layla's grandmother are with me."

She sighed. "Thank God. I'd been sick with worry. Anyway, I spoke to your father. He already knew Roman had men in the Catskills. Cooper Gray called your sister, Jo, and told her they were under attack."

"No!" Layla cried. "Any word on my daughters or Jordyn?"

Tension, thick and soupy, stole the air from my lungs.

"I'm afraid not," Kendra said. "Steven sent a team with Jo and Webb. They're an hour from the shifter compound."

I had no doubt my sister was frantic, as was Webb. Their adoptive daughter, Abbey, was with the shifters.

I banged my head against the seat.

"When will we catch a break?" Layla mumbled.

"Tripp, Steven is scrambling to find a pilot," Kendra said.

A muscle ticked in Tripp's jaw. "So the plane isn't here?"

"Sorry," Kendra said. "Steven will call you when he has an update. There's a hotel not far from the jetport. I'll secure a bank of rooms and text the address to you." Then she hung up.

I punched the dashboard with the same hand I'd broken the bones in earlier. "I need blood." My gums throbbed, and my throat was bone-dry.

I also needed to run or fuck or bash a punching bag until it exploded.

Layla lashed out with several swear words. "Who else can we call on the compound?"

Dane had a strict communication plan, making it hard to contact anyone from his pack. Two-way radios were used on-site, and only a small group of shifters had cell phones.

I went through Tripp's contacts. "We need to get ahold of Dane. He'll be able to reach someone on his compound. Tripp, you said the shifters took him to a vet, right? Rebekah is with him, then."

"Yes," he said. "Her number is in my phone."

Red flashing lights illuminated the darkened road as a fire truck came toward us in the opposite lane.

I made quick work of calling the Special Forces medic, Rebekah, but failed. Then I tried my father. I had no luck on that front either.

Silence followed us for a mile.

"How do you know Kendra?" Agnes's voice broke through the hell I was burning in.

"Long story," Layla replied. "But not one I want to talk about right now."

Agnes was the key to understanding Layla's maternal side of the family—the Drakes and the Monroes. She was also Abbey's great-grandmother. Jo would definitely be excited to learn more about Abbey's mom, Rachel. My sister had been trying to locate anyone in Rachel's family. But I agreed with Layla. The last thing I wanted to do was talk about their family tree and the tangled web of who was who. Frankly, I didn't give a fuck.

"What I would like to know, Agnes"—I swiveled in my seat—"is why my fire element isn't working."

"What the fuck?" Tripp blurted. "Did the witches take your powers?"

"I got them back, thanks to Agnes," I said. "Or at least I got my earth element back."

Tripp slowed to a stoplight. "We need a weapon to fight against witches."

Layla sniffled. "You have one. Me."

I rounded my gaze on my beautiful wife. Her cheeks were flushed, and her auburn hair was messy, as if she'd been rolling around in bed. What I wouldn't give to be tangled between the sheets with her right now. "You were amazing tonight. I'm so proud of you."

I'd been in awe, watching her as she chanted the spell that had set the fire. What a sight to see. Her illuminated yellow eyes were brighter than the sun on a scorching summer day. Her siren voice was mesmerizing as she spoke each word with purpose, passion, and force. Dare I admit that my cock was jerking in my pants at how fucking stoked I was that my wife had magical abilities? Granted, she had a lot to learn, but with Agnes's help, Layla would be unstoppable. And she was right. We did have a weapon to fight against witchcraft. Above that, if the prophecy proved true that Layla would be the Mystic, then no one would be able to touch us or our children.

Our future was looking better by the day. Maybe that happily ever after we both wanted was within our reach.

"It might take time before you're one hundred percent again, Sam," Agnes said, breaking my concentration.

Layla twisted in her seat so she could see Agnes. "One thing I would like to know. Did Orion suffer from blood deprivation?"

I looked out the windshield at the city of Bismarck and listened.

"No," Agnes started. "Given the prophecies, we knew your children were inhuman. We also knew that one or all four had to be vampires. But Orion was fussy and cranky and crying nonstop. Adam still had a supply of Sam's blood from when Sam had been his prisoner."

"So Orion didn't drink anyone else's blood?" Layla asked.

"Maeve did try hers, but he got sick."

I growled.

"And Luna?" I asked.

"Luna didn't show any signs that she needed blood," Agnes said evenly. "So we didn't give her any. Besides, we had to ration Sam's blood because Adam didn't have much of it left. Maeve believes that Orion is the one who will turn witches into vampires."

"All of them could fit the prophecy," I mumbled.

If my children were vampire witches, I wondered what that meant in relation to the prophecy.

"You're right, Sam," Agnes said. "Or none of them will turn witches into vampires. Prophecies are predictions with loopholes and can change over time. However, witches believe prophecies to be true more often than not."

Zoey Thornton, the academic, had told Layla and me the same thing. Wouldn't it be nice if we didn't have to worry about any prophecy? Maybe then we wouldn't have the threat of witches—as well as every other power-hungry and curious human and supernatural on the planet—hunting us.

"Let's hope that neither prophecy has any substance to it," Layla said. "You know, maybe Dr. Vieira can run lab tests to see if any of our children's DNA mixed with a witch's can prove that a witch would turn into a vampire. He can use me as the witch subject."

I was digging the way she was thinking. "Great idea."

Tripp was nodding. "For sure."

Jo would be all over this since she was studying to become a doctor with a focus on genetics.

I checked on my beautiful daughter, more to shake off the effects of the last several hours than because I was worried about her. Instantly, my chest loosened.

Her violet orbs glimmered in the dark cab of the SUV. Her thick raven hair curled at the ends, and she seemed happy as she sucked on a pacifier.

For the moment, she was a balm to my frayed nerves. I pushed everything out of my mind but her. I still couldn't believe she was my blood. That Layla and I had made this amazing inhuman being.

"Hey, baby girl," I cooed in a voice that sounded foreign to me, basking in a bath of unadulterated love.

Layla held on to Luna's hand. "I will die if anything happens to Ellie and Rorie. I want all this shit to stop. No one has any right to our children. Why the fuck do they think they do?"

Layla's anxiety was amplifying my own. I reached around the seat and touched her leg. Electricity charged up my arm and kick-started my heart. "Jordyn will protect our daughters with her life." I had every confidence in Layla's sister. She might've screwed up a couple of times in the past, but she was dedicated to Layla and me. "The pack will protect them too. Cooper won't let anything happen to anyone on the compound." I tried to infuse as much assurance into my tone as I could. Not only for Layla's benefit but for mine too.

Luna spat out her pacifier, fidgeting in her car seat.

My heart swelled with a love that was both overwhelming and terrifying. I had failed to protect her, and that felt like a dagger to my chest. But for fuck's sake, I would not make the same mistake twice.

# 10

## SAM

We were hunkered down in a motel that required more repairs than a dilapidated home. The carpet in our room was riddled with burn marks. The walls were stained with brown spots, and a hot shower turned into a cold one when I'd stepped into it.

Despite these shortcomings, Layla, Orion, and Luna were safe and with me. I couldn't say the same for my other two daughters, Ellie and Rorie. Layla and I were sick with worry, not knowing what the fuck was happening in the Catskills. I wanted to tear out my hair, but I couldn't. I had to be strong for my wife, which was a monumental feat. Her panic was jumping off her and heightening my own—a double whammy that felt like my insides were going through a meat grinder.

From the time I'd woken up in the cage until we drove into the motel parking lot, three long, excruciatingly painful hours had ticked by. Layla and I still had more panic-filled time ahead of us as we waited for word from the Catskills.

"Jo and Webb and whoever went with them should be there

by now." Layla was sitting on the edge of a queen-size bed, wrapped in a towel and worrying her bottom lip.

Orion and Luna were asleep with pillows surrounding them on the other queen-size bed behind Layla.

As for me, I was in a chair across from my wife, lacing up my boots. "I'll check with Tripp and see if he's heard anything or if Dane is here at the motel yet."

When we'd pulled into the hotel parking lot, Sergeant Rebekah Whyte with Army Special Forces had phoned Tripp to fill him in on Dane's condition. The good news was that Dane was fine. He'd been shot in the stomach in wolf form and had a hard time shifting. Once the vet removed the bullet, he returned to human form. His prognosis was good since shifters healed quickly, although not as fast as vampires.

"I hate waiting." Layla sounded like she wanted to scream.

I buckled my belt, went over to the bed, and tugged Layla to her feet. "Come here, baby doll." Once her warm face was against my bare chest, a much-needed sigh escaped me. I smoothed a hand over her damp hair. She'd showered before I did while I watched Luna and Orion.

She clung to me tightly. "I'm exhausted, Sam. But I'm also sick with worry." Her voice trembled. "I want to disappear where no one can find us."

I guided her face to look up at me, and my pulse stuttered. Her eyes, once a bright shade of electric blue, appeared dull and fatigued, while her skin had taken on an ashen hue.

I had time to think in the shower about our next steps from here. "We'll look for a place as soon as we can. But for the fore-seeable future, the naval base will be our home until this war is over." Dane ran a tight and secure ship, but he and his enforcers weren't my SEAL team. "I know we left the naval base because of the mob of humans outside the gate and I had guardians on my ass. But I would feel better with the Vampire Navy SEALs protecting you and our children. We also have the military police and another SEAL team in Viking II."

She snuggled into me. "I do miss our apartment and the new nursery we never had a chance to use. To add to your point, we also need Dr. Vieira while the kids are growing. Which brings up a list of questions. Will they be walking earlier than human children would? I also want to know what their DNA results show. Are they all vampires or witches or both? Or is Orion the only vampire? Then there are both prophecies. And dare I say I'm curious what's happening with Rianne? Not that I want to see her. I don't. I'm also wondering about Carly."

I chuckled, feeling dizzy as she babbled all that. "Slow down, baby doll." At the mention of Rianne, I tightened my hold on Layla.

She eased away, biting a nail. "I'm sorry. My mind is racing with all these thoughts and questions. Not to mention, will other witches hunt us down to kill our child who's tied to the prophecy?" Her chest lifted. "My emotions are on a roller-coaster ride too. I'm angry, worried, in awe of my powers, and freaking out that our children are not safe yet." She slid her warm hands up my chest and neck, then dragged her nails along my unshaven jaw, searching my face. "Remember our handfasting ceremony and the vows we exchanged?"

I curled her hair around her ear, perplexed about how that fit into the conversation. "Of course. I'll never forget that memorable day." I swallowed and then regurgitated the exact words I'd spoken to her as she'd stood before me. Maybe hearing them again would quell her anxiety. "No matter where we come from, who we are—mortal or immortal, human or vampire—or what we believe, love is the great unifier. *Our* universal truth. My world is a better place with you in it." I placed her hand and mine on my heart. "You are the yin to my yang, the brightest star in my universe, and I give you my soul." I lifted my brow with a grin. "Those words?"

She cried, "Yes. I've been sitting here thinking of that day. How lucky I am to have met you. I couldn't imagine a life without you. As I said to you at the altar in front of family and friends, your ability to love me unconditionally is the most precious gift you could ever give me." Her lips trembled. "Our journey so far has been bathed in chaos, yet through it all, our love shines the brightest and always will." She brought our joined hands to her chest. "My heart will only beat for you. I'm honored to be your wife and partner." She rose up on her toes and placed a gentle kiss on my mouth. "I would like to add that you're my rock in times of weakness, my beacon of hope in the darkest of times, and you're my entire universe, Sam Mason."

I cupped her cheeks and captured her lips in mine. The kiss was sloppy, wet, hard, soft, and passionate. And before my brain caught up with my actions, I was flicking the towel off her. Nothing mattered for the moment except pleasing her.

I gripped her tight ass and mashed her body against my erection.

Her moan echoed through the quiet room as she crawled onto the bed and spread her legs.

What a fucking beautiful sight. Her damp auburn hair framed her face. Her tits were full, her nipples standing in perfect peaks, and her cheeks were flushed.

My cock jerked furiously against the fabric of my jeans as my eyes flashed from green to silver, my fangs clicking into place.

I was the luckiest fucking vampire in the world, and I was desperate to be balls deep inside her. But this little tryst wasn't about me, just her. She needed a distraction, to feel pleasure, not pain.

I grasped her ankles and gently pulled her to the edge of the bed.

"Strip, vampire."

I shook my head, kneeling. "No. This round is just about you."

She rested on her elbows, not protesting, pressing her feet on my shoulders.

I licked my lips, then one fang, tracing a circle around her inner thigh with a finger. "What's your pleasure, baby doll?"

"You know what I want," she said in a sultry tone.

I adjusted my painfully hard dick in my jeans. "I want to hear you say it."

She regarded me through hooded lids and lustful wonder. "I want you to bite me and do that move with your tongue where you lick really fast as you drink." She opened her legs wider, shoved a finger inside her channel, then pulled it out.

I sucked on that finger like I was a starving animal, and I was. I was beyond hungry to taste, feel, and smell every inch of her. Her signature cherry scent mixed with the hotel's coconut shampoo she'd used. No matter. I was digging the coconut fragrance too. The juices on her fingers tasted like sweet nectar, and my eyes rolled back in my head. Then I went wild, striking hard and fast, sinking my fangs into her creamy thigh.

She flinched but kept quiet, looking behind her at the other bed where Orion and Luna were.

I could hear Orion's and Luna's slow beating hearts and their deep breathing, telling me they were asleep. I gently pushed on Layla's stomach, urging her to relax. As I drank, I flicked my tongue faster and faster as her savory essence cooled the fire in my throat. Once I had my fill, I licked the puncture marks before capturing that swollen nub between my teeth.

She barely squealed.

"Relax," I whispered again.

"I feel like we shouldn't be doing this in front of them."

I flattened my tongue on her wet folds. "I could stop."

She checked on our children again. "They're sleeping." Then she gripped my head. "Eat me, vampire. I need this."

She didn't have to tell me twice. I feasted on her as I licked and sucked and fucked her with one finger, then two. "You're so fucking wet." That tingle in my lower spine warned me I was reaching that moment right before I blew my load, and a laugh broke out in my head. I wasn't even inside her nor was her mouth around my engorged cock, and here I was, ready to orgasm in my jeans.

I inhaled and exhaled.

"That's it, vampire. Harder."

*Fuck me.* Her erotic tone felt like she was stroking my cock.

"Play with your tits," I commanded, adding to my own torture.

She moistened her fingers in her mouth before she took her taut nipples between them, pinching and rolling. Her face was beet red, her mouth forming an O.

I finger fucked her as my tongue danced on her clit.

She locked her ankles around my neck, my face plastered against the most delicious spot ever.

Bunching the blanket in her hands, she rocked her hips, keeping a rhythm with my tongue.

"I'm almost there, and I want to scream so loud," she said through heavy breaths.

"Come for me," I commanded as I stuck my tongue in her channel and licked my way up to her extremely swollen nub.

When I did, she bucked and squirmed with soft moans.

I kept up my assault while she rode out her orgasm. As her body began to loosen, I rose and bent over, pressing my hands into the bed on either side of her, and indulged in her tits, only driving myself to the edge of an orgasm.

She latched on to my hair, pulled herself up, and smashed her mouth to mine. "Mm. You know what I would like?"

I nibbled on her tongue. "My cock?"

She lit up like lights on an airport runway. "I'm dying for him."

I was jonesing for her to suck me off, but then knuckles rapped on the door.

She flew off the bed, grabbed her clothes, and darted into the bathroom.

# 11

## SAM

A hint of car exhaust and the smell of trash from a dumpster somewhere nearby wafted in the cool August air as I stepped out of the motel room.

The white-haired alpha's red eyes glowed in the muted light as he leaned against the hood of Roman's SUV, which was parked only feet from my door. I wasn't a fan of the outside entrances of motels, mainly because of safety. But we were only here until the pilot arrived, which was hopefully soon.

Dane had both hands in his jeans pockets, one leg bent, his foot pressing into the bumper, wearing a scowl—his signature expression. The alpha always seemed to be in a pissed-off mood, but he'd had a rough night like the rest of us.

I didn't want to act like a dick and not ask him how he was feeling, but I needed to know if he'd called his brother Cooper. "Did you just get here? Did you talk to Tripp?"

My insides were trembling like a fast-moving marching band as I waited for him to speak.

It seemed Tripp was agitated as well. He was stomping up and down the parking lot near the road with his phone to his ear.

If any of the motel guests were peeking out the window, they would probably wonder why we weren't tucked into our beds at three in the morning.

A crease dented the spot between Dane's eyebrows. "Tripp told me, then I called Cooper immediately. Your girls are fine."

A loud sigh escaped me, sounding like a hissing steam engine. "Thank fuck." I poked my head into the motel room. "Layla," I called.

She was just coming out of the bathroom. "Sorry, my stomach is acting up. So?" She hurried outside, leaving the door cracked open.

"Ellie and Rorie are fine," I said.

She squealed. "And my sister?"

Dane fixated on Layla, long and hard. No question he had bad news on Jordyn.

I tucked Layla into my side.

He blinked once. "I'm afraid it's not good. Our doctor is doing everything she can to save her." A large gust of wind blew out of Dane's mouth. "Tripp is on the phone with Steven now."

Layla turned into my chest, her body racked with sobs. "She doesn't deserve any of this. I should've never left her."

I rested my chin on her head. "She's in good hands with the shifter's doctor." I shot Dane a questioning look. "What happened?"

He shrugged, frustration washing over him. "I only got bits and pieces. Roman sent thirty men. But not all of them work for him. I guess the man who picked up Adam Emery tonight is supposedly Draven Murphy, whoever the fuck that is. Conrad would know more."

My eyebrows came together. That wasn't good.

Draven Murphy came from one of the oldest vampire families in Europe. Like his counterpart, Roman, Draven ran a thriving blood cartel business. The two had butted heads several times with Draven stealing major clients of Roman's. Both were nutjobs in different ways. Whereas Roman liked to play games with his enemies, Draven attacked without question. He had a penchant to behead anyone who pissed in his direction. Which led me to believe that was where Adam got the idea to chop off heads.

Layla sniffled as she faced Dane once again. "What happened to my sister?"

Dane crossed bulky arms over his chest. "She was fleeing to a cave we have carved into the mountains outside the compound. I don't know the details of how it all went down. But two vampires were hot on her tail. Jordyn was shot twice and also suffered a blow to the head. Part of her injuries were from Abbey's magic. Jordyn got caught in it when Abbey was waving her hands and sending the bloodsuckers to their deaths over the cliff."

Layla snapped her jaw shut, shaking her head, squeezing her hands together to the point that the blood was pooling in her fingertips.

Instantly, images of Layla hanging over that cliff outside Dane's compound brightened before me. My heart had literally stopped that night I'd found her barely hanging on over the chasm, thanks in part to a powerful dream walker, the seasoned witch known as Maeve Monroe. She'd forced Layla to sleepwalk almost to her death simply because she needed my wife dead to break the connection with our children. That had been the first step toward Maeve becoming the Mystic.

I held Layla tightly as she sobbed. "Any other casualties?" It sounded to me that Abbey was fine, although a ten-year-old killing someone, even a vampire, had to be hard on her.

Dane growled. "We lost five shifters. We have three vampires in custody. Several are dead, and we think eight fled."

Layla shuddered. "I want to be there now. Jordyn needs me. Who has Ellie and Rorie?"

"I believe Jo does," Dane said.

For the moment, I took comfort in knowing Ellie and Rorie were in good hands with my sister.

Tripp waltzed over and handed me the phone. "Your father wants to talk to you."

"Pops, give me a second." I didn't wait for him to answer as I lowered the phone and kissed Layla on the ear. "Will you be okay?"

She nodded. "I'll be in the room. Please ask your father to send a pilot as fast as he can." She turned on her heel, went inside, and shut the door.

I was completely gutted. Layla couldn't lose Jordyn. My wife had lost too many family members already. I wasn't sure Layla would ever recover if Jordyn didn't make it.

I walked away from Tripp and Dane as the two began talking. Then I heard a door open, and Conrad's voice filtered out on the August breeze. I guessed he and Olivia had returned from tailing Adam and Draven Murphy.

I raised the phone to my ear. "Hey, Pops."

"I finally have a pilot en route now," he said. "He should land at the jetport in two hours. That's the best I can do."

"Thanks, Pops." I crossed the parking lot to a sidewalk along the road.

"Look, son. We don't think Jordyn is going to make it. You need to prepare Layla."

*How the fuck do you prepare anyone for death? You can't.*

My boots scuffed on the sidewalk that ran alongside the motel. "Dane said Jordyn was shot twice and took a blow to the head."

"Sadly, Abbey's magic was wild and uncontrollable," my dad said. "Jordyn was thrown several feet, and she landed on her backside on a large rock. Not to mention the two bullets. She's being medevaced to our Boston medical facility. Dr. Vieira is in a chopper now, en route to Boston. We also have a surgeon from Mass General and a good friend of Dr. Vieira's meeting him at our facility. Please let Layla know we're doing everything we can to save Jordyn."

A ball of emotions was clogging my airway. Just when I thought we were nearly out of the woods—bam! Another blow to the heart. "How are my daughters? Do you know?"

"I do. I'm here at the scene in the Catskills. I decided at the last minute to accompany the team. Rorie and Ellie are great, and they are absolutely precious." He choked up. "I'm sorry I haven't met them sooner."

I quietly cried as I walked down a darkened street lined with airport businesses. "Don't beat yourself up. I've hardly spent any time with my family. I can't wait to see them and you."

"Son, I'm relieved that you and Layla got out of there with Orion and Luna. I'm also glad that we didn't lose anyone on the team. Adam has threatened to start sending me body parts if I don't release his brother and Carly. He's already sent me a picture of Matthew's head."

"Adam practically shoved Matthew's head in my face."

"We don't bargain with enemies," he said. "Given all that has happened since Layla delivered my grandchildren, we have a lot to catch up on, son. We're also not about to figure out Adam's next move today. I have fifty heads of state in the country that have large teams behind them. We will locate Adam. Of that, I have no doubt."

When I came to the end of the road, I glanced up at the star-ridden sky as the moon cast a glow in the distance. "You sound like a weight has been lifted off your shoulders."

"I don't have the Council of Elders to deal with anymore. And I'm building my team with those I trust, and Samuel, you'll be part of that. It's a new era for us. It won't be an easy road, but with the right people in place, I believe we can build strong relationships with those humans who run this country."

"What role do you have in mind for me?" I was curious.

"Webb and I are still tossing around a couple of ideas," he said. "But don't worry about that right now. I'll have two cars waiting when you land. I love you, son. I'll see you later today." Then he hung up.

My father was right. We were entering a new era. A scary one, in my book. Now that humans knew that vampires existed, I believed they were our biggest threat. Their population far outnumbered ours, and I wouldn't be shocked if hunters came out in droves. I wasn't afraid for me or Layla either, to a certain extent. Now that she was a witch, she could protect herself. It was our children's lives that would keep me up at night, and by the time they reached their teenage years, I would probably be the first vampire ever with a full head of white hair.

**12**

---

# LAYLA

Dark, angry clouds skated by outside the plane's window, appropriate for the storm raging inside me. Time seemed to move infinitely slowly. Each passing moment felt like an eternity, each second ticking by with agonizing sluggishness. As the plane jetted across the country below us, my mind raced with it as I thought about Jordyn fighting for her life. No one had to tell me that she stood a good chance of dying, and somehow the weight of that knowledge made me feel as if I were the one who was about to take my last breath. The conflict within me was palpable, a struggle between hope and despair, faith and doubt. I could only wait and pray that she would make it through, hoping against hope that she would emerge victorious in this life-and-death battle.

I briefly closed my eyes, trying to focus on the myriad of other things and questions bouncing around my brain like a bowl of out-of-control jumping beans.

I couldn't wait to see Ellie and Rorie and reunite them with their brother and sister, who were behind me with their daddy. Sam wanted to watch them while I relaxed.

The only relaxation I would enjoy would be a five-year vacation with no enemies hunting us, no one trying to kill me or anyone in my family, and no one out to steal my children.

It would also add to my comfort if Roman Brown had burned to a crisp and was now walking in the fires of hell. Though, knowing that asshole, he probably did survive, just like he bragged he would. *"Fire will burn me to the bone, but I'll walk out of here a skeleton. I've done it before."*

In between my thoughts, I'd been catching bits and pieces of Sam, Tripp, and Dane's conversation. They were talking about how to take down Adam, the potential issues we were facing with humans, and a host of other topics, including Dane's brother Ross. Dane was extremely nervous after hearing about Matthew Costner's death. If in fact Ross was Adam's prisoner, Dane was afraid his brother's head might be next. Nerves were definitely heightened all the way around. Anyone on our team could be Adam's next victim.

I swung my gaze from outside the window to my grandmother. Agnes was snoozing in the seat across from and facing me. As I studied her, I wondered what life would've been like if I'd known her growing up. Maybe back then, my sisters and I would've been practicing magic from an early age. Which led me to think that if I was a witch, did that mean Jordyn was as well? Rianne even? How would that play out if Rianne became a witch while she was a monster? That wasn't something I had any desire to see.

Nevertheless, the years hadn't been kind to Agnes. Her short hair was a silvery white. She had deep wrinkles marring her face and neck. I would guess she was in her early sixties but certainly not a frail woman. The yoga pants she'd borrowed from me accentuated her slender waist and wide hips, and the T-shirt she was wearing hugged her small bustline. She did look better now that she wasn't wearing soiled pajamas.

All of us were clean after hot showers and fresh clothes. Sam and I had packed our luggage in Conrad's car before we'd stormed the farm, and the vampire scout had shown up at the motel not long after Dane had given us the bad news about Jordyn.

Agnes opened her glossy brown eyes. "I can feel you staring at me."

"Sorry. You look like my mom."

She gazed out the window, crossing one leg over the other. "When your mom was growing up, lots of folks said the same thing."

"I resemble my dad, but my sisters are more like our mom."

"No one in my family or my husband, Derrick, had red hair. So I figured as much." She sat up straighter. "Thank you for allowing me to stay with you until I can figure out what to do with my life now that Maeve is gone." A hint of sadness threaded through her tone.

I sympathized with her over the loss of her sister. Maeve was just as evil as my paternal grandmother, Harriet Aberdeen, had been. Actually, more so, since Maeve was a witch. Still, when I jabbed a syringe of that genetic-altering serum into Harriet, I thought it would've felt good to see her take her last breath. In a way it had, but a part of me had wanted to puke. Taking a life was never easy, especially a family member's. But in a supernatural world where the cliché eat or be eaten was so flipping real, Harriet wouldn't have stopped gunning for my babies and their DNA. She'd thought they were her saviors for her incurable blood cancer.

"Maeve would've killed you and me," I said.

"I know." Agnes picked lint off her yoga pants. "She would've had Patricia do her dirty work."

A thought surfaced about Patricia. She had helped kidnap Orion and Luna. She'd confessed she was at the house in Maine that night. Was she the brown-haired woman in my recurring dream? She had to be even though the woman had red eyes. Or maybe they were reddish orange.

"Anything wrong, Layla?" Agnes asked. "You're wrinkling your nose."

"Just thinking of something. When I found out I was pregnant, I started having dreams of a young boy with green eyes on a dark road. Over time, the dreams began to reveal more. But there was always the same young boy. Not long before Orion and Luna were kidnapped, a brown-haired woman showed up in that dream. I never saw her face except her red eyes. I assumed it was my sister Rianne since she'd taken the serum. Maybe it was Patricia. I know witches have orange eyes, not red. Am I making sense?"

She frowned. "It saddens me that Rianne chose the dark side."

Agnes and I had a small window to chat while we'd been waiting for the pilot to arrive. After I told her what happened to Jordyn, she'd asked me about Rianne. I ended up explaining how my sisters and I had gotten to this juncture in our lives.

"As Jordyn would say, Rianne chose her path." I briefly glanced at the dark clouds outside the window. "I'm so overwhelmed with everything, and as I look back on my dreams, I can't help but wonder if I could have prevented Orion and Luna from being kidnapped."

She leaned forward slightly. "Layla, you can't blame yourself. You also can't rely on dreams. I'm not saying don't pay them any mind but just to take them with a grain of salt. In our world, they're windows into the future. But they don't reveal every detail. For example, the seer who envisioned the prophecy only saw an inhuman child born to a Monroe witch turn the Monroe coven into vampires. Nothing further in that vision was revealed. So we still don't know if it includes all witches or if we will lose our powers or when that would happen. We assume and speculate, and we run scared or act like Maeve and other witches, wanting to kill so that the prophecy doesn't come true."

"I understand. I'm just looking back at the signs. The little boy in my dream looks like Sam. Is he Orion? If so, is my son trying to warn me about something in the distant future? He'd said I had to help his sister."

She crossed one leg over the other. "Maybe. Maybe not. Layla, your children are safe now. Take a breath. I'm here to help and guide you. I know you probably have lots of questions about witchcraft, and we'll get to them."

We certainly had many things to discuss, and right now we had plenty of time since we were on a plane.

"We don't land for another hour," I said. "Maybe we can talk now."

"Sure. Where do you want to start?" she asked.

I bit my lower lip. "While we're on the topic of dreams, will I be able to dream walk like you?"

I recalled Sheriff Stan's administrative assistant, Grace, explaining the difference between a dream walker and a shared dream. *"Dream walkers make deliberate efforts to walk into a person's consciousness and gain control over their space, and the powerful ones can control your actions, whereas a shared dream is done without control."*

"Possibly," Agnes said. "But that feat takes years of practice, and first you need to understand the basics. For example, the difference between a blood spell, a nonblood spell, and your natural witch ability."

I could feel my eyebrows drawing down. "When you say natural, you mean my mind control? I had that ability when I was pregnant. It wasn't my strongest, but I assumed my children gave me magical powers."

She shrugged. "In a way, they did. But they couldn't have unlocked your true potential. If you hadn't drunk my blood, then whatever powers you had while pregnant probably would've died off."

"So why do some spells need blood and others don't?"

"Ah, yes. The Monroes are blood witches. We activate our powers by the blood of an older Monroe witch. As you have done by drinking mine. So some of our spells will require blood to work. Whereas the nonblood witches can't perform the spells we do, like the one you used on Maeve. And the one she'd been about to cast on you would've boiled you from the inside out if she'd given you her blood."

I shivered at the thought, then something occurred to me. "Abbey is a Monroe. But her mom is dead. So how does she have magic?"

She bobbed her head. "I've been thinking about that. The only way is that Rachel had to have given Abbey her blood at some point before Rachel died. She probably wanted to make sure Abbey had her powers. After all, Rachel was in hiding, and she probably feared for Abbey's life, and she wanted to be sure Abbey had a way to protect herself."

That certainly made sense. I couldn't help but think, what if my mom had accepted who she truly was? Then she could've used her powers to help my dad kill vampires. But I couldn't change the past. I was just grateful that I had Agnes's help.

"Thank you for saving me and Sam," I said.

She pinned her brown gaze on me. "I'm happy I had the chance. And I will do whatever is necessary to help in any way I can, Layla." Her tone was heartfelt.

I leaned into the space between us and held out my hands. "I would like that very much." As much as I needed her so I could grasp my newfound powers, I also would like to build a relationship with her.

She held my hands, her eyes brimming with tears. No words needed to be spoken. It was a quiet exchange of feelings between two relative strangers bound by a shared bond of blood.

Letting go of her, I sat back. "Agnes, I know life might be awkward for you around vampires. But everyone in my extended family are the best creatures you'll ever meet. I also haven't thought about where you'll stay. But rest assured we'll figure something out."

While I hadn't been a good reader of people in the past, especially with those I trusted, Agnes deserved a chance. Not to mention, she'd proven herself so far. Plus, she was Abbey's great-grandmother, and Jo would want a chance for her adoptive daughter to meet someone who shared the same bloodline.

"I'm not worried," she said. "I'm just grateful. I want to get to know you, Jordyn, and Abbey."

Turbulence rocked the plane.

"Fuck," Sam growled.

My strong and powerful husband hated flying. He'd claimed it could be a death sentence for a vampire. It could for humans as well.

Agnes gripped the arms of the chair. Seemed she didn't like flying either.

"Sam, are the babies okay?" I peeked around my seat at him.

He was across the aisle and behind but facing me. His handsome features were tight. "They're doing better than me."

"Bloodsucker is afraid to fly?" Dane chided. "Well, now."

Sam threw Dane the finger.

I could only see the backs of Dane's and Tripp's seats.

I blew my hubby a kiss before returning my attention to Agnes.

"I'm not a fan of flying either," Agnes said.

"I have more questions to distract you," I said.

I could ask all about her past and my mother's as well, and I would love to hear stories about my mom growing up, but it would be best to save that topic for when Jordyn could be present. *Please let Jordyn get to hear the stories.*

I clasped my hands in my lap. "While I believe in the supernatural, I'm having a hard time wrapping my mind around the idea that I could be the Mystic. For one thing, I know I fit the definition since I had quadruplets. I also know that a Mystic has the power of a coven. But so what? If I hold the title, what can I do with all that power? Raise the dead?"

She paled. "First, dark magic should never be performed. There are severe consequences. The saying 'a life for a life' is true if a witch raises someone from the dead."

"As much as I would love for my mom and dad to be alive, I wouldn't do such a thing. But if I'm hearing you right, a Mystic has the power to bring someone back to life?"

She rubbed her arms as if she was cold. "Yes. Which is one reason the witches are scared. But our knowledge about a Mystic is thin at best. The last known Mystics were in the seventeenth century. In today's world, we don't know what to expect, which is another reason our community is apprehensive. Are you the Mystic?" She shrugged. "If Maeve's vision is true, then I believe you are. I'm not a scholar on the topic. It would be best to bring Zoey Thornton into the fold. After all, she teaches on the subject of prophecies at Sacred Flame Academy. I can call her and see if she can sit down with us."

"That would be great. I'm sure she'll love to hear from you anyway." After all, Zoey and Agnes were friends. At one time, Agnes had considered sending her daughters, Vanessa, my aunt, and Meredith, my mother—to the school.

Sam's woodsy scent announced him as he joined us with Orion in his carrier. My son was wide awake, his green eyes bright and happy as he sucked on his pacifier.

I reached in and picked him up. "How are you, little one?" I cradled him in my arms. "You feel like you've gained weight." Or maybe I was feeling weak since I hadn't slept.

Tripp and Dane joined us as well, both sitting in the seats across the aisle. Tripp brought Luna and her carrier with him.

Sam rested a hand on my leg. "Sorry, I didn't mean to interrupt. I think all of us would like to be better informed about the Mystic."

Agnes regarded her captive audience. "To be a Mystic is an honorable role for a witch, according to my mother. It's been whispered through the ages that a Mystic is a healer and has the foresight to see into a person's soul."

I reared back. "Heal? How?"

Aside from the plane's engines, a pin drop could be heard.

"I don't know," Agnes said. "Again, Zoey is a good person to talk to about this."

I thought about what my mom had said to me when I'd died and had seen her in the afterlife. *"The world needs you. You and Sam are instrumental in making sure humanity survives."* I wondered if my role as the Mystic was a way to ensure mankind flourished.

I kissed Orion on his thick head of hair. "Do you know how one becomes the Mystic?"

"I only know what Maeve learned through her research," Agnes said. "Apparently, there was a witch in the seventeenth century who killed the one destined to be the Mystic. Similar to what Maeve was about to do with you, Layla. Anyway, Maeve learned that she needed to break the connection you have with your children. Then she needed a coven of witches along with your children to help her perform the ritual. Whether that's how a true Mystic comes into her powers, I couldn't say."

Tripp leaned his elbows on his knees, watching Agnes with shock and awe. Dane, too, wore a distinct look of *what the fuck.*

"Now that Maeve is out of the picture," Sam said. "She's not a threat to Layla anymore. My concern is—will a child of mine turn witches into vampires? You've been around a long time, Agnes. I understand that the Monroe witches are not well-liked because of this prophecy. Will we have witch hunters coming after our children?"

"There's always that threat," she said. "Prophecy or not."

Sam's nostrils were flaring. "We'll have the entire world after our kids."

Tension blew through the cabin, though the plane ride was smoother now.

Tripp cleared his throat. "I'm curious about something off topic. Sam filled me in on how you and Maeve met Fred Emery two years ago when he was looking for Abbey. But tell us how Maeve got wind of Layla and the quadruplets. From our end, we had two moles within our organization feeding Roman information about the quadruplets. So how did Maeve know Layla was a Monroe witch?"

Agnes flicked her gaze at Tripp. "When Maeve had the vision six years ago, she thought her daughter, Patricia, might become the Mystic. Then, her vision wasn't that clear. After Maeve learned that Abbey was a Monroe, she added Abbey to her list. But two months ago, Maeve woke up frantic and excited. She'd seen who the Mystic would be. The woman had auburn hair and sharp blue eyes."

Sam scratched his unshaven jaw. "But she didn't know that woman was Layla."

Agnes shook her head. "No. Maeve kept in contact with the Emery brothers because of Abbey. In a call she made to Adam over a month ago, she wanted to know where he and Roman were in their plans to kidnap Abbey. That was when Adam told her that Sam was now a father to quadruplets and that Abbey wasn't as high on his priority list. The babies were. From there and through questioning him further, Maeve found out Sam had gotten a red-haired, blue-eyed lady pregnant. My sister didn't believe in coincidences. After Adam told her all about Layla, he put Maeve in touch with Harriet Aberdeen. She shared everything about Layla's life, as well as Meredith's, and told her how Meredith died of breast cancer. After that call, we knew everything about Layla, Sam, the Vampire Navy SEALs, Jordyn, Rianne—you name it."

Sam and Tripp snarled when they heard Harriet's name.

I did as well while playing with Orion's feet. "Harriet is dead now." Yet she was still a fucking thorn in my side.

The pilot came on the overhead speaker. "Folks, we are making our descent into Boston. Please make sure you're in your seats with your seat belts fastened."

Once everyone, including our children, was safely strapped in, I sighed as a queasiness began to swirl inside me. Before we'd boarded the plane in Bismarck, Steven had sent a text to Tripp telling him that Jordyn was going into surgery. That was well over four hours ago. My pulse began to race as I wondered if Jordyn was still alive.

**13**

---

# LAYLA

**T**wo guards were posted at the gate leading into the underground garage of the vampires' Boston medical facility. Once they confirmed who we were and waved both vehicles through, a metal-grated barrier rolled down from above and sealed us in.

The bulletproof Escalade that Sam, Orion, Luna, and I were in wound around the corner, the tires screeching and echoing. Agnes, Tripp, and Dane were in the car behind us.

Once again, time seemed to stand still as we slowly passed a row of cars. Even the journey from the airport to the medical facility crawled at a snail's pace because of an accident and bad weather. An August summer storm was wreaking havoc over the city.

I bounced my foot as I sat in the back seat behind the driver with Orion and Luna next to me. "Where are we going?" I was itching to wrap my arms around my daughters, Ellie and Rorie, and to see Jordyn.

As the plane had touched down, Tripp's phone had pinged with a message from Steven. Jordyn had made it through surgery, though her condition was still critical. I'd been so relieved that I'd cried, squealed, and threw myself at Sam. She wasn't out of the woods yet, but my sister was a fighter, and that was the hope I would cling to for now.

Sam regarded me from the passenger seat. His mesmerizing green eyes sent a wave of calm through me. "There's an elevator on the other side. You'll see it soon enough."

Steven, Jo, and Webb came into view as they stood by the elevators. Jo was dressed in scrubs and a lab coat. Steven and Webb were decked out in their signature Vampire Navy SEALs uniforms—black T-shirts, cargo pants, and military boots that were spit shined.

Finally, the driver of the Escalade stopped.

I unclipped my seat belt when Steven opened the door, reached in, and extended his hand.

"Is Jordyn okay?" I asked as I climbed out on trembling legs.

Steven wrapped strong arms around me. "Nothing has changed since I sent Tripp that text."

I held on to my father-in-law, burrowed my face into his chest, and cried.

He petted my hair. "Shh. She's in good hands with the medical team here."

Voices echoed in the cement-enclosed space as "Welcome home" and "Good to see you" zipped around.

After Steven and I broke apart, Jo gave me a teary-eyed grin before she was squeezing me to her. "I'm so glad nothing terrible happened to you." She leaned away. "Ellie and Rorie are doing great. They're with Dr. Vieira. He's examining them. It's more of an overdue monthly checkup than anything."

The black-haired beauty was reading my mind, a supernatural talent that not many of us liked but a weapon that came in handy during interrogations with our enemies when they wouldn't talk.

"Orion and Luna definitely need to have a full exam," I said, sniffling and dashing away tears as I finally got my bearings.

"They will," she said. "This must be Agnes." Jo walked over to my grandmother, obviously eager to meet the woman who held answers to Abbey's past. "I'm Jo, Abbey's adoptive mother," she said to Agnes.

I tuned them out as Webb joined his wife, and the three began chatting.

Dane was leaning against a car at the far end of the garage with his phone to his ear.

Tripp was holding Luna in her carrier, and Sam had Orion.

I closed the distance from the Escalade to the elevator where Sam, Steven, and Tripp were standing.

"This is your grandson, Orion," Sam said to his dad.

As soon as Steven picked up his grandson, the hardcore features of the imposing elder Mason softened to mush. "Hi there. You sure do look like your dad."

My son resembled not only his dad but also his grandfather—green eyes and black hair, although the shades of green varied between Orion and Sam. Whereas Sam's were a forest green, Orion's eyes were more of shamrock color.

I couldn't stop the tears as I watched my father-in-law dote on my son.

Then Steven traded Orion for Luna and pressed her to his chest, securing her with his large hands. "No one will ever hurt you, precious one."

Sam watched in emotional fascination as he tucked me close to him. "I've never seen my dad that way."

Our heartwarming reunion was shattered when a phone chirped, startling me.

Jo pulled her cell from her lab coat pocket. "It's Dr. Vieira. He wants to know if the group arrived yet."

Steven kissed his granddaughter and returned her to her carrier as Webb, Jo, and Agnes ambled up.

"How is my niece?" Sam asked, regarding Webb.

"She's deeply shaken up." Webb, the stoic brown-haired and blue-eyed vampire who was normally known for his blank expressions, had anger stamped on his unshaven jaw.

No ten-year-old should be fighting in a war. I imagined Abbey had to be sick to her stomach after killing those bloodsuckers even though they were our enemies. My first kill as a vampire hunter had me peeing my pants and throwing up.

"Alia is with her," Jo added. "And Alia knows Matthew is dead." She looked sorrowful as she spoke. "I'm brokenhearted that we lost Matthew."

"And Alia's father, Victor?" Tripp asked as he pressed the elevator button.

"Still no word from him," Webb replied.

"We can talk about all this later." Steven nodded at Webb. "Grab Dane, and then you head with him and Tripp to the conference room. Sam and I will meet you there after I show Layla to Jordyn's room. Jo, can you take the babies to Dr. Vieira? I want to talk to Sam and Layla for a moment."

"Of course, Dad," Jo said. "Agnes, why don't you come with me? I would love to chat and also for you to meet Abbey."

Several minutes later, after the elevator doors closed, Sam, Steven, and I were alone. Steven scrutinized Sam and me with a deadpan expression—a far cry from his emotional display with Orion and Luna.

"What is it, Pops?" Sam squeezed me to him as if he wanted to protect me from whatever Steven had to say.

As an empath, Sam could read another's emotions like Jo could read someone's mind.

A feeling of dread crept into my chest and settled like a ten-ton boulder in my stomach. I couldn't bear the thought of more bad news. Hell, I couldn't even imagine what else could go wrong. And yet, with everything that had already happened, how could I expect anything else? I knew whatever he was about to say had to relate to something that affected both Sam and me. But Jordyn had made it through surgery, and my children were home. Unless he was about to tell us that Rianne had somehow escaped from prison.

"Please tell me that you're not about to say Roman Brown is alive," Sam said.

Steven scrubbed a hand along his chin. "We don't have confirmation on him yet. Layla, your uncle Jack and aunt Tabitha will be flying in to see their son, Noah. Jack will call when he makes their flight arrangements."

I slumped my shoulders, relieved that he didn't say Roman was breathing. Although that wouldn't surprise me. But also, the news of my aunt and uncle coming to visit wasn't earth-shattering. I hadn't seen Aunt Tabitha since the day Sam and I had gotten married. They'd paid a visit to the naval base to retrieve my uncle Ray's body and their son Junior's as well. Ray had died of a heart attack, and sadly, my cousin Junior had lost his life in a car accident.

My aunt Tabitha was a strong individual. In my book, she had to be to put up with my crotchety uncle Jack and six kids. Plus, she'd fought off vampires many times. Regardless, her emotional backbone had cracked several times after losing Junior, and even though she hadn't seen Noah since he'd surrendered his humanity, my aunt would never be the same again.

Sam and Steven were talking about Noah, and as I came out of the fog I was in, I heard the word *painless*.

"I'm sorry," I said. "I wasn't listening all that well."

"Dr. Vieira feels it's time to end Noah's life," Steven said. "Which is why I reached out to Jack. We feel he and his family need to know the next step. Noah is at the point he doesn't know who he is anymore."

Growing up, Noah and I had mostly butted heads. He was a class A jerk, but he was family. Yet he'd sided with the enemy, just like my sister Rianne had. That didn't mean he had to die, but the physical state he was in as a feral monster was no way to live.

I hugged myself. "Has Rianne's condition progressed to the point of Noah's?"

"She's on her way there," Steven said. "She's changing quickly. She's stronger, her features are more pronounced, and she's losing the ability to shift into human form. Dr. Vieira's studies on both Noah and Rianne have produced very similar results despite Rianne's supernatural bloodline. He suspects that Rianne will eventually not know who she is, just like Noah."

I'd put my heart and soul into trying to talk my sister out of taking the serum. But she was adamant about becoming a super-natural soldier in order to eradicate vampires—Sam Mason in particular. Her main goal was to kill my husband, and she felt the only way to do that was to be like him.

"We should end her suffering," I whispered, feeling pangs of sadness in the pit of my stomach.

Steven clutched the sides of my arms, setting his soft gaze on me. "Dr. Vieira wants to wait a little longer as he runs more tests on Rianne. For the time being, I don't want you to worry about her."

I craned my neck to look up at Steven. "Thank you. I'm so grateful that you're in my life. I couldn't have asked for a better father-in-law."

"You're family." He pecked me on the forehead. "I love you, Layla, like you were my own daughter."

I hugged Steven. "I love you as well. You've opened your heart and home for me when you had no reason to, considering I was your enemy."

Steven gestured for Sam to join us. "Come here, son."

Once we were tangled in a warm embrace, I couldn't help but cry. I hadn't felt this loved or felt like part of a family since well before my mom passed away. Sure, I had my sisters and dad at the time. But we'd lost our connection to one another as each of us dealt with the pain of loss. Then my dad was taken from us, which had been the second hardest blow to our hearts.

"I can't tell you how proud I am of both of you." Steven sounded choked up. "And never forget that I will always be here for my family. And Layla, that includes Jordyn."

A host of emotions were making me one hot mess, and I cried harder as the two formidable vampires tightened their hold on me. I was home with a family that I wouldn't trade for the world.

## 14

## LAYLA

We were finally on our way to Jordyn's hospital room. Steven and Sam chatted about the vampire government, enemies, Intech, Adam Emery, Roman, and military stuff.

Given the recent news about Noah, Jack and Tabitha flying in, and Rianne's outlook, I couldn't help but reminisce about the past and some of the good times the Aberdeens had had over the years.

In particular, the family gatherings at the holidays when we would sit at the dining table at my uncle Jack's ranch, talking, laughing, and planning the next hunt. For everyone's faults and flaws or the arguments we'd had or even the hatred we might have had for one another, no one deserved to die. Yet, here we were. My uncle Ray was dead. I killed my grandmother, Harriet. Ray's wife, Deb, blamed me for her husband's death and wanted me in a coffin. Noah wasn't human. I'd lost my mom to breast cancer, and my dad had been murdered by Fred Emery. Then there was Rianne. It gutted me that she wasn't human anymore. It ripped my heart right out of my chest that we would never be close again. Aside from my mom, everyone's plight was because of Adam Emery and Roman Brown. Even Jordyn was suffering at the hands of those evil fucking assholes.

"Layla." Sam's soft but husky voice brought me out of the past as we reached the nurse's station. "Where did you go?" He wiped a tear from my cheek.

*To hell and back.*

"Just thinking." I rounded my gaze on a brunette nurse in pink scrubs. "Wendy?"

She'd been one of the nurses on my birthing team and had worked alongside that bitch Beverly, who'd been responsible for leaking my children's information and their whereabouts to Roman Brown.

"Layla, it's great to see you again." She stood at the edge of the nurse's station with a stethoscope around her neck, and her pink-painted lips curled at the corners.

I wasn't sure how I felt about Wendy. She'd been nice, but considering what Beverly had done, I had a bad taste in my mouth, even though Wendy hadn't been part of Beverly's scheme.

Steven must've felt my apprehension because he said, "I promise both of you, Wendy is trustworthy. I've read her mind."

"No offense, Pops, but that doesn't mean much anymore," Sam bit out. "Vampires are becoming experts at blocking you and Jo."

She rolled her shoulders back. "I'm so sorry about what happened to Orion and Luna."

Sam's jaw hardened. "Why? Did you do something wrong?"

Her brown gaze flickered to Steven for help.

Steven sidled up to Wendy as though he was her protector. "Son, ease up."

Wendy held up her left hand, and the one-carat diamond on her finger sparkled beneath bright lights overhead. "It's okay, Elder Mason. I feel horrible about what Beverly did."

"Where is Beverly?" I asked.

I couldn't recall what punishment Steven had exacted on the nurse. He'd killed Norman Collier, the guardian who'd been caught red-handed in the nursery that night at Jo's house in Maine.

"She's in prison at our Boston complex," Steven said. "No need to worry about her. As far as Wendy goes, I want both of you to know that she's accepted an offer to work for Dr. Vieira. Her employment will be temporary, pending an evaluation process. Wendy is also studying to become a pediatrician, and with the expansion of the infirmary, we need the help. We've also hired Dr. Martin."

My mouth parted. "My human ob-gyn doctor?" I liked Dr. Martin, who was good friends with Dr. Vieira.

"The same one," Steven confirmed. "Look, we need to start integrating more with humans if we're going to succeed in this new era. I also have plans to build a school on the naval base. With the soldiers' families returning to their homes, I want a safe haven for them and their children until such a time when they don't feel too threatened to come and go as they please."

Sam rubbed his neck. "I guess we missed a lot. Does any of what you just relayed have to do with the role you have in mind for me?"

Sam had mentioned the phone conversation he'd had with his dad at the motel in Bismarck. He was more than curious what position his father intended for him as Steven led the vampire nation.

"We'll talk in more detail about the new organizational structure that I have in mind and where you fit into it later today," Steven replied. "For now, I'm sure Layla would like to see her sister. And Samuel, you're welcome to stay with Layla, but I would prefer if you joined me and the team in the conference room."

I gripped his arm. "Go with your dad. We'll see Ellie and Rorie when Doc is finished with their exam, and you can stop by and check on Jordyn later."

There wasn't much he or I could do for my sister, and from the conversation he and Steven had been having on our way here, I could tell my husband was anxious to catch up on what was happening in North Dakota. After all, Olivia, Ben, Kraft, Kendra, and Conrad were scouting the state for Adam Emery. Plus, I was dying to know if Roman *was* dead.

Sam rested a hand on my lower back. "Will you be okay? I know you can probably kick my ass now with your witch powers, but if you need me to hold your hand, I will go with you to see Jordyn."

I just adored my husband for thinking of my emotional well-being. I gave him a quick kiss on the lips. "I love you, vampire. Go with your dad."

After we parted ways, Wendy and I navigated in the opposite direction from Sam and Steven.

"I hope my fiancé and I have that deep love you and Sam share," Wendy said.

I really didn't want to make small talk. It wasn't only taxing on my psyche, but it was hard to chat with her, knowing she had worked alongside Beverley. If Steven wanted us to give her a chance, then she had to start earning our trust. Nonetheless, I believed she had to have known something about Beverly's actions.

"Did you know what Beverly was up to?"

Wendy brushed her brown bangs away from her eyebrows. "Sadly, Beverly never gave me any indication she was up to something. I understand she was vetted and her background check was clean, just like mine and the other nurse, Amy's. But... she was excited about a new man in her life. She'd been dating him for a few months. She didn't share details about him or who he was."

As we turned a corner down another hallway, I asked, "Didn't you work with her here at this facility?"

"Yes. We weren't close, if that's where your questioning is going. We were on opposite shifts. She did, however, volunteer to work on your birthing team." Wendy touched her chest. "I didn't. I had a final exam that I was cramming for when Dr. Vieira came to me. He thought being on the birthing team would be a good learning opportunity, and he trusted me. He and my parents are good friends."

I could see why Steven had gone to bat for her, not only because he'd read her mind, but he trusted Dr. Vieira's judgment.

"If I had to guess, one of your parents is a doctor?"

Her head moved up and down. "My father owns a well-known law firm in Boston. As a vampire, he caters mostly to people in our community. My mother is a surgeon at Mass General here in the city, and she was the one who operated on your sister Jordyn."

I made a mental note to thank her mother if I had a chance to meet her.

When we reached the double doors, Wendy hit a large silver button on the side wall, and the doors opened.

"Wendy, I want to be very frank. You don't want to make an enemy out of my husband and me." I felt compelled to say my piece, especially if she would be working in the infirmary on the naval base.

"I can assure you I will never betray the Masons. That's not who I am or how I was brought up. The Banks family code of honor is to help those who can't help themselves."

Much like the Vampire Navy SEAL's mission statement. Still, for all I knew, she could be blowing smoke up my ass.

She gently touched my arm. "I hope over the coming months, you'll see that I'm trustworthy. For now, I want to prepare you before you see Jordyn. She's hooked up to a ventilator and an EEG machine to monitor brain activity. Since she hit her head and she's in a medically-induced coma, the EEG is necessary. So don't freak when you see the green cap on her head that has probes attached. Dr. Vieira will explain more about her prognosis when he comes up."

Suddenly, the outside world and our conversation vanished as we walked into a modest-sized area with three rooms and a nurse's station. Directly ahead was a sign for the operating room.

Each step I took as I walked alongside her felt heavy and painful, both in my legs and my chest. I didn't know what to expect when I saw Jordyn. The last time I'd seen someone I loved in a hospital bed fighting for her life, it had been my mother. And the deathly sight of my mom as she fought to breathe and talk during her last moments before she passed was forever imprinted on my brain. I wasn't sure I could even see Jordyn without falling apart.

The second I looked through the window into the last room we came to, tears flew out faster than I could stop them, and air rushed from my lungs as if someone had punched the wind out of me.

As Wendy had detailed, Jordyn was hooked up to machines— a ventilator, vitals machine, IV—and she had that green cap on her head.

I swallowed the dryness in my throat as I went into the room and up to Jordyn's bedside.

Wendy followed on my heels, staying at the bottom of the bed.

"Will she be able to hear me?" I asked.

"She might be able to hear sounds and voices. But she won't be able to respond. Talk to her. Let her know you're with her. It might help her recovery."

I held my sister's hand while her chest rose and fell. The

vibration of the machine kept her breathing and my heart beating.

"Again, Dr. Vieira will go over everything with you. If you need me, I'll be at the desk right outside."

After Wendy left, I shuddered violently as if someone had thrown me into the cold waters off the coast of Antarctica. I shouldn't have put all the responsibility on Jordyn to protect two infants against bloodsuckers. What the fuck had I been thinking?

"I'm so sorry this happened to you. I should've been there with you."

*Stop blaming yourself. You couldn't have predicted what would happen.*

Regardless, guilt and regret rode me hard, punching me in the gut and twisting my insides until I couldn't breathe.

Inhaling deeply, I dragged the only chair in the room from the corner to the side of the bed and sat down.

"I promise, sis, if you make it, I will make sure you don't go through anything like this again." I knew I couldn't exactly stick to that promise, but I would sure as hell try.

I would give anything to see her happy and away from vampires and any supernatural creatures. Sadly, neither she nor I could run away or disappear. As Agnes had written in her letter to my mom, we couldn't ignore who we were, where we came from, or the supernatural world around us. If we did, we would put ourselves and our loved ones at risk.

"Well, sis. I'm officially a witch." I giggled through tears. "Can you believe that? I can't."

I was anxious to know her DNA makeup and if she could be a witch like me. For a while, she had no desire to know her DNA makeup. Mainly because she'd seen what I'd gone through. However, she'd recently expressed that she'd wanted to know if she had the same blood type as me—Vel negative—the one that made it possible for her to get pregnant by a vampire. My sister had the hots for Sawyer, the Vampire Navy SEAL's tech guru. So she felt that if she wanted to sleep with him, then it was best she knew.

I didn't know much about him except that the handsome vampire with kaleidoscope-colored eyes seemed like a genuine guy—honest, quiet, intelligent, and a perfect match for my sister.

I glanced up at the high ceiling as if my mom was up there, looking down over us. I was sure she was. When I'd died and seen my mother, she'd told me she was watching over me.

"Mom, if you're listening, please help Jordyn through this. I want her to be happy. I want her to find a life where she can settle down, marry, and have kids." Jordyn wanted little rug rats running around.

Dr. Vieira's voice filtered in through the open door before he entered. The intelligent and caring resident doctor, who was an amazing vampire inside and out, was wearing a surgical cap and scrubs.

I popped up from the chair. "Dr. Vieira," I said on a sigh.

He gave me a quick hug and studied me with weary brown eyes. "Welcome home. You had all of us worried."

Warmth spread through my chest at the realization that he cared. "It's good to be here. Of course, I wish it was under better circumstances."

He rounded the bed. "Agreed. But your sister is a fighter."

"That's the Aberdeen way," I teased.

He removed his surgical cap and stuffed it into the pocket of his scrubs. "Your sister has a long road to recovery. The next couple of days will be critical. We removed two bullets. One had nicked her lung, and we pulled the other one from her lower back." He pointed to a spot on his body between his spine and waist. "She also took a severe blow to the back of her body, including her head. She had a small brain bleed that complicated things. The fact that she made it through surgery is a miracle, in my book."

*Holy hell. He was right. A miracle for sure.*

"The coma is necessary to give her body time to heal," he said. "As she improves, we'll slowly pull her out of it. But I do want to prepare you, Layla. It's possible she might not have use of her legs." He held up his hand. "Jordyn's lead surgeon, Dr. Banks, feels she might have some nerve damage that could be temporary around the lower spine, both from the bullet and the blunt-force trauma to her back."

Despite the word *temporary* in that sentence, I practically fell into the chair, pressing my knuckles into my chest, willing the prickly pain to go away. I didn't think I could shed any more tears. Yet there I was, silently crying.

"She doesn't deserve any of this." Then something hit me. "What about the healing blood?" The magical potion had sped up my recovery time and worked wonders after my C-section.

"I have given her a dose," he said. "That will help the wounds. But I can't say the same for nerve damage or the swelling in her back. Time will tell, of course. From here it's up to Jordyn."

I wanted to unleash my banshee scream as frustration, anger, and many other emotions had me in a ball of knots. It seemed every day I was fighting, running, praying, and trying to save a loved one.

Jordyn needed positive vibes, not crying and brooding. I considered her more headstrong than me. She was always the light in our dark times. She was the one who made Rianne and me laugh when the two of us were in our doom-and-gloom moods.

"I hate this, Dr. Vieira."

"Believe me, I do as well. The best thing you can do is get some rest. When was the last time you slept?"

I lightly chuckled. "Sleep isn't in my future."

He gave me a doctorly yet fatherly look. "I order you to. And don't tell me again that you're fine. You're not, Layla."

*Busted.* "I want a break from the madness. Something has to give."

"I have good news for you," he said. "Your children are healthy and wonderful. They've gained an average of four pounds. They've grown anywhere from two to three inches in five weeks. Their progression is surpassing a human baby's, which falls in line with how fast they grew inside the womb. I would speculate they'll be crawling soon and probably walking by eight to nine months."

I laughed hard, and it felt great. "They'll be teenagers before long."

"One thing is certain: we'll have our hands full with them."

"We?" I tilted my head.

A deep furrow appeared between his eyebrows, contrasting sharply with the exuberant grin stretching from ear to ear. "You and Sam aren't parenting alone, Layla. I'm here to help. Besides, you realize that you have a large support network here."

"I do. It's hard for me to absorb all that has happened—good, bad, and indifferent." The outpouring of love since I'd arrived at the medical facility was overwhelming. But it was also a beacon of hope and the pillar of strength I needed to fight in the coming days or months or years. And I knew we had battles ahead of us, particularly if witches came out of the woodwork because of the prophecy.

"Dr. Vieira, have you confirmed yet if my children are all vampires or witches or both?"

"Preliminary results show that they're all vampire witches," he said. "I pulled blood from them today just to confirm my findings. If you remember, we had some mix-up in samples right after they were born. I don't suspect the second set of data will show anything different than the first, but I just want to be sure."

"Vampire witches." I rolled those words around on my tongue. "Ellie and Luna haven't had blood yet like Rorie and Orion. Is that normal?"

He chuckled. "Nothing about your children is normal. And considering I don't have experience with inhuman babies, I can't give you an answer. However, I would guess that it's just a matter of time before Ellie and Luna show signs they need blood. All four have the vampire gene, and each of them have the blood type of a witch."

"Vel negative?" I asked. "Like me?"

"Yes and no. Once I have the complete set of results, I can go over that with you and Sam. For now, just try and relax."

"I'm not sure I can. If they're all vampires, then which one will turn witches into vampires?"

"Breathe, Layla," he said. "Now that you're a witch, at some point when I have more time, my plan is to run some lab tests combining your children's DNA with yours. I can't guarantee the results will tell us the answer you're seeking, but I'm curious about the genetics of your children in general."

Of course he was. I was the second case of a woman in the last eighty years to have given birth to inhuman babies. The last case was Emily Crawford, who'd given birth to twins, but Emily had died during childbirth. And to date, we didn't know if those twins were alive or anything more than that they had been born. Her case file had some pages missing, and we'd searched high and low for them—with no luck.

Doc started for the door. "I have a conference call in a few minutes. Alia has offered to watch your children. They're in a hospital room with her. I suggest you visit with Jordyn for a few minutes longer, then join your children. There's a bed for you to sleep in next to them. Wendy will show you the way. And Layla, no arguments. You're no good to Jordyn if you don't take care of yourself. Do you understand?" He nailed me with a doctor's glare.

I wanted to argue, but he didn't give me the chance as he waltzed out in a hurry. Then again, I knew I wouldn't win against him.

Above that, I was feeling drained, and my eyelids were heavy. Maybe I could sleep for a couple of hours. I was also dying to see Ellie and Rorie. If anyone could put a smile on my face, it was my children. Plus, I didn't want to burden Alia Costner. She had her own issues to deal with, especially the death of her son Matthew.

I kissed my sister on her forehead. "I'll be back later."

Then on doctor's orders, I went in search of my children.

## 15

## SAM

Webb was absorbed in his laptop, addressing an urgent email. My dad left to take a call from Jonah, a vampire guardian who worked for my father. Tripp had done the same, only he was talking to Sawyer, and Dane was also on the phone, catching up with his brother Cooper.

I was the only one without a role to play. If the meeting didn't start soon, I was leaving. I wanted to be there for Layla if she needed me. I also wanted to see my kids.

The sound of Webb banging on his laptop keys competed with the earsplitting thunderclaps outside the conference room window. A summer storm was raging over the city, producing a dazzling show of lightning that illuminated the ominous darkened sky.

It was midafternoon, and traffic was stopped on the street below and also jammed the freeway farther in the distance.

From where I stood high above the city, I imagined the fragrant odors of damp vegetation and petrichor that churned up during the first drops of rain—scents I loved.

Webb sauntered over, slipping his hands into the pockets of his black cargo pants. "I just love thunderstorms. They energize me." He had the ability to manipulate water, earth, and fire but not air.

Those of us who had elemental powers needed Mother Nature to keep our abilities sharp and deadly.

I stared out at the rain coming down in sheets as pedestrians scurried to flee the harsh weather.

"Did you ever think that the entire world of humans would one day know that we existed?" Some had known about us but not the entire world's population.

"It was just a matter of time," he said. "And no matter how much we planned for something like this, we really aren't ready. Our disaster-preparedness guide certainly helped our soldiers and families on the naval base. But we have a long road ahead to bridge the gap between us and humans. Hell, we're just starting. I believe it will be easier now that your father is in charge and the Council of Elders has been disbanded."

"And what about the two elders who were caught working for our enemies?" I asked. "My dad said the evidence against them had been astounding."

"Those two have been shipped to our prison in Puerto Rico," Webb said. "The other elders who were on the council are no longer a part of our governmental team. We're watching them closely though."

A flash of lightning made me blink. "And the human government? Last I heard, they wanted to eradicate all vampires."

He chuckled. "They can try. But they won't—at least not in the foreseeable future. We've agreed to work together to show unity, and that includes taking down Adam Emery."

I gave my brother-in-law a sidelong glance. He hardly showed signs of fatigue, even during the worst of times. But his skin was pasty white. I could also feel the emotions that were keeping his shoulders stiff and his jaw tight.

All of us were walking time bombs, ready to explode at the next round of bad news or death of our brethren. I wanted to believe we were immune to the feelings that came with death or the pain we felt seeing someone we cared about grieve and suffer. But as vampires, our emotions were heightened to a level that could decimate us if we allowed them to take over our psyches. I had it even worse. I was an empath, and the emotion of others hit me like a Mack truck speeding down a highway at two hundred miles an hour.

Silence hung over us and was only broken by the rumble of thunder and the flash of lightning. Both of us were deep in thought as we watched Mother Nature unleash her fury across the sky.

"Tell me about Sacred Flame Academy," Webb said.

"There's not much to tell. Layla and I were only there for a few hours, if that. However, the campus is secluded in the mountains in the state of Washington. School wasn't in session, but there were guards at the gate."

He crossed an arm over his chest and clasped his other arm. "As much as I want to keep Abbey close, I can't. Jo can't either. Abbey needs to be around people like her and to learn from those who can teach her how to handle her craft. Alia told us that Abbey's magic was out of control when she unleashed her powers on those two vampires she killed. Sadly, Jordyn got caught in Abbey's crossfire, which was why Jordyn suffered more than just gunshot wounds."

"Maybe Agnes can help Abbey," I said. "Agnes did a great job of schooling Layla, which is the only reason we're here."

Although it sounded to me like Abbey had stronger powers than Layla. Then again, I couldn't compare the two. Abbey had a vampire father. Layla didn't.

"Regardless," Webb said, "It's time that Abbey is around

others her age with similar supernatural abilities, and she needs that social structure."

"Sometimes I wonder why Abbey isn't considered inhuman like my kids."

He guffawed. "I asked Doc that question just this morning."

I could feel my forehead creasing. "And?"

He threaded his hands through his brown hair. "It's not just magic that categorizes your children as inhuman but the fact that their growth process is faster and they're drinking blood as babies. And if Doc is correct, your children will have fangs, either when they start teething or when their adult teeth grow in. Abbey certainly doesn't fall into those two categories."

Shaking my head, I let out a hearty laugh. "Teething and fangs will be a challenge." I had no idea how to deal with a teething baby, but I guessed I would eventually find out.

Tripp waltzed in, sandy-blond hair tied at the nape of his neck, bronze eyes clear as if he'd taken a power nap, and he set his laptop on the table. "Webb, have you filled Sam in on the Midnight Raiders and the Mystic yet?"

I returned to my seat across from Tripp. "I remember the name Midnight Raiders. One shifter on Rebekah's team brought them up. What do they have to do with the Mystic?"

Webb flipped through several written pages of his notepad as he dropped into his chair. "Captain Greer of the Midnight Raiders leads a small unit within the Marine Special Forces. Her secret tactical squad of witches polices the witch community and keeps wars from breaking out among their kind. Much like us. Word has spread to her about Maeve Monroe and the way she'd planned to become the Mystic. The captain is also aware of the prophecies related to the Monroe witches."

"I'm guessing the Midnight Raiders know about Layla and my children," I said.

If he even mentioned that this tactical team was planning on removing my wife and children in some way, I would blow the roof off this building.

"They do," Webb continued. "The supernatural military is a small community, and word spread quickly after Layla gave birth. The Midnight Raiders have been training a second team ever since they got wind of the prophecy about the Mystic when it surfaced six years ago."

"For what?" I held my emotions in check.

"To *protect* the Mystic," Webb said. "Apparently, this powerful witch will lead her kind into a brighter and better world." He held up his hand. "Those were the captain's words."

"What does that mean?" I asked.

Tripp grabbed the back of his neck. "You heard Agnes, Sam. Some Mystics are healers. What if the message Layla's mother gave her was right? What if Layla is the Mystic, and that's the way she'll keep the natural order in balance? Or maybe she already has by preventing Maeve from becoming the all-powerful witch."

I cracked my knuckles. "You mean from dark magic?" Zoey Thornton feared that if Maeve was successful, the world would be a much darker place. Maybe Tripp had a point.

"Whatever," Tripp added. "Think about it. If Maeve had succeeded, you know we would be fighting many more wars than we could imagine."

Maybe so. "Did the captain say anything about the other prophecy?" That was my main concern. "Does she think that a child of mine can turn them into vampires?"

Webb picked up a pen off his pad. "No." His tone was emphatic. "She claims her scientist can prove it. They've been testing vampire DNA together with a witch's for years."

"Okay." I shrugged. "But the DNA is not my children's. So how can this scientist come to that conclusion?"

"I can't answer that," Webb said. "But I've put the captain in touch with Dr. Vieira. In fact, I just sent her Doc's info thirty minutes ago. I'm confident Doc will figure out if any of your kids can turn a witch into a vampire. Right now, the Raiders aren't our enemy. They assured me they're on our side. In the meantime, our immediate concerns are Adam Emery, Draven Murphy, and assigning new roles as we reorganize the vampire government." His phone vibrated on the table.

That was my cue for a quick break. I needed to sate my hunger, but I also wanted a moment to clear my head.

The Midnight Raiders might be on our side, but if by chance they were wrong about a vampire turning witches, I had no doubt they had a protocol in place to eradicate anyone who threatened their existence.

"I'll be right back," I said as I left the room.

Once in the hall, I released a heavy sigh as the electricity blinked on and off. I was sure the storm had something to do with the flicker of power, but a fleeting pain in my gut said maybe not.

# 16

## SAM

After taking a short bathroom break and grabbing a six-pack of blood, I returned to the conference room, but there was no sign of my father.

I popped the top on a bottle as Tripp and Webb did the same. No sooner than we'd toasted like three old friends kicking back at a bar, I heard my father's voice then Dane's.

My dad strode in, jaw tight, body tense, and with a very familiar-looking box.

"That isn't what I think it is," I remarked, raising an eyebrow.

The white-haired alpha snarled, "It's a head."

"I know," I replied. "I've seen that same style of box with Matthew's head in it."

My father's green eyes transformed in an instant, flashing like quicksilver and glittering with a fierce intensity that cut through the air like a sharp-edged blade.

Webb was on his feet with his drink in hand. "Please tell me the victim isn't anyone on our team."

My father set the box down on the long conference table, muttering swear words like the sailor he was.

Dane's wolf was showing signs—glowing red eyes and long canines—that he wanted to come out to play. Or rather, gut Emery and eat him for dinner.

My father marched over to the six-pack, yanked a bottle out, and knocked back half of it. After he swallowed his last mouthful, he said, "Victor Costner."

Shocked gasps came from Webb, Tripp, and me.

Webb placed his blood on the table, the sound exploding in the room. His anger was unmistakable as his skin turned ten shades of red. "Fuck me sideways. In all my years of knowing Victor, no one could best him in a fight or play him. How did this happen? I know he was AWOL. We speculated that he probably took off to find his grandson Matthew."

If I were to write Victor Costner's epitaph, it would read: A warrior, an expert swordsman, a great father, and a loving grandfather.

I wasn't a fan of Victor, but I respected the hell out of the vampire.

My father finished off his blood and tossed the empty container in the trash can by the door. Then he padded across the carpeted floor to the window, balling his hands into fists, seemingly ready to punch a hole through the glass. He'd known Victor for over a hundred years. While they'd butted heads many times, they admired each other.

The four of us were quiet as we eyed one another, giving my old man time to ease his anger and heartache as we took our seats.

"Victor usually wasn't stupid," my dad finally said. "I'm not sure I can break this news to Alia. She just lost her son and now her father."

A pressure cooker of tension built to a point I was sure would blow us out of the room or through the window if my father couldn't tame his fury. The empty chairs were shaking, and once again, the lights overhead flickered.

Now I knew why the electricity had blinked on and off earlier. My father must've been the source when he opened that box.

Dane placed his phone on the table and cracked his knuckles. "The note from Emery inside the box states that more heads will be sent if his brother and Carly aren't released. I'm afraid that if Ross is Emery's prisoner, he might be next."

I sipped on my blood. "Adam doesn't want Carly herself. He knows she's not human anymore. She has something he wants."

"Patrick's files," Webb announced. "After Rianne injected Carly, she'd had enough. She transferred all Patrick's data and her own to a thumb drive, then wiped every piece of data from Intech's servers. She went as far as having her tech assistant load a virus into the computer system."

My eyebrows rose. "She and Rianne hated each other. But why would she ditch Adam? They were tight."

My dad came over and gripped the back of the leather chair beside Webb. "Carly's relationship with Adam declined severely when he brought Roman, Harriet, Noah, and Rianne on board. After she helped us rescue Layla from Intech's West Virginia facility, Adam hit the roof. Carly knew her days were numbered."

"I always knew I could coax her into joining our team," I mumbled.

"She's not on our team." Webb's tone was matter-of-fact. "And given her condition, I doubt she will ever be. But I believe she's trying to make amends."

"Do we know how Adam is making the serum if he doesn't have either Carly's recipe or Patrick's?" Tripp asked.

My dad finally folded his big body into the chair. "In her haste to leave the West Virginia facility, she left a notebook behind. It only contained the latest experiment data that she was working on. Nothing more."

Dane, who was across from my father, said, "None of this has anything to do with a plan to take out Adam Emery or brokering a deal with him so we don't have more heads showing up. If he wants Carly or the data and his brother, then give it to him in exchange for Ross. Steven, we need to act now. If we don't, your team and my shifters will be next."

Calm, cool, and collected, my father stared at Dane as he chewed on the inside of his cheek. "You want me to give our enemy data that will help him build an army of supernatural creatures? I won't do that."

"Then give him his fucking brother!" Dane all but shouted, his canines gleaming from beneath his upper lip.

"If he has Ross, what's to say he hasn't already killed him?" Webb asked. "Then we trade Fred Emery for nothing."

"But we won't know that until we make the deal," Dane said. "At least see if Adam will bite. I would like hard confirmation that Ross is his prisoner. Plus, if you open up talks, it might buy us time to find the fucker before he chops off more heads."

"He has a point," I said. "Set up a face-to-face meeting with him, Pops. We can draw him out."

Tripp and Webb were nodding in agreement as well.

A muscle jumped in my father's jaw. "It's a hard no on an in-person meeting. It's too risky. But it wouldn't hurt to talk to Adam by phone. So far we've just exchanged emails." He sighed. "Every move we make needs to be well-thought-out. We cannot have an all-out war, especially if Draven Murphy and his clan are involved with Adam. We can't lose sight that we're under the human microscope either."

The only sound in the room was the rain lashing against the windows.

As I listened, something occurred to me. "Have any of you

thought about why Adam is threatening us to secure Fred's release all of a sudden? Think about it. He made a plea at his news conference for Fred, sure. But he only did that as an afterthought. Adam's lead-in was all about him and bragging about his new prototype program. Also, he had Matthew Costner then. He could've made the deal to exchange Matthew for Fred, and he didn't."

"Interesting observation, son," my father said. "Then what does Fred have that Adam wants?"

"What if Fred also has Patrick's files?" Tripp asked. "That's the only thing that makes sense since Adam hasn't shown any love for his brother until now."

"Carly didn't mention anything about Fred," Webb said. "Then again, Dr. Vieira didn't ask her if anyone else was in possession of Patrick's files. I'll get right on that."

Dane seemed to have lost his edge as his phone dinged. He lifted his cell off the table, tapped on the screen, and blanched. Then in a flash, he kicked the chair backward as he flew to his feet, roared so loudly that my eardrums felt the pain, and took off.

None of us moved.

"What the hell just happened?" Tripp asked.

My heart was in my throat. "I'll find him."

I tore out of there, sniffing Dane's mutt scent as I tracked him through the building, into the stairwell, and then to the underground garage.

The alpha was still upright in human form but punching his fists into the cement wall near the elevator, grunting and growling.

"Dane." I kept my distance. "What happened?"

He spun around, baring his canines, eyes glowing red. "Ross is dead because of you."

I raised my hands as my vampire reared its ugly head.

"Whoa! I blame myself for many things, but I'm not responsible for Ross." Anger laced my tone. "And you had dealings with Roman way before we ever met." I was trying to keep my cool and not rouse Dane's ire and his wolf any further. Yet it was all I could do not to make the first move.

Saliva dripped from his canines. Bones snapped into place. His clothes ripped open. His phone dropped to the ground, and in seconds, I was facing off with a white wolf who, on all four legs, stood snout to nose with me, and I was six-and-a-half-feet tall.

"I don't want to fight you." I might stand a chance against his wolf with my elemental powers, but as furious as Dane was, he could tear me to pieces.

He followed my line of sight as I slowly squatted down and picked up his phone. An image of Ross's detached bald head and hazel eyes stared back at me.

The only time I'd met Ross was when he'd accompanied Dane to the naval base. We'd agreed to help the Gray Pack uncover why one of their own had died from the drug in the tranquilizer darts that the Aberdeen sisters had used the night at the vampire club when they'd tried to capture me alive. In exchange, Dane had agreed he wouldn't seek vengeance against the Aberdeen sisters for killing his pack member.

Dane stared at me, growling low as I read the writing on the note in the picture sent with the head. *You shifters seem to be in bed with Steven Mason. Shame on you. This is what happens when you obey the wrong master.* It was signed by Adam Emery.

"What a fuckwad. The wrong master? He's delusional."

Dane angled his wolf head, showing those sharp teeth.

Whether he was ready to rip off one of my limbs or he was reacting to what I was reading, I didn't know, but I read Cooper's text beneath the photo. *I'll call you in a bit when I'm done running off my rage.*

I touched my chest. "I'm so fucking sorry, man. I truly am." My gut twisted and tightened as fury settled in my veins, not at Dane but at Emery.

Before I could stop him, Dane was running through the garage.

I chased after him, reaching him just as the grated barrier was opening. Dane bared his teeth at the guard.

"Dane," I said. "Wait."

The barricade wasn't all the way open, but that didn't stop the wolf from slipping through the four-foot opening.

"I'm sorry, sir," the guard said.

Dane became a blur as he ran as hard as the wind was whipping around in the summer storm.

I waved the dude off. "He would've torn you to pieces." That was the truth.

## 17

## SAM

After that explosive encounter, I needed to run myself, which was a great idea. I was itching to work out in a gym —something I hadn't done in quite a long time. I returned to the conference room with the intention of informing my father that if it wasn't urgent for me to attend his meeting, I would be with Layla. Afterward, I was going for a run unless the medical facility had a gym.

My brain was about to burst from learning of the Midnight Raiders, seeing Victor's head in a box, trying to come up with a plan to stop Adam threatening us further, and now discovering Ross was dead. My heart hurt for Dane. But I was also vibrating with the itch to end this fucking war with Adam Emery once and for all.

As I approached the conference room, I heard a very familiar voice—one that only amplified my ire.

"I take it you got Victor's head," Adam Emery said. "Did the alpha shifter receive my gift yet?"

Gritting my teeth, I stalked into the room, clutching Dane's ripped clothes and cell phone.

126

My father raised a finger to his lips as he pointed to his cell phone on the table. He was probably reading my mind because I was ready to spit venom at Adam. Instead, I sat in the chair Dane had been in and tossed his clothes onto the leather seat next to me.

Webb was crushing his pen. Tripp's jaw was granite.

I passed Dane's phone around, sharing the pictures of Ross and the note.

"I have a good mind to send Fred's head to you," my father said in a venomous tone as he glanced at the image of Ross on Dane's cell.

"You know you won't do any such thing." The cockiness in Adam's voice made me want to slash his throat. "If you do, you don't stand a chance with the humans in this country. I'll show the world that you and your precious Vampire Navy SEALs are predators and that all of you should be wiped off the face of the earth. You won't win this war, Steven."

My father glared at his phone as if it were Adam. "If you hate vampires, then why are you working with Roman Brown and Draven Murphy?"

"I never said I hated vampires. I just despise the Masons. Your brother Patrick was a great man and my closest friend. My goal is to honor him. I promised him that after I was successful in building my army of supernatural soldiers, I would kill you and those you care about. I'll start with your son, Sam."

I opened my mouth to volley a threat, but Tripp held out his arm and shook his head at me. I snarled at my lieutenant and best bud next to me. I really wanted to say what was on my mind.

"Adam, don't think for a second that you'll succeed," my father said in a tight voice. "Hiring Roman or Draven isn't your smoking gun. Let's face it—Roman is dead, which means you're down to Draven. The Murphy family doesn't want a war with me. Draven knows that. Don't you think he would've tried before now to take out me or anyone on my team?" My father chuckled, the sound deadly. "Draven's objective is money. That's the only reason he's agreed to whatever deal you two have."

The sound of a train could be heard in the background.

The four of us exchanged knowing looks before Tripp typed out a text to someone.

"It seems, Steven, you know all. But I hate to break it to you —you have no idea what's coming. Now, release Fred and Carly, and the bloodshed *will stop for now*." He emphasized the last four words.

My father was digging a fang into his bottom lip. "Carly came to us of her own free will. She's free to leave anytime. But she doesn't want to. And I know she has Patrick's files, and that's the only reason you want her. But what I'm trying to figure out is why you're coercing me to release your brother after the several months that he's been my prisoner. Why now?"

I bounced my foot, waiting anxiously to hear Adam's response. I wasn't expecting him to give us a truthful answer.

"I understand that you had no love for Patrick," Adam said. "But I do for my brother." Then the call ended.

The four of us sat there, not saying a word for a long minute.

Webb had broken his pen in two, and he lobbed one half of it across the room toward the trash can. "That went as I expected. Nowhere."

"What do you think Adam meant by 'you have no idea what's coming'?" I asked. "Do you think his experiments are working?"

"Maybe he is creating more Noahs and Riannes," my father bit out. "Maybe he'll use those as his army for now."

More Noahs and Riannes would be a shit show. Humans would probably be more frightened of the hybrid monsters than vampires.

"Sir, I have Sawyer finding train stations and railroads in North Dakota," Tripp said.

"I take it we have confirmation that Draven is partnering with Adam?" I asked Tripp.

"Affirmative," he said.

My father pushed to his feet, grabbed the last bottle of blood out of the six-pack, and popped the top. "I'll call Baxter Murphy, Draven's father. I doubt I can convince him to knock some sense into his son. Baxter is as cunning and money hungry as Draven. But it's worth a shot."

If Adam didn't have either Roman or Draven, then he might be dead in the water until he found another vampire guinea pig with lots of money. Or at least one with an army to fight against us.

During a lull in the conversation, I said, "Not to change the topic, but Dane shifted and took off into the city. The guard had no choice but to let him through the gate. I doubt I could've stopped him either."

My dad took a swig of blood. "Just what we need—a wolf the size of a horse running around Boston. Let's hope we don't have repercussions from that."

How could we not? Humans were on high alert now that our existence was out in the world. I didn't think Dane would harm anyone, but given the state of mind he was in, an angry wolf might unleash his wrath on the first human to walk into his path.

The room was becoming claustrophobic. "I need to see my wife and kids." If anyone could take my mind off things, it was definitely them.

"Not so fast, son." My father finished off his drink and returned the empty bottle to the box. "I would like for you to accompany me tonight to an interview I'm doing with Violet Keller from CBC 4."

I reared back. "You want me to go on TV?" That, I wasn't expecting. "Is this the role you had in mind for me?"

My father anchored himself behind the high-back leather

chair. "No. Webb, Tripp, and I want you to run our training department for new recruits."

Fuck yeah. "That, I'll take." It was way more appealing and would also keep my weapons and fighting skills sharp. "I'm the wrong person to make public appearances. Layla would be better. The nation loves her."

"Layla's preoccupied right now," my father said. "Look, this is a chance for humans to get to know you and change their perception of you."

My reputation with humans—or rather, their first impression of me—was that I was a monster thanks to Rianne. She'd announced at Adam Emery's news conference that I'd kidnapped Layla and compelled her into falling in love with me.

"Public appearances are not my thing," I argued, although I'd promised the reporter, Tim Cox, an exclusive if he brought me leads about the whereabouts of Orion and Luna. But he hadn't come through on that part.

"This is our chance to control the narrative," Tripp said. "Which has always been Layla's strategy. But your father is right. This is your chance to show humans you're not a monster."

"Our goal tonight, son," my dad said, "is to announce how we'll help those who have suffered at the hands of Adam Emery. There are several families grieving because a loved one died from Adam's prototype program."

Tripp's phone trilled, nixing our conversation for the time being. "It's Olivia." He slid his phone to the middle of the table and hit the speaker button. "Steven, Webb, and Sam are with me."

"We just finished our meeting with local authorities. Good news and bad." Olivia's voice was light, her tone businesslike. "Bad news first. A firefighter, two police officers, and a paramedic were found drained of blood on the property behind the now-defunct barn. A witness saw a naked man with blond hair walking along the road behind the farm. The witness added that the man appeared disoriented and had burn marks on his body."

Tripp and I said in unison, "Motherfucker."

Then I laughed. Of course Roman would survive.

My father growled. "Is it Roman?"

"From the picture the witness took, it's hard to say," Olivia said. "Firemen recovered the bodies of two females and a male from the farmhouse that burned down. They didn't find a fourth."

Maeve, Patricia, Warrick, and Roman had been the only ones in the house when Layla set it ablaze.

"What's the good news?" Webb asked.

"The chief of police has an APB out for the vehicle Adam is in," Olivia said on a sigh. "Conrad and I managed to snag the license plate number. The human authorities here are on our side. Whatever we need, they'll oblige. The chief told us that protests are breaking out in Bismarck to hang Adam Emery. His offer of one hundred thousand dollars hasn't been paid to anyone who'd signed up for his program. Family members of victims are livid."

"Many more protests are going on around the country," Webb added. "Not just in North Dakota."

"Anything else, Olivia?" my father asked.

"Yes, sir. The chief also explained that while he liked Maeve and Warrick, he suspected that they were into something illegal. During the last month, there were countless deliveries to the farm —trucks unloading equipment, furniture, people coming and going. He had men watching them, but as it turned out, those cops took bribes from Warrick to keep their mouths shut."

I pushed my chair away and leaned my elbows on my knees. "Which was why the cops didn't show up last night when all the gunfire was going off. Agnes told us after the fact that Warrick was in tight with some of the police officers."

Voices in the background behind Olivia grew louder. "What are our orders from here, lieutenant?"

Tripp scraped a hand along his jaw. "Hang tight until the morning. If nothing new surfaces, then return to base. I'll have a plane waiting at the jetport. Check in with me this evening. One last thing—Adam is chopping off heads. You need to be more alert than ever. We've confirmed Draven Murphy is with him."

"Copy that," Olivia said before Tripp's phone's screen returned to an image of a tree-lined road covered in snow.

If Tripp had his way, he would live in the mountains and in a place that had long winters with snow year-round.

Webb rose and stretched in the process. "I'm not surprised Roman might have survived. Abbey has been having dreams of him capturing her."

The idea of Roman succeeding in his sinister goal to get his filthy hands on my niece filled me with an intense urge to hit something. Not to mention what he'd told me in the farmhouse basement. I debated whether to share that with Webb, but in the end, I decided he needed to know, as did my father and Tripp.

"Roman knows Abbey will be the first female vampire able to procreate." I stared at Webb. "Matthew told him. This knowledge has only enhanced Roman's desire for Abbey. The asshole doesn't want to sell her or her DNA to the highest bidder. He wants her. He wants to have kids."

Webb picked up a chair and hauled it across the room. "Motherfucker in hell."

Silence ensued after the explosive sound of the chair hitting the wall.

My dad shoved his hands through his hair. "All of us are under quite a bit of stress. If Roman made it, he's a problem, but he's not the only one right now. Adam is our priority. Webb, we have three of Roman's men whom we captured in the Catskills. Head over to the council admin building and interrogate them. Take Jo with you to read their minds. They might have information on Adam as well as know a place Roman would hide."

Webb seemed to perk up at the idea. "Copy that."

"I'll have Sawyer question Carly about Fred." Tripp packed up his laptop.

I was on my feet when my father held up his hand. "Wait, son. You and I aren't finished discussing the TV interview."

Here I thought I could escape going on national television. Then again, I wouldn't—or couldn't—say no to my father or my team. If my appearance helped in any way, I was all for it.

After Tripp and Webb left, I said, "I'll do the interview, but let's not make it a habit, please."

"That's not my intention," he said as he circled the table and came up to me. "I plan to ask Layla to be my liaison between us and the humans. But right now, considering Jordyn's condition, she needs to be with her sister."

I grinned so hard my lips hurt. "That's fantastic. She would love that."

"Good. I'm glad that's settled." He started for the door. "Walk with me. It's time I break the news to Alia about her father. But I want you to do something for me."

I didn't envy him on that front. My deepest sympathies went out to her. Losing her son and father in a span of a few days was soul crushing.

I snagged Dane's phone and left his ripped clothes behind before I met my dad in the hallway.

"When Dane returns, I would like for you to talk to him about joining us," my father said. "My plan moving forward is to have leaders from different packs and also witches from covens work with us as we navigate our way into blending in with humans. It's only a matter of time before humans learn of shifters and witches."

"Why don't you ask him? You're building your new organization. You're the man in charge."

"Because, son, I already asked him, and he said no. I believe you can convince him."

"I'll try, but I don't believe Dane likes working with anyone," I said.

Whether Dane did or didn't adapt to the new path we were on, no amount of effort to build a relationship with humans would work until Adam Emery was out of the picture.

**18**

---

# LAYLA

$T$he pews were packed with people as I followed a woman down the aisle while others around me swiveled their heads as I passed. Whispers droned, and I could hear someone say, "She doesn't belong here."

I tapped the lady on the shoulder in front of me. "Ma'am, whose funeral is this?" I was assuming someone had died, since the sea of parishioners was decked out in black suits and dresses.

The lady turned and lifted the veil off her face.

My gasp echoed through the church, bouncing off the stone walls and high ceilings painted with religious figures. "Mom?"

She quickly glanced over her shoulder with a perplexed look as if I were a stranger.

Organ music began playing, and the occupants in the pews rose, their clothes rustling together.

My mom slipped into an open seat several rows from the altar, then caught my arm. "My child, darkness is coming. You must prepare. You are their light."

My eyebrows knitted as the organ music grew louder. "What do you mean?"

As if someone had magically transported me toward the altar, I was

135

*kneeling in front of the priest. I searched for my mother behind me, but the faces of the parishioners were blank—no eyes, noses, or mouths.*

*The priest darted his steely gaze to the coffin beside him.*

*Rising to my feet, I followed his line of sight.*

*The second I saw the body in the coffin, I screamed at the top of my lungs.*

*"Layla." A faint and raspy voice cut through the sounds of cries and wails. "Baby doll, wake up."*

Someone shook me as the coffin began to vanish, and my scream trailed off.

"Layla." Sam's voice was louder now and panicked.

I jolted upright, shivering, sweating, and disoriented.

My husband's handsome features slowly took shape. Lush green eyes—the color of a forest after a hard rain. Hair as dark as a moonless sky. Lips that would tempt a saint. And his woodsy scent that drifted into my nostrils and eased the memory of the nightmare.

He tapped my face. "Hey, was someone trying to kill you in your sleep again?"

I rubbed the chills from my arms. "No, I was already dead."

One thick eyebrow lifted. "Come again?"

I swung my legs over the bed in a room tucked within an unused wing of the medical facility. It had all the standard furniture and accessories along with four cribs, a bathroom, and a window with a view of a building across the street.

"I'll tell you about it in a minute." I needed a second to digest what I'd dreamt. "First, have you seen Jo? She offered to watch the kids while I took a quick nap."

Sam handed me the piece of paper in his hand. "The note on the dresser says she's with Dr. Vieira in the lab. The babies and Agnes are with them. I just came from Jordyn's room, and Wendy told me where you were."

I slumped against my husband. "There's a possibility Jordyn might be paralyzed."

He traced circles on my arm. "Let's not go there."

It was hard not to think the worst. "Can we find a place on this planet free of pain, enemies, and suffering?" I knew that was an impossible feat. I also knew our happily ever after might not be that house on the beach and a life where we didn't have to hide our children or run. But a girl could hope.

"Baby doll, if I could give you everything you wish for, you know I would."

"I know." My tone was low and sad. "It doesn't help my psyche when I see myself lying in a coffin with my neck mangled and an ear missing. Normally, I wouldn't think twice about my dreams, but mine now have some truth to them." My fingertips skated over Roman's bite marks, and I could feel the rough scabs and ridges. "I pray Roman's ashes are blowing in the wind."

Sam growled, his muscles snapping taut.

I pursed my lips. "What is it? He's not dead, is he?"

A muscle ticked in Sam's unshaven jaw as a pensive look washed over him. "We don't think so."

I placed a gentle hand on his face and guided him to look at me. "What else happened in your meeting with your dad?"

He went over to the window. "Ross's head showed up, as did Victor Costner's."

The news punched air from my lungs, pangs of sorrow stabbing my chest. I crossed the room, feeling chilled and heartbroken. "Where's Dane now?" I untangled his curled fingers and held his hand.

He tipped his head at the window. "Out there somewhere. He shifted."

Taxicabs lined one side of the street. Cars slowed down at traffic lights. Pedestrians held umbrellas, waiting to cross streets, and delivery trucks were double-parked.

For the longest time, we stared out at a bustling city of four million people, who were going about their days and none the wiser to the problems in the supernatural world. Then again, they knew vampires existed, though not shifters or witches.

The door opened, and Jo and Abbey breezed in.

Sam wiped the despair off his face, replacing it with a huge grin as Abbey ran toward us. Her blue eyes were rimmed in red, as were Jo's.

I had no words, and I felt as though I was becoming numb to the tragedies around me. It was like a never-ending cycle of grief and pain, and the gravity of it was crushing me under its merciless grip. I had lost so many people in my life, and each time it happened, whether the person was close to me or someone on our team, a part of me died with them.

I was trying to hold back tears, afraid that if I cried I wouldn't stop. But when Abbey wrapped her arms around my waist, I lost my composure.

I held her tightly as she sobbed. "It's okay." I suspected she was distraught over what happened to Jordyn.

"I'm sorry," Abbey said. "I didn't mean to hurt Jordyn."

I squatted down and swiped gentle fingers over her rosy cheeks. "You didn't do anything wrong."

"My magic was too hard to control." Abbey's bottom lip wobbled.

My heart shattered in two at the overwhelming sadness in her tone, but more than that, it pained me to see that she blamed herself for Jordyn's injuries. The black-haired, blue-eyed ten-year-old carried the weight of the world on her shoulders.

I fixed her striped shirt where it was curled at the hem. "You're my hero. Never feel bad for protecting loved ones."

Abbey flattened a small hand on my face and glued her gaze to mine before she pulled away, blinking rapidly.

"What is it?" I asked the young seer who saw the future of those she touched. "Did you see something bad?"

The first time Abbey had attempted to read my future, she'd seen nothing. However, Rianne had been a different story. When she touched my sister's face, Abbey had seen Rianne killing me. That prediction hadn't happened, although I'd come close to dying by Rianne's hand.

She shook her head, her ponytail swinging side to side. "It's nothing."

Abbey didn't like to share her visions, and I would prefer not to know. Yet given my recent dream of my dead body in a coffin, I was curious if she'd seen the same thing.

"You know, Abbey," I said, "I just had a bad dream." I didn't want to describe the details and freak her out.

She stared at me in shock, her bright-blue eyes glistening with unshed tears. "Were you dead?"

My heart lurched as icy terror clutched my veins. I swallowed hard. "I was. Is that what you saw too?" I couldn't bring myself to breathe.

She nodded, her neck muscles straining with fear and dread. "Yes."

Sam inhaled sharply, standing motionless beside me. I couldn't bear to see him freaking out. Unfortunately, looking away wasn't an option.

He helped me to my feet. "I think we've had enough bad news for one day."

"You mean a lifetime," I teased, trying to infuse some light into the darkness hanging over us.

His narrowed gaze told me he wasn't impressed with my comment. The imposing vampire was an ice sculpture and white as a fucking ghost.

I pushed down my fear, rolling back my shoulders. "Vampire,

I'm not going anywhere." I had to say something—more to convince myself than him.

Abbey feigned a smile at Sam. "On a brighter note, I'm going to Sacred Flame Academy."

I had to applaud her for changing the subject.

Sam finally snapped out of his haze. "I think you'll like the school."

Jo strode over, her raven locks cascading over one shoulder. My beautiful sister-in-law had changed out of her scrubs and into tan capris, a black blouse, and black flats. "Not so fast, Abbey. Your dad and I haven't decided yet. We need to talk more about it."

Abbey's face crumpled, desperation etching into her frown. "But, Mom… you heard Agnes. It would help me control my magic, and I can learn a lot."

"You know she's my grandmother, and you and I are related," I said to Abbey as my mind shifted, and a cog on a wheel clicked into the place. I knew we shared the same maternal relatives, but I hadn't had a chance to really grasp that knowledge.

"I know. We're cousins," Abbey said with a big smile. "I like Agnes a lot. She's sweet."

I nodded. My grandmother reminded me so much of my mom. Both had a tender and caring side to them.

"I like her too," Jo added. "She and Dr. Vieira have hit it off. Oh, and Dr. Vieira is spoiling your children."

It seemed the resident vampire doctor would make a great godfather to the quadruplets. Actually, Ellie, Rorie, Luna, and Orion would probably have an entire team of godfathers and godmothers.

"Thank you, Jo, for watching them while I napped."

Jo clutched Abbey's shoulders. "Whatever help you need, I'm here. Abbey and I are meeting Alia. She needs us more than ever now. But we came in because Abbey wanted to see Layla."

Sam crouched down to Abbey's level. "I'm proud of you."

She hugged her uncle, then after we agreed to meet for dinner, Jo and Abbey left.

My husband closed the distance between us, exuding an aura of danger and menace, causing those butterflies in my stomach to take flight.

I inched away from him, my heart fluttering. The idea that I was trying to escape my husband had me laughing.

"Something funny?" he asked, not even grinning.

As he was about to back me into a wall, I scurried away and giggled. "Want to play hide-and-seek?"

Finally, the vampire cracked and let out a belly laugh. "We're in a medical facility. Not the woods."

I smirked as I stood in the doorway. "The wing is empty."

We both needed to lighten up. There had been too much heartache and destruction.

He stalked up to me. "How about another time? Right now, baby doll, if I don't feel you against me and just hold you, I'm going to explode."

"I'm sorry about the visions Abbey and I had."

His hands shaped my hips. His mouth was on my ear, and strands of his hair tickled my neck. "I don't want to talk about it. I'm tired of bad news after bad news."

Goose bumps blanketed my entire body. "I know what you need." I pushed him—or rather, he let me.

After I closed the door, I felt along his groin and squealed and squirmed over discovering that he was hard and ready.

He moaned, nibbling on my ear as I unbuckled his belt. I loved his cock in my mouth. I loved hearing the sexy sounds coming from him and seeing the pain and pleasure wash over him as I took him deep.

He grabbed my wrists, lifted my arms over my head, and

pinned me to the door. "As much as I'm dying for you to suck me off, I think we need to wait until we're home."

He was probably right. "Then kiss me, vampire."

He shoved his tongue into my mouth, took, tasted, and teased, kissing me like he was starving for something more, and I had no doubt he was. I knew I was hungry for him—to roll around in our own bed, naked and sweaty. We hadn't done that in forever. The last several times we had any type of sex was in a tent, in the woods, and in a motel.

He dragged his lips down my neck.

"I need you, Sam. I need us in our own place with our children in their nursery. I want to take bubble baths with you and long, hot showers. I want to lounge on our couch and watch our kids play."

He rubbed his nose over mine. "I know you don't want to leave Jordyn, but soon I can head home and freshen up our apartment. I won't be able to do that quite yet. I have to accompany my dad to a TV interview tonight."

"Seriously?" Shock rode my tone. "Why? I mean, I'm excited for you, but what is the interview about?"

He buckled his belt. "My dad is going to announce how we can help those who'd been affected by Adam's genetic-altering program. He wants me there because he thinks it's a good opportunity to change the perception humans have of me."

"Make sense. That means we can control the narrative."

"And my dad is going to ask you to be his liaison between us and the humans."

I squealed. "I would love that role."

I hadn't had a job to call my own since I'd met Sam, and even before that time, I hadn't had any steady employment.

"You will be fantastic at it." He traced a finger over my eyebrow. "I love you, baby doll. Why don't we go see our kids, and I'll fill you in on other things."

"You mean our vampire witches?"

He angled his head. "Have you talked to Doc?"

I fixed my wild hair into a messy bun. "Yep."

As we left the room, we talked about our children, the Mystic, and everything that had happened in his meeting.

By the time we entered the lab and set our sights on four beautiful precious beings, I didn't care about the Mystic or Adam's threats. The only thing that mattered was giving Orion, Luna, Ellie, and Rorie our undivided attention.

Sam strutted over to the four strollers by a lab bench where our children were watching Dr. Vieira wave a bubble wand around.

Sam lifted Ellie up. "I've missed you, baby girl." He peppered kisses all over her face, then hugged her like she was the only person in his world.

If anyone could reduce the arrogant, formidable Sam Mason to a puddle of water, it was his children.

I picked up Rorie, and the minute she was in my arms, I felt complete. Even more so when I laid eyes on Luna and Orion.

We had our children back. For the first time, I felt that sense of family as love poured out of Sam and me.

**19**

---

# LAYLA

Seven long days had passed, and Jordyn remained in a life-and-death battle. When I wasn't at her bedside, talking her ear off, or reminiscing about the good times we'd had growing up, I was busy with my children. I'd also volunteered to sift through bags of letters that were coming in after Violet Keller's interview with Sam, Steven, and Eugene Delgado, a human government representative.

Steven had officially offered me the liaison position, and I couldn't be happier. In preparation for my start date, which was still up in the air, I thought reading through the correspondence would give me a chance to understand the mood of the public. In turn, I could advise Steven on ideas and strategies that might help foster a relationship between us and humans.

I'd already read through a bin of letters, and so far, the common themes had been that they were shocked that vampires existed, they loved Steven and Sam's message to help those who couldn't protect themselves, and they hoped Steven, Sam, and Eugene could stop Adam Emery.

On top of that, I'd also read several letters from women and

144

some men who were in love with Steven or Sam. That didn't shock me. They were both handsome. I also wasn't surprised to read how Sam had a growing number of followers. Initially, he'd gotten a bad rap from many folks around the country, thanks in part to Adam Emery. However, people feared what they didn't know. At first, humans had seen a man with fangs on television who had been accused of compelling me into falling in love with him.

On the other hand, we also had naysayers who thought vampires were an abomination who should be wiped off the face of the earth. We certainly had our work cut out for us, and our strategy needed to focus on turning the cynics into believers. One way to do that was to make sure we followed through on everything we promised.

I opened my brand-new laptop Steven had given me and powered it on. Then I moved my piles of opened letters to one side of the table, ensuring that I didn't disrupt my filing system. I had three stacks—read again, save for Steven to read, and file away. I didn't want to throw any letters out yet.

The city lights of Boston twinkled outside the window. The room was eerily quiet until my cell vibrated on the table.

I opened the text app.

Sam: *Baby doll, I made it to our apartment. Things on the naval base seem normal except we still have a group of humans outside the gate. I don't think they'll leave anytime soon. But we do have more guards around the perimeters and on rooftops. I feel comfortable that you and the kids will be safe here. I'll call you later. Love ya.*

My cheeks flushed as I sent him several heart emoji, then a text.

Me: *Has Greta shown up with all our belongings yet?*

The she-wolf we'd stayed with at the shifter compound had offered to personally bring us all our stuff we had at her cabin. Her trip also involved Dane. He'd shifted and had taken off into the city a week ago. Since then, he hadn't returned, and he hadn't shown up at his compound either. Cooper had said it wasn't unusual for Dane to disappear for a few days when something bothered him. But Dane's pack was worried, and considering Greta was an expert tracker, she'd volunteered. How she would find Dane was beyond me. The three-day rainstorm in Boston had probably washed away his scent. Not to mention how difficult it would be to find Dane in a large city such as Boston.

Sam: *She just arrived.*

I turned my attention to my computer as I slid into a soft leather chair.

Agnes was watching the babies in my room in the unused wing of the medical facility with two guards outside my door. It wasn't that we didn't trust Agnes. In fact, Jo had read Agnes's mind the minute she'd stepped out of the SUV when we'd arrived, and Jo had continued to do so anytime she was with Agnes.

According to Jo, Agnes's emotional pain ran deep, and she was desperate to be a part of my life as well as Jordyn's and Abbey's. Sam had been apprehensive about trusting in mind reading. Those who knew about Jo's or Steven's supernatural ability could easily find a way to block them. But Agnes's thoughts matched her actions, and she also knew she had to prove herself if she wanted to be a part of our lives.

Regardless, we were being overly protective even though the building was heavily guarded. None of us wanted to take a chance if we had another mole.

I brought up the video of Sam and Steven's interview.

I'd been distracted during the live show. Luna had started crying that night, then Ellie followed suit. Both had been showing similar symptoms for the last several days to the ones that Rorie had when we'd been at Jo's house in Maine—warm to the touch and crying even after they'd been fed. I suspected they were hungry for blood, and it turned out that I was right. Now I was adding blood into all their formulas.

I had my pen and pad poised to take notes as I fast-forwarded past the small talk at the beginning of the segment.

Violet Keller sat in a fabric chair while Steven, Sam, and Eugene were seated on a couch angled toward Violet.

"Steven," the brunette reporter said. "What you're telling us is that humans can't become vampires by being bitten from someone like you?"

Steven nodded, his black hair tied at his nape, shining in the studio lights. "That's correct. As natural-born vampires, we have nothing in our physiology that can make a human into one of us. The recessive gene we're born with only allows us to turn if we so choose. Even then, there could be factors that prevent us from becoming immortal. We need our vampire father's blood to make the change. If he's dead, then we can't activate our recessive gene."

Like his dad, Sam wore his hair in a low ponytail, looking deliciously scrumptious in his white shirt that was open at the collar. No tie for Sam. They made him feel too claustrophobic. Both Steven and Sam had their shirtsleeves rolled three quarters of the way up their forearms, displaying large-faced, black-strapped watches that were designed for military missions.

I was so caught up in ogling my husband that I'd missed Violet's next question, so I toggled back a few seconds.

Violet leaned in slightly toward Steven. "Which means that if a vampire chooses not to activate their gene, then they'll grow old and will eventually die like a human. Correct?"

"That's right," Steven said.

Violet curled her dark hair around her ear in a flirty sort of way. The pretty reporter was dressed in a red skirt that crept above the knee, showing off her long, tanned legs and red-and-black pointy-tip heels that had to be at least three inches high. "If your people have a choice on immortality and the vampire father is alive, why wouldn't they choose eternal life?"

Sam's dimples were showing as he chuckled. "One reason is family. Natural-born females can't have children if they turn."

"This is all very interesting, and I have many more questions related to how you grow your population, but we are pressed for time. And I want to discuss a problem we're seeing in this country." She set her attention on Eugene. "Mr. Delgado, what is the human government doing to halt Adam Emery's genetic-altering program? It's been deadly to several humans, as we know from interviews they've done with the media. But is Mr. Emery and his corporation, Intech, still in business?"

The hefty man in a sharp suit and shiny shoes sat up straighter. "I can't divulge classified information. What I can say is Camden Industries and Intech Corporation had been supplying weapons and technology for our military forces. We have severed ties and dissolved all contracts with them. We're also working closely with Steven Mason and his organization to provide for those families who have recently suffered from the genetic-altering program."

Violet's short, bobbed hair fell forward as she briefly lowered her gaze to the notecards in her lap. "Sam, your father explained a little about your physiology, and it's not the folklore humans have read in books or watched on TV. So tell us, how exactly does Adam's program change a human into the animallike creatures we've seen so far? To give our viewers a reminder of a product of the program, on-screen are before and after images of Rianne Aberdeen."

I shivered seeing my sister as a normal human, then as something that would probably scare a tiger. Her cheekbones and forehead extended outward. Her nails were sharp and long, curling toward her fingertips, and her canines sent a chill through me.

"I'm not an expert on the genetics of Adam's program," Sam

said. "But the animallike image of Rianne is proof that the program does not produce a vampire or what Adam deems super soldiers. More importantly, we know of two other victims like Rianne. They've come to us for help. Unfortunately, the outcome is short-lived. In fact, death can be instant if the candidate has a compromised immune system or suffers from an incurable disease. If not, then it's only a matter of time. Anyone on the program *will* die."

"There's no cure or a way to reverse the process?" Violet asked.

"Not at this time," Steven said. "Will there be? It's hard to say."

Violet crossed her ankles. "I want to go back to the natural-born concept. You were born human with a distinctive gene that can turn you into an immortal creature during puberty. How do you think vampires evolved? Is it the same as human evolution where genetic variations started to adapt? And what is a vampire's purpose on earth?"

Sam and Mr. Delgado looked at Steven.

Steven grinned. "To answer your first question, we would need a lot more time to discuss the evolution of a vampire. But like humans, we arose from a species of organisms that developed through the natural selection process. As for your second question about what our purpose is on this planet, I would ask you the same. What's a human's purpose? Why are humans here? For that matter, why are animals, insects, etc.? You get my drift."

Violet's manicured eyebrows lifted as she smiled at Steven. "Point taken. We only have time for one more question. How do the vampire and human governments plan on stopping Adam Emery?"

"All we can say on the matter is, we're in talks right now about that," Steven said. "I would like to reiterate that we will take care of those victims' families who have been affected by

Adam's one-hundred-thousand-dollar offer to sign up for his program. How? Well, we're also in discussions on several different options to help the victims. We realize that whatever we do won't bring back loved ones, but we hope that our efforts will help in some way."

"Any final comments?" Violet asked.

"Yes," Sam said. "To add to what my father said, our mission is and has always been to protect those who can't protect themselves, which includes humans as well as vampires. We have laws and a military just like our human counterparts. We want peace. We strive for freedom, prosperity, and to raise our families in a safe environment. We're not the enemy."

"Over the coming months," Steven said, "Our plan is to start a dialogue with humans and listen to how our government can help them."

Violet straightened. "This interview has been informative, and I thank each of you for joining me tonight. I know there are more questions my viewers have that we haven't touched on." She faced the camera. "If you have questions for Steven Mason, Sam Mason, or Eugene Delgado, you can email them or send your letters via our postal system. The information is scrolling at the bottom of your screen. Until next time, I'm Violet Keller, CBC 4."

I clicked out of the video and jotted down a couple of notes, underlining the one about contacting Violet. She'd given her viewers the TV station's email address, and I wanted to ask if she would forward their emails to me. If we were to get along with humans, then I needed to read every piece of correspondence.

I picked up the envelope from the top of a stack of letters I had ready to read next. The beginning paragraph read:

*Dear Steven,*

*I'm in love with you and your son. It's not just your looks but also your genuine concern for humanity. If you want to help humans, I suggest that you start with low-income housing and infusing some new blood into the welfare system. I work for the city of Atlanta and would be happy to take you on a tour of those neighborhoods in need of help.*

I bet Ms. Lydia Erickson would love to do more with Steven than give him a tour, if the perfumed paper was any indication of her intent. I placed her note in the pile that I'd categorized as to be read again.

I continued going through letters, losing track of time as I yawned and checked my phone—ten p.m. I rubbed my neck, stretching. I tore open another envelope. I would read one more letter, then I would call it quits.

*Dear Steven,*

*After watching your interview the other night, I'm quite impressed with you and your son. I still can't wrap my mind around vampires and the reality of your kind. But having said that, I have seen quite a lot in my time on this earth. You remind me of my old senior chief in the Navy. He had a way of engaging his audience and commanding respect without slamming down the hammer. I applaud you and hope that you do help those families who've suffered at the hands of Adam Emery.*

*I'm a retired Navy SEAL, and I've been putting my skills to use to learn more about who Mr. Emery is. You may or may not know this, but Mr. Emery wants you to believe he's not in Chicago. I know for a fact he's been trying to set up shop in a new building in the city. However, the property isn't in his name but that of his brother, Fred Emery. Adam's hands are tied until his brother either signs the building over to him or Fred is released from your custody.*

*If you would like more information on Adam's activity in the city of Chicago, you can reach me at the phone number listed below my signature. Thank you for your time.*

*Retired Navy SEAL Petty Officer First Class Grant Vega.*

I was so absorbed in highlighting Grant's contact information that I didn't hear Steven come into the room until he cleared his throat.

"Layla, it's late," Steven said. "Surely, you have to be tired of reading letters by now."

I closed my laptop. "Not at all. But I was about to pack up for the night."

He sank into a chair across from me. "Have you found a topic, other than Adam Emery, that we need to focus on first?"

"I'll summarize my suggestions in a report for you."

He smirked, reminding me of Sam. Whereas my husband had two dimples, Steven had one. "You're excited about your liaison role, aren't you?"

"Very. I don't know how I've gotten so lucky as to have you as my father-in-law. The first time I met you, I almost peed my pants."

A hearty laugh escaped him. "If I recall, you didn't back down, nor did you wet yourself. But you're an Aberdeen. I haven't met anyone in your family who ran from me."

I relaxed in my chair. "We were brought up to not show fear, but facing off with a vampire certainly did a number on the nerves."

"Your ability to hold your head high despite adversity is what will make you shine as my liaison," he said. "I appreciate your efforts to collate a report for me, but can you give me the highlights while we're here?"

I examined my organized stacks. "We need to focus on ensuring we follow through on helping the victims of Adam's program. That's priority number one. The second is figuring out how you can assure the people that a vampire won't kill them. Those two topics are front and center. However, this letter is also worth addressing now." I slid the correspondence from the retired Navy SEAL over to him.

While he read Grant's message, I wrote down a few more issues to prioritize.

When he finished reading, he looked at me. "This is definitely worth checking out. We haven't had any hot leads on Adam's whereabouts. However, we now know why Adam is desperate for me to release Fred from our prison. Carly confirmed that Adam had Fred store a copy of Patrick's genetic-engineering files in a safe location no one but Fred would know. Adam was afraid that if he was ever confronted by his competitors or enemies, they would try to torture him for the information. And Fred's thumb drive has Carly's data on it as well."

"Does that mean Adam won't be producing any more monsters?" I asked.

"Hard to say. He has a new scientist, and he also has a notebook with Carly's notes that she'd left behind. I believe he will continue to try."

"How is Carly doing, by the way?" I asked. We had so much on our plates that my cousin-in-law wasn't on my priority list.

"The serum is affecting her at a slower rate than it did with Rianne and Noah. That's all I know at this point."

My phone vibrated. It was probably Sam. But when I saw Dr. Vieira's name on the screen, my heart stopped.

"Dr. Vieira is calling." I hurriedly answered. "Is Jordyn okay?"

"She's awake," Dr. Vieira said. "I've been slowly weaning her off the medication for the last several hours to bring her out of her coma."

Steven had a broad grin on his face, as he could hear Dr. Vieira.

I was crying happy tears. "I'll be right there."

I was out of my chair in a flash with my phone in hand. "Is it okay if I go see her?" I didn't want to be rude or interrupt our conversation.

"Go," he said. "We'll have plenty of time to talk later."

My pulse raced faster than ever as I flew out of the room and through the medical facility like a witch with wings.

# 20

## LAYLA

I was out of breath by the time I pushed through the double doors into the wing where Jordyn was. Isaac, the nurse on duty, jumped out of his seat at his desk.

The vampire with curly blond hair and lean physique was shorter than others I'd been around. He was a sweet guy who liked to keep everyone laughing and upbeat. He'd told me his boyfriend always rolled his eyes when Isaac told jokes. I appreciated Isaac's warm, friendly, genuine disposition. It had been refreshing amid the dreariness around here.

"Your sister has a guest." Isaac waggled his eyebrows. "A very hot and handsome one."

I stopped short. "Sawyer's here?" I asked myself more than Isaac.

Jordyn had the hots for the Vampire Navy SEAL's tech guru. I knew Sawyer was working on leads that he had. Maybe he'd driven the two hours from his tech cave at the naval base to meet with Tripp. I knew he hadn't tagged along with Sam. I'd seen Tripp with Steven and Webb shortly after Sam had left.

Then again, Isaac could be talking about Webb or Tripp.

They were both handsome. But I didn't see any reason for them to visit Jordyn. Tripp wasn't a fan of my sisters either.

As he circled his desk, he gestured with his head toward Jordyn's room. "Come on." He extended his elbow. "You look like you could use an anchor."

I inhaled slowly, catching my breath and hooking my arm through his. "How long has Jordyn been awake?"

"About an hour. Dr. Vieira started to wean her out of the medically-induced coma about four hours ago. He didn't want to alert you until he had a chance to run a quick exam and adjust any pain meds."

"She's fine, then? Can she walk?"

My stomach churned and roiled at the possibility that her freedom and independence could be forever stolen from her if she didn't have use of her legs. The anger at the senselessness of the violence that had brought us to this point, the frustration at the cruel randomness of fate, and a deep, gut-wrenching sadness at the thought of what she might have to endure had weighed heavily on me since Doc informed me of Jordyn's outlook if she made it through.

"Whether she can or not is something you'll need to discuss with Dr. Vieira."

The emotions spinning inside me came to an abrupt halt when I glanced through the window of Jordyn's room, and my jaw hit the floor. Tripp was sitting next to Jordyn's bed, fidgeting with his phone as if he was nervous, which was totally odd and confusing. He didn't even like my sister. Plus, I had yet to see Tripp anxious about anything.

Isaac leaned into my ear. "Isn't he swoony?"

The formidable sandy-blond vampire with eyes of the color of shiny pennies was nice to look at, but he wasn't my type.

"I just love a man in uniform," Isaac whispered.

The Navy SEAL uniform was an eye-catcher. I loved to see

Sam in his, especially with weapons around his waist and legs, hair tied back, biceps showing through the T-shirt with the Vampire Navy SEAL emblem sewn onto it, although Tripp's patch was different today. This was the first time I noticed the name Jupiter Sentinels.

My bewilderment lessened. "I don't think your boyfriend would appreciate you drooling over another guy."

"Pfft," he said. "That handsome creature with your sister is nothing but eye candy."

Tripp didn't swing Isaac's way. Come to think of it, I'd never seen Tripp with a significant other, so maybe he did.

Regardless, it was great to see Jordyn with her eyes open. No ventilator but an oxygen tube in her nose. She was still on the IV and tethered to the vitals machine, but at least she was wide awake. That was a celebration in and of itself.

"Is she still hooked up to the EEG?" I imagined she was, which was the reason for the green cap on her head.

"Dr. Vieira won't take her off the EEG for another day. He's being cautious. He'll explain everything when he finishes his phone call." He stabbed a thumb at the desk down the hall. "I have paperwork to finish."

I was tempted to probe Isaac more on Jordyn's outlook, in particular if she could walk, despite what he'd already said about it. But I knew nurses couldn't divulge too much about a patient's condition. Frankly, I wasn't sure I wanted to know right now. Jordyn was awake, and that was all that mattered for the moment.

"Hey, sis," I said as I entered.

Tripp jumped out of the chair faster than the speed of light.

"Layla." My sister's voice was rough and scratchy. Definitely because of the ventilator. "Tripp was just telling me you, Sam, Orion, and Luna were here."

I kissed her on the cheek. "I came as soon as Doc called me. I would throw my arms around you, but I don't want to hurt you." Happy tears cascaded down my cheeks, and I was feeling as though I could breathe easier now.

"I need to go." Tripp touched Jordyn's arm. "I'm really happy that you made it. If you need anything, let me know."

My eyebrows climbed to my hairline. Tripp had a heart and cared. I'd personally seen that side of him. But his actions and words weren't aligning with his dislike for Jordyn. Granted, it meant everything to me that he took the time to see her. I was sure he could feel and see my confusion. After all, he was an empath like Sam.

"Thank you, Tripp," she said.

We watched him swagger out of the room before Jordyn said, "I thought he hated me."

Even though I wasn't planning on broaching the topic of Tripp, she'd just given me an opening.

I sat in the chair that was still warm from Tripp. "It was sweet of him to visit you."

Her eyebrows knitted. "Tripp seems different from the last time I saw him at Jo's house in Maine. Did something happen?"

"Not that I know of." I tilted my head. "Different how?"

She shrugged. "The man I saw today wasn't an ogre. But I know he doesn't like me."

"I think we've all changed since we stormed that farm in North Dakota."

I knew I wasn't the same person anymore, not only because I was a witch with powers, but I had a sense of purpose and belonging and felt more empowered and alive than ever before.

"I know I'll never be the same after what I went through." She picked at her nail.

"Do you remember? I understand you hit your head pretty hard."

"I do." She licked her chapped lips. "I can't think of a

moment when I was overwrought with fear as strong as what I felt running from and fighting those vampires. Sure, I was afraid when we hunted them as kids, but we had Dad, Uncle Jack, and Uncle Ray with us."

I rested a hand on her cold arm. "You don't have to talk about it."

She brushed me off. "It's okay. I want to. But when I was fleeing with Ellie and Rorie, I kept thinking, if I die, I can't protect them." A tear cascaded down her cheek.

"They're doing great, by the way." If I knew my sister, she was about to blame herself. "You did everything you could."

"Maybe." She lowered her gaze to her lap. "I'm sure I'll have nightmares, but I need to tell you what happened. I need to get this weight off my chest."

I got comfortable for the intense conversation, unwilling to argue if my sister wanted to share. She was the type who liked to nip things in the bud, talk through what bothered her, and once she did, she could move on. Not that she would forget. After what she'd been through, it would take time before her emotional well-being returned to normal, if it ever did.

"I was running with Ellie. Alia had Rorie. Dane's grand-mother, Nina, and Abbey were ahead of us. There's a cave on the outside of the shifter compound that they use as an emer-gency shelter. Cooper had given me a gun, but the shifters don't use cobalt bullets because they don't usually fight off vampires." She paused for a breath. "We had a bloodsucker hot on our tails. But I couldn't do much while carrying Ellie. So Nina took her. I ran in a different direction to throw the vamp off from following Nina. He and I shot at each other until I had no more bullets."

Silence stretched between us as she dashed away a tear.

"He kept shooting, and I ran as hard as I could until I jumped over a branch," she said. "When my foot caught, I felt this piercing pain in my back. I fell, thinking that was it. Then

Abbey came to my rescue. She stood in front of me and unleashed her magic. She screamed as her hands and arms moved in all directions. I couldn't see what was happening to the vampire behind me. Whatever she did gave her time to help me. But she couldn't. All I was able to do was roll over onto my back. I told her to get help. No sooner than she left, another vamp came out of nowhere. As I sat up, I felt the bullet hit my chest." She touched a spot on the right side of her upper breast. "After that, I don't remember anything, not even hitting my head on a rock. Dr. Vieira told me my head injury was from Abbey's magic. She must've come back for me."

I was glued to her every word as I gritted my teeth. "Apparently, she did. You got caught in Abbey's line of magical fire. She's been blaming herself for what happened to you."

Jordyn inhaled deeply. "No, she shouldn't. I owe her my life."

I puffed out my cheeks. "I think she'll feel better knowing you've pulled through. I should've been there with you."

She pursed her lips. "I know the Aberdeens are famous for blaming themselves for shit that they shouldn't. I'm guilty of it as well. But I made my choices. That means *I* own them. Not you. I could've walked away that day when you found out you were pregnant and you urged me to start a life away from vampires. I thought about it, but I chose not to. Also, you can't forget that you were on the hunt to find Orion and Luna. You can't be everywhere at once, sis."

The tension in my shoulders was starting to take its toll on me. "You're right. But I want you to think about your own life. I want you to find your man, have kids, travel the world, and do something fun. Please, Jordyn."

"What about you? You can't take care of quadruplets by yourself."

I touched my heart. "I love you, Jordyn. You've always been there for me," I said in a choked tone. "I'll find a nanny or two.

For now, I want you to concentrate on healing and your future." I waggled my eyebrows. "What about asking Sawyer out on a date?"

She giggled or tried to. "Don't make me laugh. It hurts." She held her stomach. "I don't even know if he's interested."

"Maybe we could ask his sister Harley," I said.

I hadn't seen the strawberry-blond vampire in what seemed like ages. I adored her. We'd become fast friends the first day I drove onto the naval base with my sister Rianne, who had been compelled by Sam at the time.

"I can do my own investigating," Jordyn said. "We're not in grade school anymore."

I giggled, and the act felt freeing and liberating.

"Your turn," she said. "Tell me about the rescue mission. Did you meet the white-haired witch who is supposedly our grandmother?"

I'd spoken to Jordyn via phone a few times during my travels to Montana, Washington, and North Dakota. But the last time we'd spoken had been the day before we'd stormed the farm.

"Are you really in the mood to hear what happened?" I wasn't sure I was ready to relive the events, but she needed to know several things that transpired, especially my new witch powers.

"It's not like I'm going anywhere," she said.

I curled my legs underneath me and was about to start when I heard Dr. Vieira's voice. Then the possibility of her not being able to walk again stung my brain. Surely, she would've told me by now if that were the case.

Shoes scuffed on the floor as Dr. Vieira waltzed in, his brown eyes dancing with delight. "Layla, has Jordyn told you the good news?"

"I was waiting for you," Jordyn said to Dr. Vieira. "And we were talking about other things."

I laughed. "Are you referring to her ability to walk? If so, I was tempted to ask her, but I guess I wasn't ready to know. So…"

"Jordyn has feeling in her legs," he said.

I squealed. "That's the best news ever. Is there a *but* coming?"

"No," Jordyn answered. "I might need physical therapy for my back. Dr. Vieira gave me a dose of the healing blood, so that should help speed up the recovery process for my wounds. As far as my head goes, Dr. Vieira will set a final scan before I head to the naval base. Right, Dr. Vieira?"

Doc tucked his hands into his lab coat pockets, chuckling. "You are correct, Jordyn. But as we talked about, once we're back home, I want you to stay in the infirmary for a few days."

I was silently shedding tears. I couldn't have been happier at that moment. The fact that my sister was alive was a miracle. It was also a sign that she had a purpose to fulfill, and it wasn't as my nanny.

Happier times were ahead of us. I had to believe that.

# 21

# LAYLA

I'd been walking on air for the last three days since Jordyn came out of her coma. To see her smile, laugh, and talk about her dreams had taken away all the bad that had happened to us. Until Dr. Vieira broke the news to her that she had the same blood type as me, Vel negative—then her bubbly attitude took a downturn.

I thought she would be happy to know that she could get pregnant by a vampire. Not that she wanted to, but she had expressed interest in knowing one way or the other in the event that she slept with a bloodsucker.

"Do you want to talk about it?" I'd asked her.

"I need to process that I have the potential to have a vampire baby," she'd said.

To take her mind off the news, I'd filled her in about Agnes, what happened on the farm, how I became a witch, the Mystic, my new job with Steven, Sam's new position as the Vampire Navy SEAL's training instructor, how her nieces and nephew were vampire witches, Rianne's prognosis, and everything in between. We'd laughed and cried for hours on end.

That cheerful feeling followed me all the way to the naval base, as the second we'd driven through the emergency gate on the backside of the base, I felt a sense of peace wash over me. We were home. My family was whole again, and for once, fate seemed to be on our side.

I squealed when Sam opened the door to our apartment—or as he called it, the penthouse suite. I wouldn't use that term. To me, a penthouse was on a very top floor of a high-rise building and overlooked a city like Boston. We were only on the fourth floor, and our view outside was of the base prison.

I lugged Ellie and Luna into the apartment in the carriers, which weighed me down. Thank God we had an elevator in the building. "I can't believe we're actually here."

When I'd packed up to leave for Jo's house in Maine close to seven weeks ago, I honestly thought the building wouldn't be here if we ever returned. Intruders had wormed their way onto the base that day. With the large mob of humans that had been outside the gate, I wasn't confident that many of the structures would be standing—or that we would be either, for that matter. Although if my dream and Abbey's vision came true, then my days were numbered.

I couldn't control the outcome. So I kicked the last thought to curb and padded deeper into the open floor plan as the moon cast a glow through the wall of windows.

We'd left Boston later than the rest of the team. Sam, Greta, and Tripp wanted to scour Boston for Dane.

Sam set Orion and Rorie on the couch in their baby carriers. "Greta helped me clear away the dust and cobwebs."

I followed suit with Ellie and Luna, then unhooked my bag from around my chest. "The place looks amazing." I inhaled the fresh pine scent wafting in the air, making a mental note to thank Greta.

She'd stayed in Boston to continue her search for her alpha.

Cooper and the Gray Pack were on edge that Dane might be hurt and couldn't shift—or worse, he was dead. According to Cooper, if Dane could shift, he would've done everything he could to call.

I flicked on the light in the kitchen that overlooked the spacious family room. Formula and baby bottles were organized on the counter. The stainless steel appliances sparkled, and a chalkboard sign leaning up against the backsplash near the stove read Welcome Home and was signed by Greta.

Sam skirted the island, swaggering in and wrapping his arms around me. "I just love seeing you happy. It's been too long since we've been able to kick back. I know we have a busy week ahead, but we'll steal time here and there. Plus, we have nights together in our own bed." He waggled his eyebrows.

I buried my face in his chest, absorbing his sandalwood scent. "That last part sounds amazing." I pressed my hands into his six-pack abs. "You might have to settle my nerves before my first day tomorrow."

He gave me a roguish grin. "Anything your heart desires. I'm here to please you."

"First, you'll have to pinch me. I can't believe I have a job."

He chuckled, the sound melting my heart. "My father is thrilled to have you as his liaison. And you'll do great with your first TV interview."

"Nothing like throwing me straight into the fire," I said playfully.

Steven had thought it might be too soon for me to dive into work given Jordyn's condition, and I had the babies to care for. I didn't want to wait. Jordyn was on the mend, and my grandmother Agnes had agreed to babysit. She was staying with Jo, Webb, and Abbey at their house on base. I was reserving Sam's old bedroom for Jordyn when she was released from the infirmary.

Sam combed his fingers through my hair. "You'll be a natural on TV. Right now, we should get the kids to bed so we can do something I've been thinking about on the drive here." He guided my hand to his groin. "It involves him."

I whimpered, feeling his cock grow against my hand.

His fangs slid out as he dragged his lips up my neck to my ear. "And this spot right here. I want to taste you so fucking badly." He rubbed a hand along my inner thigh.

I whimpered again as butterflies tickled the lining of my stomach. There was nothing more erotic than him piercing his incisors into my flesh and drinking from me.

Tonight was a chance for Sam and me to really reconnect in our own bedroom, bed, and en suite and unwind without worrying about anything other than him and me.

"We should put the babies to bed. Then we can start with a bubble bath."

"Baby doll, I'm not sure I can wait to fuck you."

I pouted, thrusting my hips into his erection. "No foreplay first? And don't forget what you just told me. 'Anything your heart desires. I'm here to please you.'"

"Your wish is my command, queen." His lips curled at the corners, his dimples winking at me.

I giggled. "I might have something in mind for our first round of foreplay, then."

The vampire wasted no time in collecting two of our children and beelining it for the nursery.

I giggled as I ambled over to the couch and lifted my two daughters, who were sleeping, and met Sam in the nursery.

He was already kissing his son on the head before he placed Orion in a crib. "I love you, baby boy. You are the stars, the moon, and the universe."

To see my powerful husband melting over his children

brought tears to my eyes, even more so when he lifted Rorie out of her carrier and rubbed his nose over hers.

"Aurora Mason, our little witch." He smoothed a hand over her red hair and peppered gentle kisses over her face. "You look like your momma," he said, setting Rorie in her crib. "I'm still in shock and awe that I have children and a beautiful wife. I never imagined myself as a father." He rubbed a hand down her back. "I love all of you so much it hurts."

I cried and laughed at the same time, words escaping me as I held Luna in one hand and Ellie in the other.

He proceeded to take Luna from me.

I was mesmerized, unable to move or tear my gaze away from the sight of Sam with his beloved children. Every fiber of my being seemed to vibrate with emotion at the sheer beauty of the moment, an uplifting feeling that left me breathless and overjoyed.

Maybe I was consumed with an overabundance of feelings, but I swore I could sense the magic in the room. The sensation was a cross between tingles and light, feathery touches dancing along my skin.

"Sam, do you feel the energy in the room? Or am I just too sentimental right now?"

Once he'd cooed and whispered sweet nothings to our raven-haired, violet-eyed beauty, Luna, he took Ellie from me. "There's definitely magic. I can feel yours. In fact, your eyes are glowing yellow."

"They are?" I had no idea.

"Remember, heightened emotions can trigger your magic." He played with Elara's—or as we called her, Ellie's—red curls, admiring his daughter, who had blue orbs the color of the ocean off Bora Bora.

I had to somehow work on being more aware of myself. I certainly couldn't have my eyes change color on TV. *Holy hell.*

That would stir some new viral videos. But that was a worry for another day.

While Sam tucked Ellie in, I sighed as I took in the nursery. The room itself was magical with the gray walls, the hint of blues and pinks in the curtains, musical crib mobiles of safari animals, the gray-and-black elephant rug, two rockers beneath the window, and stuffed animals scattered about.

Sam came over and draped an arm around me. "I feel your tension, baby doll."

"I keep having moments of relief, but when I think of them growing up, fear grips every muscle in me. I want them to have an ordinary childhood—play dolls or trucks, sports, learn music if that's what they're interested in, or anything other than supernatural shit."

He guided me to face him. "We will make sure they have as normal a childhood as possible. But we can't shield them from who they are. Plus, we need to teach them how to control their powers, how to fight, to protect one another, and in doing so, they'll be better equipped to face whatever dangers are dropped in front of them."

I shivered. "A mom can dream of a peaceful existence for her children."

My parents had tried to give my sisters and me a quiet upbringing without the bloodshed or rushing into a state of emergency because a hoard of vampires had overtaken my uncle Jack's ranch. But prior to us learning that vampires were real, our home had been bathed in love—family dinners every night, my sisters and me riding horses, playing in the yard, and doing all the fun things that kids do. Sam and I could do the same.

"I just want them to understand that despite their inhuman abilities, humanity is just as important to supernaturals as it is to humans," I said.

"Baby doll, we have time. They're not even walking yet."

I snorted. "They might be in a few months. Remember, their growth isn't normal compared to human infants."

"Okay, I need to take your mind off things. Does foreplay ring a bell?"

He got a snicker out of me. I gave our precious sleeping children one last look before he and I went into our master suite.

The second I was in our bedroom, I flopped onto the king-size bed, sighing and reveling in the softness of the quilt beneath me.

Sam flipped the switch on the wall, and the lamps on the bedside tables were illuminated.

I rose up onto my elbows. I'd almost forgotten what the room looked like. The walls were painted a soft blue, a large, framed photo of Sam and me at our handfasting ceremony hung over our dresser across from the bed, and an oversized chair sat in the corner.

A sharp hissing sound filled the space, drawing my attention to the entrance of our en suite.

Sam unzipped his jeans, then bent over to untie his boots.

"Are you about to give me a show?" My lady parts awakened.

"I'm about to take you to heaven." His raspy tone sent delightful shivers south to pinch my clit.

"Round one of foreplay." I adjusted my position on the bed and curled my legs underneath me. "I want to watch you strip, then play with yourself."

He obliged on the first part until he was stark naked.

My gaze took a slow and sensual hike down the length of his body, and a low purr crawled out of me, sounding like a satisfied cat being scratched behind the ears.

With my eyes, I traced the thin line of hair down to his erect cock, my tongue darting out to lick my lips.

A growl like that of an aroused wolf rumbled deep in his throat. "I want to see your tits." He widened his stance, his powerful thighs anchoring him as he slowly stroked himself, watching me watch him.

But that lustful feeling, the mood, and the moment that strung us together was obliterated when a fucking phone rang.

Sam ignored the incessant noise until the ringing stopped—only to start up again.

"Fuck," he bit out, fishing in the pockets of his jeans until he found his phone.

I returned to sitting on the bed. "Something must've happened."

It couldn't be intruders on base because the sirens would've gone off. Jordyn came to mind. Maybe Dr. Vieira was trying to reach me. My phone was in my bag in the family room.

"It's Tripp." He sighed, his erection gone with the wind. "What is it, man? It's eleven at night." He paused to listen. "Fuck. I'll be right there." After he hung up, he threw on his jeans. "We've only been home less than an hour, and the shit has hit the fan already."

My pulse skyrocketed. "Please tell me that we don't have to flee again."

He shrugged into a T-shirt. "It's Dane. Cooper found a YouTube video of some fucking human who is holding Dane in his garage. Wolf Dane, that is. It seems he can't shift for some reason." He laced up his boots. "Greta is picking him up, and she's on her way here. Apparently, he is in bad shape. That's all I know so far."

We knew something had happened to the alpha, but I wasn't expecting this scenario. I didn't even want to think about the reactions from humans, especially if the video went viral like Sam's had. After those folks in the hospital parking lot had snapped photos of Sam with fangs, my husband's handsome face was on every news station coast-to-coast.

I followed him out of the room. "I hope Dane is okay."

He tied his hair in a low ponytail with a leather strap. "Me too. I'm sorry, baby doll. I'll be back as soon as I can, then we can pick up where we left off." He gave me a quick sloppy tongue kiss. "I love you." Sam was definitely grumpy and worried.

After he left, I closed the door, leaned against it, and blew out a sexually frustrated breath. It was time for a drink, and I didn't mean water. I recalled seeing a bottle of bourbon in the pantry when I'd been pregnant.

As I wound my way through the kitchen, a dozen things instantly sprang to mind.

Not only was I starting my new job tomorrow, but the week ahead was filled with a list of events. Zoey Thornton was flying in this week. Agnes had gotten in touch with the teacher from Sacred Flame Academy, and Zoey only had a small window of time before the fall semester started. I had loads of questions about the Mystic, and Jo and Webb wanted to chat with Zoey about the potential of Abbey attending the witch academy.

On top of that, Captain Greer of the Midnight Raiders had set up a meeting between Dr. Vieira and her resident scientist, who believed that a vampire couldn't turn a witch. But the scientist hadn't conducted any experiments combining a witch's DNA with my children's. Even when she had the opportunity to run tests, the Midnight Raider's scientist was confident that the results would still confirm her original findings because of a dream she'd had.

I was anxious to see the results. Hell, I was praying that prophecy had no merit to it. It would be one less headache. More importantly, we wouldn't have witches hunting our children.

I ducked into the small closet that housed mostly paper towels, canned goods, formula, dishes, cases of water, and a safe. The bourbon was on the top shelf next to a bag of coffee.

I snagged the bottle, twisted off the cap, and took a swig. No glass needed. The burn jolted me before warmth slid through my veins.

*One day at a time, girl. One problem at a time.*

I went over to the wall of windows, sipping the alcohol and hoping nothing was seriously wrong with Dane. The alpha was becoming family to me. He'd gone out of his way to help us rescue Orion and Luna. Plus, my heart hurt that Dane had just lost his brother Ross. On that note, I drank again, wincing from the sheer burn of the alcohol.

Darkness crawled through the courtyard below, broken only by the moon's light casting an eerie glow on the sentry standing guard outside the prison building. Instantly, a sense of déjà vu enveloped me. The last time I stood in this spot, I'd spied Jordyn running through the courtyard in a failed attempt to get past the guard and inside to see Fred Emery. That asshole had affected my sister's psyche more than I had realized. Not only had he smashed her face into a parked car that night I'd been kidnapped by Roman at the local hospital in Fall River, but Fred had also come onto her when she'd interviewed with Intech last February. To add to her hatred for the man, Fred had also confessed to murdering our father.

Tonight, I felt the same ominous chills that were skating down my spine, but this time that prickle had more to do with my other sister, Rianne. She was in one of those prison cells in the basement of the building. The magnitude of just how close she was suddenly clouded my excitement to be home.

As I drank from the bottle, I replayed what Steven had told me about Rianne in the underground garage.

*"She's changing, growing stronger. Her features are more pronounced, and she's losing the ability to shift into human form. Dr. Vieira's studies on both Noah and Rianne have produced very similar results despite Rianne's super-natural bloodline. He suspects that Rianne will eventually not know who she is, just like Noah."*

I clung to the bourbon like it was my salvation when in fact I hoped it was Rianne's. I wanted to turn the clock back and try for the hundredth time to knock some sense into her. I missed her despite how infuriating she could be. I also couldn't forget all the wonderful times we had as sisters—laughing, teasing, partying, and loving each other. I wanted more of those days where we rode horses together or talked about her flying jets for the military. Her dreams were never to be realized, and that broke my damn heart.

I wished there was a cure or a way to reverse the genetic-altering process, but I was reaching for a miracle thinking that way. Now, I just didn't want her to suffer, especially if she was in pain or didn't know who she was.

Maybe it was time to end her life. But was I the one to make that decision?

# 22

## SAM

I stalked through the building, feeling frustrated as hell with blue balls to match. Just when I thought I could relax and unwind with my wife in our home, things went to shit. I'd planned on fucking her the way she liked, but I wouldn't have argued if she wanted to watch me jack off.

As soon as I shoved open the back door of the building, the fishy salt air from Mount Hope Bay about knocked me sideways a step. The moon was bright in the night sky, casting its rays down over the water in the distance.

I scanned the car-filled parking lot, looking for Tripp as a sense of foreboding sizzled like sparklers in the humid breeze.

I hoped nothing serious had happened to Dane. I didn't know a great deal about shifters. But it had crossed my mind that losing his brother Ross might be a reason Dane couldn't return to human form. Something that gut-wrenching fucked with the psyche, and maybe he wanted his wolf to take over. If he did, he could lose his humanity altogether. As much as Dane and I had a rocky start to our relationship or lack thereof, I considered him a friend and part of my family now.

I checked my phone for a message from my lieutenant, making sure I didn't miss a text telling me that he'd changed the location. Or maybe I hadn't heard him correctly, and he'd meant the front entrance. After all, my mind had been on my wife.

I'd started to take a walk around the building when Tripp called my name. I pivoted on my heel to find him strutting down the walkway from the opposite end of the building, wearing ripped jeans, a Navy SEAL T-shirt, and his military boots. As usual, his phone was glued to his ear. The man was always putting out fires. Despite his casual attire, he had his dagger in a sheath around his leg and a gun holstered to his hip.

I listened to the voice on the other end, which sounded like Cooper.

One tap of the screen and Tripp held out his cell. "Coop, I have Sam here with me. Can you repeat what you just told me?"

"My tech guys have been scouring the net for any chatter about a white wolf in the city of Boston. Earlier today, we found a YouTube video of a guy showing off a white wolf. This Terrell Watson thought the wolf had wandered into the city from the wild and was lost."

Tripp and I exchanged what-the-fuck looks. Wolves in the wild weren't as large as Dane.

Cooper made a noise in the back of his throat. "Terrell found Dane on the wharfs in Boston. According to Terrell, Dane seemed sluggish and disoriented, which tells me something is physically wrong with him. His wolf would never go near a human unless he was being attacked. Although, he had hitched rides from Chicago with truckers after he'd escaped Intech with Sam. He'd had the chip in his head then."

Dane and I had both been prisoners of Intech. Not only did Carly Aberdeen take our DNA, but she had also implanted microchips in the backs of our skulls for the sole purpose of controlling us. Adam Emery's program to build super soldiers and use them as robots had been a failure. I had my chip removed, but to my knowledge, Dane hadn't.

"Dane never had the device taken out," I stated.

"My brother is one stubborn motherfucker. I've tried to coax him into having it surgically removed. But he's not a fan of anyone cutting into his skull."

"Can't blame him there, dude," I said.

Creases marred Tripp's forehead. "You think the chip is fucking with him, then?"

"Possibly. Maybe the freaking thing engaged somehow." Cooper sounded as though he wanted to tear out someone's insides. Probably Adam Emery's, if I had to guess. "According to Greta, Dane hasn't been shot. There are no signs of deep wounds. My gut says it's the chip."

That brain-to-machine device had certainly fucked me up— to the point that I landed in a coma. Not to mention, when I rescued Layla from the clutches of Intech, her bitch of a sister, Rianne, had managed to turn on my microchip in the hopes that she could order me to kill Layla. I would have if Layla hadn't gotten through to me.

"Dr. Vieira isn't arriving until the morning," Tripp said. "But Peter Landon, the scientist who originally developed the microchip, is on our staff now."

"I remember him," Cooper said. "Our resident doctor, Dr. Hammond, is heading your way. I'll text you her ETA. If it is that fucking device, she's the best one to do surgery. I would be there, but I can't leave. We're still cleaning up after the fiasco with Roman Brown's men. I understand he might be alive. Actually, I hope so. Because I'm hunting down that motherfucker and taking an axe to his head once and for all. Then I'm going to do the same with Adam Emery." He growled like the wolf he was.

"We'll be right by your side," I added.

"One last thing, Coop," Tripp said. "This Terrell guy, is he going to be a problem? That video might go viral. I don't have to tell you that humans are on edge with vampires after all of the publicity. Their curiosity is on high alert now. I wouldn't doubt that a headline might someday read: 'Vampires Exist. Can a Human Shift into a Wolf?'"

He sighed. "I'm not going to lie. We're finding other videos on the Internet of Dane in Boston. But we've already hacked into Terrell's computer and wiped his video."

Tripp's jaw flexed. "Give us an update about when Dr. Hammond will be here." Then he clicked off. "I knew when he took off into Boston, we were going to have a problem. We can't put out that fire. We have too much shit of our own to deal with. Can you call Jo and ask her to meet us in the infirmary while I alert the guards at the gate to allow Greta through? Then I'll have Peter escorted to the infirmary."

I would bet my father and Webb also knew that Dane trotting around Boston as a humongous wolf would garner attention. If the news hadn't already reported anything on a white wolf in Boston, it wouldn't be long.

I did as Tripp commanded, creating distance from him as he began talking to the sentries at the front gate.

My sister's cell rang once, and Webb answered. "What happened, Sam?" His voice was rough and scratchy.

"I should ask you the same thing. Where's my sister?" The fact that I was talking to him and not Jo gave me reason to pause.

"Abbey had a terrible nightmare. Jo and Agnes are with her now."

"Another one about Roman kidnapping her?" I asked, grinding my molars, although her recent vision of my wife being dead had hit me between the eyeballs. What scared the fuck out of me was that Layla had a dream with the same outcome.

"I'm not sure yet. Tell me what happened," Webb ordered.

"We found Dane. Greta is bringing him in now. He can't shift. We need Jo's doctor-in-training skills."

"Can we have one fucking day without the shit hitting the fan?" His annoyance and ire rang through the line loud and clear as he hung up.

I was beginning to believe that my immortal life would never include a day to bask in the sunshine. Right now, we had to help Dane. We owed him. He'd opened his home to us, fought with us, and could've died rescuing Orion and Luna.

Thirty minutes later, Jo was pressing her stethoscope to the wolf's chest. Dane was on a lab bench, his breathing shallow. He was dirty, there were spots of blood on his white coat, and his red eyes seemed dilated.

Across from my sister was Peter Landon, who was opening a silver hard-shell suitcase. The wiry older man with salt-and-pepper hair adjusted his glasses higher up on his nose. I hadn't seen the scientist since he removed the chip from my skull, and I would never forget that day I'd almost become permanently blind.

As I stood between Greta, the petite brunette she-wolf, and Tripp, who had his arms crossed over his chest, I took a trip down memory lane.

*I sat in one of those vitrectomy chairs—or in layman's terms, a kneeling chair.*

*Peter pulled on a pair of nitrile exam gloves. "I'm going to inject a small amount of sodium hydroxide into the base of your skull in the area just below where the chip is located. The chemical will dissolve the glass surrounding the chip, and in turn, the contents inside will break apart and flush into your bloodstream."*

*Doc pinched the bridge of his nose. "You might feel like you're burning from the inside out, but it won't be as bad as if you had cobalt in you. The good news is—sodium hydroxide won't kill you. The bad news is—it could damage some brain cells."*

*Jo had her mouth slightly ajar, standing in my line of sight next to Peter. I didn't need to feel her anxiety. Her expression said it all.*

*"Before we start," Doc continued, "we're going to hook up an IV containing your blood to help flush your system faster, and, at the same time, it should heal any damage to your internals, including your brain cells."*

*"Hooyah!" I bit out the navy's battle cry in a sarcastic way rather than what it was originally intended for—to build morale. "Let's do this."*

*Once the IV of blood was streaming through my veins, Peter primed the needle that had to be six inches in length. PTSD slapped me across the face, reminding me horrifically of the needles my uncle Patrick had used on me— and the one Carly had used more recently.*

*My fangs throbbed for release as anticipation scraped my nerves. I might live off the fear of my enemy but not off my own. Losing my loved ones was my number one fear. Coming in second was flying. Rounding out third was needles.*

*"One last thing," Peter said. "Your occipital lobe that controls your vision resides in the back of your brain. It's possible your vision could be compromised. Since you're a vampire, it might only do temporary damage, like what happened to your hearing, which returned."*

*"Wait one fucking second. You chose now to tell me this?" I eyed Doc. "That's why you're sweating?"*

*Doc donned a pair of exam gloves. "Sam, the chip is damaged, which means it can't engage anymore. We could leave it in."*

*Jo shook her head. "If I were you, I would remove it. You'll have peace of mind, knowing that the chip won't shift again."*

*I was the one sweating now. "From the start, I've wanted to take it out regardless of whether it's working or not. I should heal anyway, right?"*

*Doc bobbed his head. "You should, but there is always that chance you don't. I know I sound unsure. That's because I haven't dealt with the vampire brain."*

*"Just do it," I said.*

*Once the procedure was finished, I sat up, opened my eyes, and my heart came to a screeching halt. "I can't see."*

Thanks to Dr. Vieira's quick thinking that day, he'd injected a dose of shifter blood mixed with Abbey's blood that he'd discovered healed like a charm. That was the only reason I wasn't blind.

Greta was snacking on her thumbnail and fixated on the metal headgear in Peter's hands.

I leaned into her. "It looks alien, doesn't it?" If I never had to see that piece of crap Peter was holding again, it would be a miracle. "Peter, after tonight, I vote for you to melt that thing."

Tripp's phone sounded with a text. "It's Webb. I'll be right back."

Peter powered up his laptop, ignoring my comment. "It's possible the chip moved. Just like it did with yours, Sam. Other than surgery, we could try a procedure I used on Sam to dissolve his device with sodium hydroxide. But until I know more about shifter physiology, I don't want to risk it. Greta, when you shift, is the process controlled by the brain or more on instinct?" Peter asked.

The she-wolf lifted dark eyebrows. "Emotions, instinct, and a full moon can spur it on, but that's more for the younger wolves," she said. "Healing-wise, our process isn't as quick as with bloodsuckers. You have to keep in mind that we're not exactly immortal. Also, our kryptonite is wolfsbane. As far as sodium hydroxide, I wouldn't give you the green light to use that on Dane. You can consult with Dr. Hammond when she arrives."

"Jo, can you hold the headgear steady on Dane, please?" Peter asked. "I want to check if the device has been activated. Then do an MRI."

"You can't send him to a human hospital," I said. "But maybe a veterinarian."

"Our new wing now has an MRI machine," Jo said, like I should know this.

I cocked an eyebrow. "I've missed a bunch since I've been gone."

Jo held the headgear steady. "Dad is moving ahead as fast as he can. We break ground in the spring for the new school as well. He's also purchased a parcel of land outside the south gate where the abandoned textile company is. We'll be expanding even more."

And all it took for us to change and grow was my ugly mug on TV, which had started a viral awakening about the fact that we existed, as well as Adam's news conference proving that vampires lived among humans.

Peter banged on a few more keys, pushed up his glasses with his middle finger, and leaned closer to his computer screen. "The chip hasn't been activated. I'm pretty sure it moved, which is affecting him."

Jo adjusted Dane's IV. "Dane has blood in his eyes. I suspect he took a hard blow to the head."

"That would definitely cause the device to move," Peter mumbled.

I dropped several expletives under my breath. Humans might be able to swallow one supernatural creature, but throw in another one, and hunters would have a field day.

## 23

———————

# LAYLA

Sam and I were winding our way from our apartment to the
infirmary. Dr. Vieira had texted me earlier to let me know
Jordyn was on-site. I had a couple of hours before I officially
started my new job working for Steven. It was a rather big day. As
my first assignment, I was meeting reporter Violet Keller. The
topics included me and the public's follow-up questions after the
interview with Steven, Sam, and Eugene. Plus, I was giving her a
tour of the naval base.

Steven suggested that I didn't need to jump into the new role
until I was settled and Jordyn was up and about, but I insisted
otherwise. I had to feel like I was contributing, and I believed in
Steven and his vision that vampires could coexist among humans.

Happy, giddy, and nervous was how I would describe my state
of mind. Those emotions had formed into one big knot in my
stomach, twisting into a super tight ball. Would I screw up the
interview? Would I puke on camera? I wasn't fond of public
speaking or having someone tape me.

I yawned as my high heels clicked along the tiled floor in the
never-ending hallway. I'd barely slept, although the bourbon had

helped to relax me. But the minute I'd fallen asleep on the couch while waiting for Sam to come home, Ellie woke me, then Luna started crying. Trying to feed two babies at once was quite the challenge, but when the four of them were hungry, it was impossible. The job of caring for quadruplets would require two nannies. Agnes and Abbey were babysitting today. But long-term, we had to find someone we could trust. I couldn't always rely on family. They had their own lives.

*I can do this. I won't screw up. Just focus on Violet and not the camera, just like you did with her in Bozeman, Montana.* I'd gone on TV simply to encourage bystanders outside the Pacific Dome Casino to clear the area. My paternal grandmother had a wild idea to do a TV interview to lure Sam to the casino rigged with C-4 in her failed attempt to kill him.

"You're going to do great." Sam's husky tone cut through the mental pep talk I was giving myself.

He, too, was beginning his new position as training instructor, and he was dressed for the part as well. His short-sleeved black Navy SEAL T-shirt stretched across his broad chest and showed off his bulging biceps. Cargo pants hung low on his hips with weapons strapped in strategic places.

My lady parts throbbed every time I set my gaze on him. To quote nurse Isaac, "I just love a man in uniform."

Sam gave me a sidelong glance, sweeping his luminous forest-green eyes up and down my body. "And if I haven't told you already, you look smoking hot in that outfit. I'm picturing you wearing nothing but those high heels while I fuck you."

My cheeks burned hotter than a furnace as I slipped my phone into my sweater pocket. Sam had been ogling me since I'd walked out of the bedroom in my black A-line skirt, a sleeveless red-and-white silk blouse beneath a soft white sweater, and black pumps with two-inch heels. While in Boston, I'd had a chance to buy three outfits in preparation for my new job.

I playfully swatted at him. "I don't need to be flustered thinking about your dick while Violet is asking me questions."

He pouted. "But we haven't finished what we started before we were rudely interrupted last night."

"Barring any more unforeseen emergencies, maybe we can resume our tryst after the babies are asleep. I'll even prance around our bedroom in nothing but these shoes."

He adjusted the package growing in his pants. "I want to fuck you right now."

As we turned a corner, I scanned the area to see if anyone was around even though I knew no one was. The fourth floor of the building consisted of our apartment on one end and the infirmary on the other, with quite a distance between.

"Dane's having surgery, right?" I asked, knowing the answer, but it would divert Sam's attention away from sex—although if he wanted to find a room and have a quickie, I would probably roll over like an excited puppy and have him rub more than my belly.

Nevertheless, the shifter's resident doctor had arrived around six a.m., which was when Sam had returned to the apartment. Between keeping an eye on Dane, Sam and Tripp had been going through reports and updates on leads—cold ones, mostly—that were coming in on Adam Emery's whereabouts. Although, that letter from the retired Navy SEAL Grant Vega that I'd given to Steven might just be the opening the Vampire Navy SEALs were looking for.

After Sawyer's investigation into Grant Vega and then speaking to him, it turned out that Grant was a building inspector for the city of Chicago. That position afforded him access to the files and records to just about every structure in the city. Which meant the building that Grant had referred to under Fred Emery's name was a valid and warm lead.

Sam snapped his fingers. "Did you hear what I said?"

I blinked. "I didn't."

He chuckled. "I'm running late, so I'll see Jordyn later. I want to check on Dane, then I have to meet Tripp and Webb."

"Of course." I pressed the large round silver button on the side wall.

The doors opened, and an air-conditioned breeze wafted out along with a sterile, medicinal odor that indicated we were in fact in a medical environment.

A sense of foreboding had me rubbing the chills along my arms as Sam and I entered the state-of-the-art facility that served as a research lab on one side and had patient rooms on the other.

We ambled down the center aisle that separated waist-high lab benches that traveled the length of the room on two sides. There wasn't a soul in sight, which wasn't unusual. Not many vampires got sick or hurt, and this place didn't have the activity that a regular wing of a hospital had. Unlike the Boston facility, the medical staff under Dr. Vieira only consisted of Peter Landon and Jo, although Peter was a researcher, not a doctor. Still, Steven and Dr. Vieira were in the process of hiring more staff as they continued to expand and integrate more with humans.

"Dr. Vieira," Sam called out.

Nurse Wendy poked her dark head of hair out of the last room. "Jordyn is in here, and Dr. Vieira is in an exam room in the new wing with Dane and Dr. Hammond. I'll show you where, Sam. I need to grab some supplies in that wing anyway."

I knew she'd accepted employment working for Dr. Vieira, but I had no idea that she'd started.

After Sam and I swapped a kiss, he and Wendy left, and I glanced around as an eerie feeling made the hairs on the back of my neck stiffen. Skirting by the lab bench, I shrugged off that cold chill, put on a smile, and went into Jordyn's room.

Her big brown eyes grew wider as she tried to whistle. "Whoa! Hot momma."

I sidled up to her bed. "Me? How about you? You're beautiful, sis. I would never know you were injured and had been in a coma."

Whether it was the sun's rays spraying in from the window or her natural appearance, her skin glowed within the pink robe over cotton pajamas.

"I'm weak but walking fine, and Wendy will be helping me with physical therapy. Doc says I can leave the infirmary, maybe in the next day or so."

"That's great news. I'll make sure Sam's old bedroom is clean for you."

"So, are you ready for your first day?"

I held my stomach. "Nervous but excited. I feel like I have a purpose to do something meaningful."

"Are you prepared if Violet asks you about your vampire-hunting days?" Jordyn asked. "And you know she'll ask you about Rianne."

I scrunched my nose. "I'll be honest and speak from the heart. We're living in a different time that's rapidly changing. People are afraid of what they don't know. That will be my lead-in, and I'll use myself and our hunting days as an example. As far as Rianne goes, there's not much to say. If people choose the path she's taken, then they need to know the consequences."

Jordyn quivered. "It makes me ill to know Rianne is a stone's throw away from us. It also breaks my heart that she chose to take the serum. But we can't let her suffer. When Uncle Jack and Aunt Tabitha arrive to see Noah, maybe we should end Rianne's misery at the same time as Noah's. Surely, Dr. Vieira has done all he can by now to study her."

I toyed with my ruby wedding ring. "I just wish there was a

way to reverse the process. I would give anything to have our sister human again."

"Me too," Jordyn said. "And I'm sorry I wasn't any help early on in trying to knock some sense into Rianne." Guilt was evident in her tone.

I knew she loved Rianne as much as I did.

"You know as well as I do, our sister is super stubborn. She wouldn't have listened to you either, Jordyn. Besides, you've said that she made her choice."

She nodded. "I know. But I still could've tried to get through to her."

"We'll talk to Dr. Vieira the first chance we get about Rianne's outlook," I said.

Silence ticked for a beat and was broken only by the beep of the vitals machine that Jordyn was hooked up to.

"I've come to a major decision, Layla." Her tone was melancholy.

I sat on the edge of her bed, facing her at an angle. I had an inkling that whatever she was about to say related to her future.

"I've thought hard about what it means for me to have the same blood type as you as well as the idea of me as a witch. You said I *could* be one because I'm also a Monroe."

When the topic came up the other day in her hospital room in Boston, she didn't want to discuss it.

"That's right," I said. "It's not something you have to do. Mom didn't want anything to do with being a Monroe."

She rolled back her shoulders. "I don't want anything to do with being a witch. I like who I am as a human. I don't want to change that. If, years from now, I have a different perspective, then maybe."

I was confused by what she was telling me because she'd given me the impression that I would be upset with her once I heard what she'd decided.

"Jordyn, I support that decision," I said. "To be honest, if I were in your shoes, I might do the same."

She grasped my hand. "I say this with lots of love. I've struggled seeing you go through everything. And while I wouldn't mind taking a vampire for a test drive in bed, I think for now, I don't need the baggage that comes with that. Sure, birth control would do the trick, and my experience might not pan out like yours. But I can't shake the fact that you died giving birth, sis. Your pregnancy wasn't a walk in the park. Not to mention, Mom had a great life without exercising her witch powers. I can live the same way she did."

"As we talked about the other day, your dream of traveling around the world should be your first priority. I want that for you."

She pushed out a breath. "Thank you. I know you support me, but there was part of me that doubted you would."

"Enough said. When we find time, we'll sit down and map out your itinerary."

An alarm blared.

I jumped a mile.

Jordyn froze. "They can't blame me. I didn't pull any alarms this time."

I wanted to laugh at her reference to what she'd done the night she tried to bypass a prison guard to reach Fred Emery. But my brain was focused on what the alarm meant—fire, intruder, or something else.

A voice came over the loudspeaker. "Please stay where you are. Do not leave the building."

I was relieved it wasn't gate-crashers, at least. The day we were invaded, the message on the loudspeaker had been "All personnel report to your stations. Intruders have compromised the compound."

I bolted out of the room and scanned the lab area. Again, no one was around, and Wendy had yet to return. I peered through the window of the double doors leading to the new wing. I didn't see anyone.

I spun around when the other set of doors, the one Sam and I had used to enter, burst open.

I flash froze in the middle of the aisle as I laid eyes on Rianne —or rather, a hairy beast. The word *run* blared in my head. Yet my legs wouldn't move. I was struggling with how she'd changed so drastically in a short amount of time. Not only that, but why was she here? How did she escape a prison cell?

"Layla," Jordyn whispered. "Don't move."

My good sister's command filtered into my left ear.

Rianne swiveled her attention to Jordyn.

The last thing I wanted was for Jordyn to get hurt again. She'd been through enough.

"Jordyn, call for help." I would like to think I could take on Rianne, but I had no weapons except my witchcraft, and even that wasn't something I could rely on because I didn't know many spells.

*You have mind control.*

Rianne sniffed the air.

No sooner than I lifted one foot, Rianne sprinted in vampire speed down the aisle like a damn cheetah who'd found her prey. I'd barely gotten two steps when she tackled me to the floor. Her canines dripped with blood. Her claws were longer than I remembered.

I crisscrossed my arms in an attempt to block her.

She scratched my hands and then ripped my sweater, her talons digging into my arms.

Searing, hot pain flashed like white lightning through me.

I dug deep for my banshee scream, but I couldn't breathe. She was extremely strong, and the weight of her body felt like that of a grizzly bear.

*Mind control. Make her red eyes bleed or something to get her off you.*

I envisioned her gouging out her eyes, but I was having trouble concentrating while fighting her at the same time.

She growled, the sound reminding me of a mountain lion I'd heard on a National Geographic show.

Kicking and squirming, I shoved her. The more I fought, the more aggressive she became as she sank her fangs into my ear and tugged hard like I was her fucking chew toy.

I screamed, but nothing came out.

Feet slapped on the tile somewhere nearby. "Rianne!" Jordyn's tone was sharp and deadly. "Get the fuck off her." She must've thrown something at Rianne because I heard glass shatter somewhere near me.

I grabbed Rianne's temples and shoved my thumbs into her eyes.

She let out a guttural roar as she swatted my neck, and once again, her deadly claws scratched deep into my skin.

I pushed and shoved with all I had as I continued to press my thumbs into her eye sockets. Nausea was creeping up and into my throat.

She rolled off me, giving me a small window to scramble to my feet on unsteady legs.

Rianne was blinking rapidly, trying to clear the blood coming out of her eyes.

Jordyn ran behind me and into the new wing.

"It's time to say goodbye, Rianne." I bowed my head, conjuring up any magic within me that I could as I imagined her stabbing herself with her long talons. Not that the act would kill her, but it would at least slow her down until help arrived.

She stood on all fours partway down the center aisle, angling her head one way, then the other, as if she was trying to figure out who I was, or maybe she couldn't see clearly anymore.

Still, my mind control wasn't working, and maybe it didn't on animallike creatures. Just my luck.

The only spell I remembered was how to start a fire. If I did that, the room would blow up because of all the chemicals and reagents stored nearby. I also had another problem. Dizziness was setting in. I was sure I was losing blood. I could feel it slithering down my neck and face as the wounds on my body felt like someone had stuck a hot poker against my skin. The sensation rivaled a thousand beestings.

Rianne's nostrils were flaring as she sniffed the air. The blood in her eyes coagulated as if she was healing right before me.

We faced off like two gunslingers at the O.K. Corral.

I swayed to one side. Too bad I didn't have the power of a Mystic. Or the ability to wave my hand like Abbey and throw Rianne around or even snap her neck with a flick of my wrist. I was a fucking witch, for fuck's sake. Why couldn't I do something?

*You haven't practiced. You need schooling.*

The only weapon I had was my banshee scream, since mind control wasn't working on her.

The second I inhaled, I heard Sam's voice. I glanced past Rianne and saw Sam rushing through the double doors in the distance.

"Rianne!" Sam roared.

As if responding to a mating call, my sister spun around.

I anchored myself to a lab bench.

Sam widened his stance, fangs out, silver eyes scorching with rage as he waited for Rianne to attack him.

She ran on all fours—literally on her hands and feet like an animal in the wild. The moment she leapt at my husband, he snapped her neck in one move. She fell like a rag doll to the floor.

I hurried over to him on trembling legs and snagged the dagger from his sheath.

He caught my wrist. "She's dead."

"I want to be sure," I said in a voice that didn't sound like me. "You never know what the fuck that serum can do."

"Look at you," he said with horror, taking the dagger from me. "You're covered in blood."

As if the last word was a trigger, I listed to one side.

He scooped me in his arms just as footsteps, sounding like a herd of cattle, pounded around us.

I barely heard Dr. Vieira shout, "Take her to a room now!" before I passed out.

# 24

## SAM

I set my wife on the bed in the first room I came to. I couldn't think, breathe, or even speak. She was covered in blood. Her ear was barely hanging on. Her skin looked as if someone had dumped acid on her face. Her sweater and blouse were ripped. She had deep scratches on her hands, arms, and neck.

My body shook. How the fuck had this happened?

Doc hurried in. "Sam, find Peter or your sister. Dr. Hammond needs help with Dane in the operating room."

Webb was at the door. "I'm on it."

"Sam, roll that cart over here." He pointed to the drawers on wheels, which in medical terms was the crash cart that housed everything necessary to save a patient.

I did as he ordered.

"First drawer, there's gauze. Start ripping open packets. We need to stop the bleeding." He pressed a stethoscope to her chest.

With shaky hands, I tore the gauze out of the packages.

"Put pressure on her ear," he said.

Suddenly, I remembered the dream she'd had when I woke her in the hospital room in Boston. She'd seen herself in a coffin with a mangled ear. Holy fuck! I squeezed my eyes shut as bile crept up into my throat. I didn't want to believe that dreams and visions came true. But in my world, they really did.

I held the gauze tight to her ear. "You think there's something in Rianne's blood that is causing the allergic reaction?" Her skin was severely red.

"Maybe." He was setting up an IV. "We've been testing her, Noah, and Carly. There are differences in each of them. It's hard to keep up with the data because it changes by the day and sometimes by the hour."

"Shit, Doc. What if she dies?"

"Why would you say that?"

"She's seen herself dead with a mangled ear," I whispered.

The color drained from his face. "Nonsense." His tone belied the confidence he was trying to portray.

Nurse Wendy came in and pushed me out of the way. "I got this."

On her heels was Jordyn, who skidded to a halt. "Oh my God!" she cried.

"Now that Wendy is here, I want you and Jordyn out," Doc ordered.

Jordyn and I didn't move.

"Sam," Tripp's voice trickled in. "Give them room to help Layla." He wrangled Jordyn out.

I was breaking piece by shattered piece as I looked at the mother of my children, my beautiful wife, who'd been so excited to start her new job. She'd been happy that we were home and about to begin a new chapter in our lives. I was right there with her.

Tripp returned and grabbed my arm. "Sam."

I didn't want to leave. I couldn't. But I was about to lose my shit, and Tripp was right. I needed to let Doc take care of Layla.

"She'll be okay, man," Tripp said.

I listened to her heart, which was beating rapidly.

Tripp nudged me. "Come on."

Reluctantly, I left, my pulse pounding in my ears. "Why was Rianne in the infirmary?" I asked Tripp.

"She was having a seizure. Doc gave the order to the chief on duty at the prison to bring her up to a secure room in the new wing just for Noah, Carly, and Rianne."

My father loomed over Rianne's dead body in front of the entrance. The tightness in his muscles was a clear indication that he was ready to snap like me. He loosened his tie. He was dressed in a suit to accompany Layla as they gave the reporter a tour of the base.

I heard voices in the hallway before Webb and Petty Officer Peterson came in.

"Tell them what happened," Webb ordered Peterson.

Peterson, a six-foot-tall vampire with a broken nose, brown hair that was covered in white dust, and a bloody face, regarded Rianne's dead body. "Everything happened so fast. One minute she was seizing, then when we reached the entrance to the infirmary, she jolted up as if she heard a familiar voice or smelled something. Next thing, she yanked her restraints off like twigs. My partner and I tried to wrangle her, but she ripped out his heart, then threw me through a wall in the hallway. I radioed for help as soon as I could but not fast enough."

"You're telling us that Rianne stuck her hand into your partner's chest?" Disbelief weaved through my tone.

Peterson nodded as he briefly regarded Rianne. "She was extremely strong."

Jordyn hugged herself as she stared at her evil sister lying next to my dad's feet. "And she was faster than vampires. When I walked out of the room, Rianne was a blur. Then Layla was on the floor. I'm dumbfounded at how everything happened in a blink of an eye. Layla and I were just talking about whether or not we should keep Rianne alive. It's too bad we couldn't save her." Jordyn sounded choked up.

I could understand her heartbreak over her sister. But no matter how hard Layla had tried to talk Rianne down off the ledge of giving up her humanity, she hadn't listened. Once that serum was in Rianne's system, there was no turning back or saving her.

"With the data we have on her, we might be able to save others in the future," my father said. "I know that's not what you want to hear, Jordyn, and I'm sorry for your loss. But by studying the genetics of Rianne, Noah, and Carly, we might be able to formulate a medical solution to stop the process, prevent it, or maybe even reverse it one day. I have no doubt there will be more people like Adam Emery out there. So it's important to continue to study any and all data from those affected by the serum so we can get ahead of the genetic-engineering war. If we don't, we'll never win, and the revolving door will keep turning and turning until we're living in a dystopian landscape."

While I agreed with my father's thought process, I prayed Layla didn't die because of it.

I returned to the doorway of her room and sucked in air. "What the fuck?"

Dr. Vieira was doing chest compressions.

I sharpened my hearing and listened. My wife didn't have a pulse. I staggered into the doorjamb, pain clutching my chest, tears stinging my eyes, and my ability to breathe was waning at a rapid rate. I had to be dreaming. This wasn't real. That wasn't Layla's limp body with white foam bubbling from her lips and a thick film of perspiration coating her wounded face.

I swallowed the unimaginable grief that clogged my throat as I stared at her in shock, feeling like my soul was being ripped apart.

"What is it?" Jordyn squeaked out, sidling up to me.

"Prepare the defibrillator," Doc said to Wendy.

Jordyn fell into me. "Is Layla dead?"

Tripp and my father came up behind us.

Jordyn hung on my arm. "I don't understand."

I didn't know what to tell her, as I certainly was having a difficult time wrapping my mind around what the fuck was happening to my wife. Layla had to have been allergic to Rianne's bite or whatever the scientific terms were.

Wendy cut open Layla's blouse, then snipped her bra in two.

Doc was giving Layla mouth-to-mouth.

I was living in a nightmare. Another fucking one. Layla had died three times the night she'd given birth. I had my heart yanked out several times that night. Not to mention the time when I found her hanging off a cliff by her fingertips in the early morning hours in the Catskills.

Doc started chest compressions again. "Steven, get your son and Jordyn out of here and close the door, please." His voice sounded as panicked as I felt.

My dad grabbed Jordyn. "Tripp, help Sam."

I jerked my arm away. "I'm staying."

Jordyn was crying as she went willingly with my father.

I wasn't sure I was breathing.

"Sam." Tripp's voice was soft. "You need air."

I needed a fucking miracle.

Tripp got in my face. "Look at me, Sam."

My best bud had been there for me the night Layla had given birth. He'd talked me down off a ledge several times. But I didn't think he could right now.

A buzzing started in my ears. Nausea churned violently inside me.

He was right. I did need air.

I hurried out as Doc and Wendy dropped words like *"Clear"* before the sound of the defibrillator wound up, making a high-pitched noise that stung my heart, making it feel like I'd walked into a hornet's nest. I pushed through the double doors, desperate to rid the tang of blood from my system, to expel the rage, the heartache, and the shock. I clenched my fists, jabbing my nails into my palms until I could feel blood pooling in my hands.

The dead prison guard lay on the floor in the hallway, his heart several feet away. My breath quickened as my mind went haywire at the thought that Layla might not cheat death this time around.

I snatched up the stretcher, and with a bestial roar, I hurled it like a javelin down the hall—an explosion of violence that was the only thing that could express the sorrow crushing my soul into a million tiny pieces. Then I sprinted to the exit, needing to run, pray, and pray some fucking more.

She couldn't die. How would I tell our children their mother was dead? How could I live without her?

I bent over the second I was out of the building and inhaled the humid August air. As my lungs expanded, my body pulsed in pain. Dragging a hand through my hair, I headed down to the water's edge, breathing in the salt air. I couldn't keep going through this emotional, heart-stabbing, gut-clawing pain over and over again. Something had to give.

I ran down a jogging path along the edge of the parking lot. Boats sat on the water in the far distance, looking like tiny specks on a map. We didn't allow civilians to come close to the naval base. We had patrol boats during the height of the spring and summer seasons to ward off anyone who didn't belong past a certain point on both sides of Mount Hope Bay.

I kept running on the path, following it around and along the water's edge. I sprinted, cried, and gasped for air. But I couldn't stop, afraid that if I did, my world would come to an end. I thought of my kids and sobbed harder than I ever had in my life.

I couldn't picture Layla gone. I couldn't fathom a moment without hearing her laugh, seeing her eyes light up when I walked into a room or when she gazed at our children. It shredded me to think that she would never snuggle up to me, wake up next to me, or say those four words that always melted me into a puddle of water—"I love you, vampire."

Sweat poured out of me, mixing with my salty tears, and by the time I'd circled the one-mile path and was coming around toward the infirmary, Tripp was on the sidewalk at the edge of the building.

He glanced toward the front entrance where the lobby was and then in my direction.

The closer I got to him, the harder my pulse pounded in my ears.

He was as white as fallen snow, and I knew. I knew he had bad news. I couldn't handle hearing whatever he had to say. Then again, he didn't have to open his mouth at all.

I turned around and walked in the opposite direction.

"Sam." The way Tripp said my name sent a sharp jolt of pain to my chest.

I raised a hand. "I don't want to hear it. I can't, man."

He jogged up to me. "Can I at least walk with you?"

I didn't answer. Instead, I just kept my legs moving. The minute I stopped would be the minute he would have to pluck my body off the ground with a forklift.

An excruciating silence followed us until we reached the end of the road.

I made the mistake of looking at him, because when I saw the tears in his eyes, reality hit me like a jet falling out of the sky. Tripp never shed a tear. Not one in my presence.

As much as I didn't want to hear the bad news, I had to. Maybe I was overreacting. Maybe he was just emotional that Layla had been severely hurt.

Breathing heavily, I stared at him, waiting for him to say what he came to say.

"I'm so fucking sorry, Sam. She didn't make it." More tears flowed down his face.

My brain was numb. "I don't believe you." Spittle flew from my mouth as I screamed in anguish, deep, gut-wrenching sobs racking my body as I yanked on my hair. "She can't be. She was just talking to me. No. No." I kept repeating it over and over again.

Tripp pulled me into a fierce embrace as his body shook along with mine.

As much as I needed an anchor, a Hail Mary, and a miracle, I shoved him away. "She's not dead." In vampire speed, I was in the building, climbing the steps two at a time. I pulled the fourth-floor door off its hinges and sprinted until I was in Layla's room.

Jordyn, Jo, Webb, and my dad were gathered around Layla's bed. Their collective emotions were too much for me to handle as an empath. I was already dealing with my own, and I couldn't take their sorrow and pain.

Jordyn sobbed along with my sister.

Webb and my father quietly shed tears.

Jo launched herself at me, but I backed away. I was suffocating. I was a strong individual. I could handle anything thrown at me—but not this. Not my wife's lifeless body.

Once again, I was on the move. This time I had to be with my kids. I had to hug and hold them.

Like a tornado moving at warp speed, I was in my apartment.

Agnes jumped up off the couch. "What happened?"

"Layla died." Abbey's voice cracked with emotion as if she knew.

Fuck. She did know. She had a vision of Layla dead, not once but twice that I knew of. Hell, she'd seen Layla's death the first day Layla showed up on base to engage my help to remove the compelling spell I had on Rianne.

I started for the nursery.

"Sam, is that true? Please tell me it's not." The agony in Agnes's tone was a knife to my gut.

"I can't." I went into the nursery and closed the door.

I could hear Agnes and Abbey talking. Then Agnes sniveling.

I tuned them out as I watched Orion, Ellie, and Luna sleep. Rorie was wide awake. Her legs were up in the air, and when she saw me, she smiled.

I melted as I wept, lifting her into my arms. "Hey, baby girl." Cradling her, I sat in the rocker, fixating on her beautiful mahogany eyes and that red hair. "You're as beautiful as your momma."

She smiled as if she understood. Maybe she did. At seven weeks old, all of them were becoming more alert, attentive, and curious about shiny things that caught their attention. Doc suspected they would be walking in a few months.

I held her tiny hand and grinned, hoping I didn't look like a freak as I continued to weep.

Agnes opened the door but didn't come in. "How did Layla die?" Her brown eyes were flickering to orange, a sign her inner witch was about to surface.

"Rianne scratched and bit her," I said, looking at my daughter. "If that was even the cause, I don't know for sure."

"I want to see her," Agnes said. "I also need to speak to Dr. Vieira. They need to put Rianne down."

"She's dead. I snapped her neck."

Agnes sighed heavily.

Then something she'd said clicked. "Why do you need to talk to Doc? Do you know something?"

She lifted a shoulder. "I'd overheard Roman and Adam talking about the serum one day. One of their test subjects attacked their new scientist. They've been through two now. The scientist died within ten minutes after he was attacked. Their saliva is highly toxic or poisonous."

"It's too late to save her." My tone was harsh and cold. "You can leave. I'm not going anywhere right now." Or ever. I might lock myself in my apartment and shut the outside world from even seeping in to ruin any more of my life or my kids' lives.

Agnes left, then Abbey glided in with tearstained cheeks and sat on the floor near the door. "I'm sorry, Uncle Sam."

It wounded me to hear the pain in her voice that made it sound as if she blamed herself.

"My dream last night was about Layla. But I only saw her lying on the bed and Dr. Vieira trying to revive her."

I hated that my niece had nightmares about the people in her life dying.

A knock on the apartment door echoed into the room. "Sam," Jo called loudly, emotion choking her voice as she graced the doorway with red rimming her silver eyes. "Whatever you need, I'm here for you."

Abbey greeted her mom with a distressed hug as I set Rorie in her crib.

The air was thick with grief, pity, and misery, and I was choking on it all.

"Can you watch the kids for a minute?" I asked Jo. I had to close myself in a dark space and not see or feel anyone's emotions but my own.

"Of course," she said, moving out of the way as I stumbled past her. "I love you, brother," she said to my back.

I wished her words helped, but nothing would take away the grief stabbing me over and over again.

Tears streaming down my face, I threw myself into my bedroom and locked the door. The second I was inside, Layla's cherry fragrance drifted into my nostrils, causing me to sob even harder.

I grabbed Layla's pillow, clutching it to my chest as I sat on the edge of the bed. I buried my face in the pillow and screamed, releasing all the torment that was drowning and strangling me—and that I had no doubt would kill me.

# 25

## SAM

*tars sprinkled the sky like confetti surrounding the crescent moon as the waves of the Atlantic slid along the shore in a musical push and pull. The ocean breeze wafted through the tiny opening in the accordion glass doors, carrying with it the scent of seaweed and fish tinged with salt and brine.*

*Layla and I were lounging on a blanket on the floor by the fireplace at my sister's house in Maine as I rubbed circles on her pregnant belly.*

*I nibbled on her ear. "A penny for your thoughts."*

*She leaned into me. "I don't ever want to leave here."*

*I knew she was worried about the future, something I had no control over.*

*"One day, baby doll, we'll have a home on a beach or close to it where our rug rats can play, build sandcastles, fish, surf, if that's their thing. My promise to you." I stood and held out my hand. It was time to pop the big question. I'd been searching for how to start and what to say all day. "Come on."*

*Once we were on the deck, my stomach tossed and turned. I didn't know why I was nervous. I was sure she would say yes. Yet, that niggle of doubt was a bitch.*

*We bantered back and forth, Layla trying to soothe my nerves, and I was as tight as violin strings.*

*"Are we skinny-dipping?" she teased.*

*I chuckled and draped the blanket over her shoulders. "Your tits would fall off, and my balls would freeze."*

*"I would hate that. I need those balls," she said.*

*I nipped at her nose. "And I need those sexy tits."*

*The ocean was calm. I was anything but as I struggled with where to start. I wanted the proposal to be memorable. I also wanted her to understand how important she was to me and how the energy of the universe fed my soul.*

*I glanced up at the million stars in the sky as she leaned against my chest, easing my anxiety. This woman who had come out of nowhere—a silent enemy I didn't even know existed until her weak attempt to capture me for some washed-up CIA agent who had a vendetta against me. But she rocked my world the second I laid eyes on her.*

*I sighed. "In high school, Jo and I had a space science class that took place in the school's planetarium, where we learned about the constellations." I pointed out and up over the ocean. "See those three stars stacked on top of one another at a slight angle? That's Orion's Belt." I used my finger to trace the outline of Orion in the air.*

*"The arrogant, sexy vampire is an astronomer. Who knew?" she said, surprise riddling her tone.*

*"I never knew my mom, but according to my dad, she believed in the mysticism and symbolism of the stars and planets," I continued. "That names held power. For example, the planet Jupiter, guardian and protector of the sky, signifies great fortune." I squeezed her to me, slightly shaking. "Since I was born with the astrological sign of Sagittarius, my mom thought it befitting that my middle name should be Jove, which is of Latin origin and means Jupiter."*

*She twisted in my arms until she was gazing up at me with those ball-gripping, electric-blue eyes. "Your mom was right. The name does fit you, Sam. Protector is who you are. But you're also kind, caring, sometimes an arrogant ass, but mine, and you love unconditionally. I often wonder why you and I are together. I've killed vampires like they didn't matter. You taught me that they do. The good ones anyway. Now here we are, building a family and loving each other."*

*I flattened my hands on her soft cheeks. "It doesn't matter to me that you're a vampire hunter. The moment I saw you at the nightclub was the very moment you grabbed my heart. I've been drawn to your feistiness, your strength, and your beauty, inside and out." The momentary blackness as I blinked told me my green eyes had changed to silver. "You care for those you love, you see the good in people, and your take-no-prisoners attitude fits us." Inching away, I slipped my hand into my back pocket.*

*Layla began to tremble.*

*I got down on one knee, and her emotions mingled with mine—an outpouring of love, although she was surprised as I presented my mother's ruby gemstone.*

*"Layla Aberdeen, would you be my sidekick, the woman who will keep me sane, a partner who will stand by my side and fight for what we believe in and those we love? Above all else, will you love my arrogant ass no matter what?"*

*She sobbed. "I would love to be your partner, the mother of your children, and to fight to the end of time alongside you. I will always, always love your arrogant vampire ass."*

*I kissed her pregnant belly as happiness blanketed me. "Did you hear that, kids? Your mom said yes." I swayed as I rose, drunk on the emotions bouncing between us, and slid the ring onto her finger. "This was my mom's ring. She wanted me to have this for my bride-to-be. The ruby is such a perfect match for your courageous and fiery personality." The ring didn't exactly fit over her swollen knuckle. "No matter how rough the seas are ahead of us, never, ever forget it's you and me and that our kids will always come first. I fucking love you, baby doll."*

*I never thought I would marry or have kids. But I was the happiest fucking vampire on the planet.*

*I kissed her with everything I had—mind, body, and soul. I would cherish this woman for as long as I could. I knew she would grow old, and I wouldn't. I couldn't say that it didn't bother me. To a point, it did. But we were living in the here and now, and fifty years wasn't on my radar.*

*"I love you, Layla. I would die without you."*

The sound of the waves turned into a banging noise that seemed far away yet so close. Then my body shook.

"Samuel." My father's voice seeped in my consciousness. "Son, wake up."

I lurched upright. "Is it Layla? Is she here?"

The room was bathed in darkness except for the sliver of light creeping in through the crack of the bedroom door.

I swung my legs over the side of the bed, glancing at my watch. I couldn't remember the exact time I came into my room, but I knew at least eleven or twelve hours had passed because it was ten p.m.

I swiped a hand through my hair. "How did you get in here?"

"I have a key. This used to be my room, remember?"

My synapses weren't firing on all cylinders yet.

My father eased down on the bed next to me and rubbed my back. "I know your pain, son, like it was yesterday," he said softly, reading my mind and feeling the agony singeing my soul. "Your mom's death was one of the worst things in my life. I didn't think I could go on. And the only thing that helped me was knowing I had you and Jo."

I threw my head into my hands. "I was just dreaming of when I proposed to Layla. We hardly had a chance to start our lives. I still don't believe she's dead. It was Rianne's bite that killed her, right?"

"Damon is pretty sure." My dad and Webb were the only ones on our team who called Dr. Vieira by his first name. "He's in the lab now, running tests."

"Did Agnes tell you about the conversation she overheard between Roman and Adam?"

"She told us about the scientist who died after he was bitten by one of his research subjects," my dad said.

I leaned my elbows on my knees. "I need to murder Adam Emery. I even want to strangle Carly. I don't care if she came to us for help or gave us Uncle Patrick's files. She's as guilty as Adam is." Part of me had a soft spot for Adam's former scientist. Layla's cousin-in-law, who'd been married to Junior Aberdeen, had helped me rescue Layla from Intech. But she'd done more harm than good even though her goal in genetically altering humans was more to find a cure for diseases than build an army of super soldiers. Regardless, no amount of redemption could make up for the many lives that had been lost.

Dane poked his head into the room. "You'll have to get behind me if you want to kill Adam."

After the shit that went down with Layla and then her death, I'd forgotten about the alpha. "You made it out of surgery?"

He felt along the wall for the light switch. As soon as the bedside table lamps were illuminated, I was wincing.

He proceeded to show me the back of his skull. His white hair had been shaved off, and he had stitches. "The chip was taken out successfully. That motherfucker won't screw with my brain ever again."

My dad pushed to his feet. "Samuel, when you're done talking with Dane, I encourage you to see Layla. Damon will need to move her body out of the infirmary before the morning."

My stomach roiled with sickening dread as the words *move her body* stole the air from my lungs with such devastating force that my heart stopped cold for a split second. Her lifeless body. That alone filled my veins with icy sorrow that numbed my entire being. I would never come to terms with the gravity of her death.

"Why don't we go see her together?" Dane offered.

My father nodded. "I'm here to watch my grandkids. Jo,

Agnes, and others will be taking shifts to help take care of Ellie, Rorie, Luna, and Orion."

Fuck. My children. I was relieved that they were too young to comprehend how serious our circumstances were. At the same time, grief churned in my gut as I thought about them having to grow up without their mother like Jo and I did. I never had the opportunity to remember what it was like to have a mother—she was gone by the time I was old enough to recall. No child should have to go without a mother's love, yet this was the path my little ones were now facing.

"I need a minute," I said. "Dane, I'll meet you in the family room."

I stumbled from the bed and staggered into the bathroom, clutching my abdomen as I gasped for air. It had been ages since I'd thrown up, but I was about to do just that.

I stepped up to the sink and propped my hands onto the counter, gazing at my reflection in the mirror. The person looking back at me was unrecognizable. My green eyes were cloudy and bloodshot. My beard had grown in, my face was ashen, and my lips were cracked and chapped.

"You have to pull yourself together for the sake of your kids, dude," I said aloud.

I wasn't sure I could. I also didn't want to see Layla's lifeless body or say my goodbyes. If I did, that meant she wasn't coming back. That meant her death was real.

I stuck my face under the faucet and let the cold water run over me. When I lifted my head, a wave of nausea washed over me. I ran to the toilet and hurled out whatever was left in my stomach. After washing up and changing out of my sweat-soaked uniform, I gave myself a pep talk before meeting Dane in the family room. But no amount of encouragement or positive words would erase my grief, and they sure as fuck wouldn't bring Layla back.

Nevertheless, I bypassed the nursery. I couldn't see my kids. If I did, I would lose my shit, and right now I needed the nerve and the strength to say goodbye to their mother.

Minutes after leaving the apartment, silence hung over Dane and me as we traveled the hallways to the infirmary. Our steps kept time with each other's, two alphas in perfect synchronization, both of us mourning the loss of a loved one—bonding us in grief.

"Sam, I want to apologize to you." His deep baritone voice echoed in the hall.

I gave him a sidelong glance. "For what?"

"I blamed you for Ross's death, and I shouldn't have. I was distraught and fucking pissed after I got the pic of his severed head. My rage is targeted at Adam Emery, not you."

"I know, man." At the mention of Adam's name, anger seeped into my veins. Maybe I needed to focus on revenge, because as I pictured Adam's death, that soul-crushing pain I'd been feeling waned for the moment. "We're killing that motherfucker together. First, we're going to torture him until he's begging for his life. Then you can have him for dinner. You deserve the final blow."

He chuckled. "I like the sound of that. But what about your vampire laws and your motto to protect humanity?"

"Killing him will protect humanity." If Adam lived, he would continue to murder humans in his quest for the perfect supernatural soldier. We had to remove the virus so it didn't spread.

"By the way, I know your team is looking for that asshole, but Cooper is too. If we find Adam before your team does, you'll be my first call. Also, your father is forming a group of leaders from the various packs and covens to join forces in deciding how we can blend in with humans. I originally said no, but I changed my mind."

I'd forgotten that my dad wanted me to talk to Dane about

that very thing. Regardless, I was happy to know that he and I were on the same page when it came to Adam.

That feeling of dread blossomed once again like a field of poisonous weeds as the double doors to the infirmary came into view, and my pulse pounded harder with each step as we drew closer.

"I'm gutted over Layla," Dane said. "And if you need me to hold your hand, I will."

I cocked an eyebrow at the alpha. "You would literally hold my hand?"

He gave me a cheeky grin. "For Layla, I would."

He just might have to—but I doubted I could see her. I wanted to remember her beautiful smile and gorgeous face and not the sight of her wounded and bloody.

Doc jerked his head up from his microscope in the distance when Dane and I entered. "Sam."

He skirted around the lab bench and marched down the center aisle. Specks of red or probably blood dotted his white lab coat. His brown hair was messy, as if he'd come in from a windstorm. It was on a rare occasion that Doc appeared frazzled and unsettled.

He touched his chest. "Please forgive me. It's all my fault that Layla died. I'm beside myself. If I had known Rianne's abilities had grown stronger in a matter of a week since Peter last tested her, I would've never given my approval to have her brought to the infirmary. I'm sick to my stomach."

I didn't have the bandwidth to process his confession nor soothe his feelings. Could I blame him for what happened? Not at all. Dr. Damon Vieira would never do anything to jeopardize anyone's life. He cared about his patients, friends and foes— supernaturals and humans. He was only trying to help a patient having a seizure. He'd done the same when Carly had hers. But he also believed in science and the importance of understanding the genetics behind these manufactured creatures so that maybe we could find a way to reverse the transformation or find an antidote to block the change altogether. Regardless, none of that erased my grief and probably never would.

I couldn't bear to feel or see his pain, so I said, "Have you confirmed if Rianne's bite was the cause?"

He straightened and slipped his hands into the pockets of his lab coat. "Yes. Her saliva is highly toxic, which didn't show up in our last round of testing. Understand that each human subject has different genetics that will affect the outcome of how the serum reacts in them. Also, the genetic mutations in these creatures are constantly changing, hence the physical appearance over time as well as the dynamics of increased strength, the changes in the brain, the blood, the saliva, and even the heart. Much like Edmund's first guinea pig, Blake Turner. Remember him, Sam?"

It was hard to forget that asshole. He'd been Jo's human nemesis in high school, bullying her every day. Edmund thought it would be a gas to have Jo's enemy turned into a monster to kill my sister. While Blake's transformation might be similar, there was one difference—the concoction my uncle Patrick whipped up consisted of only my DNA, not a shifter's.

"Was Blake's bite deadly?" I asked.

"No," Dr. Vieira said. "But Patrick's potion didn't include shifter DNA." Doc hunched his shoulders. "Still, when I do a complete autopsy on Rianne, I believe I'll find similarities between her and Blake—changes to the brain, heart, and other organs. I don't want to bore you with the details." He took my hands and squeezed. "Again, I am so very sorry."

I wrapped my arms around him. There was a whole cast of characters who had a hand in Layla's death, and I might even question myself. I shouldn't have left her alone. I should've had a guard on her. But none of that hindsight would bring her back.

He blinked away tears. "I've moved Layla into a birthing suite for now. After you say your final goodbye, I'll need to preserve her body until you decide on funeral arrangements."

Nausea hit me again. Funeral? Burying her? No fucking way. I couldn't deal.

Dane, who'd been quiet, asked, "Is Dr. Hammond still in the building?" Whether or not he was making small talk to give me time to catch my breath, I welcomed the distraction.

"She just left," Doc said. "She's staying in a guesthouse with Greta."

I glanced over the lab bench to Jordyn's empty room. "Where's Jordyn?"

"She couldn't stay here. She's at Jo's house. Your sister insisted she would take care of her."

Jordyn was grieving as much as I was, but I was glad she wasn't here. If anyone's emotions would bother me the most, they were hers.

"Come on, dude," Dane said, strutting toward the entrance to the new wing.

Once he and I left Doc, so many memories bombarded me as we passed the scrub and operating rooms. I'd sat in this very hallway with Tripp, listening to my babies being born, hearing a nurse say Layla wasn't breathing. She'd died during childbirth that day. But a miracle had happened then. Not this time.

"I don't think I can see her," I mumbled.

Dane gave me a sidelong glance. "I'm serious. I'll hold your hand. But if you tell anyone, I'll kick your bloodsucking ass."

I couldn't help but laugh. It was the medication I needed to keep my legs moving until we were at the door of the birthing suite, and I was looking at Layla's lifeless body on a gurney in the middle of the room.

I swallowed thickly and turned around to leave when Dane took my hand.

I jerked my teary-eyed gaze toward him.

"I told you. I got you." He guided me inside. "You need to say your piece, Sam. Otherwise, you'll regret it." He sounded as though he was speaking from experience. I imagined he was. He'd lost his parents and now his brother, Ross.

As we stood alongside the gurney, my heart thundered in my chest like a captive beast wanting to get free, to kill Rianne all over again. Only, instead of snapping her neck, I was desperate for another chance to torture the fuck out of her. To make her suffer like I was doing now.

Dane circled the gurney to the other side and kissed Layla on the cheek. "You were one of the toughest women I knew. Wherever the afterlife takes you, give them hell." He nodded at me. "I'll give you space. You got this. I'll check on you later."

As much as I wanted him to stay, I needed to say my good-byes alone. I sighed heavily, the air in the room stifling and suffocating.

Despite the scratches etched onto my wife's skin, the patches of burn marks, and her wounded ear, she was breathtakingly beautiful even in death.

"How did we get to this point, baby doll? I am gutted, angry, shocked, and I don't know how I'm going to live without you. I hope that by the time our children understand, I can tell them how you died or even talk about your death." I kissed the back of her cold hand. "I will always have you with me no matter where I go." Tears spilled freely as I inhaled a much-needed breath. "My love for you is immortal, and I will never love anyone again. Wherever you are, save me a spot next to you. I'm sure one day, we'll meet again." I traced a path over her eyebrows and nose, then kissed her on the lips as I bawled.

The longer I lingered, the harder it was to leave her. But if I didn't get out of this room, I would stab myself in the heart with a cobalt dagger until it burned to ash.

*Remember your children*, my inner voice supplied. *They need a father.*

I stood up taller, wiped my eyes, and rebooted my brain. After one last lingering look, I hurried into the hallway, taking in deep breaths. My legs were shaky, my stomach was knotted, and I couldn't stop the tears from flowing. I leaned against the wall and closed my eyes. I couldn't leave her. I was nothing without her.

I slid down the wall until I was in a crouched position and shoved my hands through my hair.

*You have to go on, man. Layla would want you to.*

I didn't know how. I couldn't think straight, and the pain in my heart would never go away.

*Get your ass up and go see your kids.*

I swallowed thickly as I rose, blinking the tears away. I needed air. As I started to leave, I turned and walked back to Layla's room. I had to see her one last time. The second I laid eyes on her from the doorway, I bawled once again.

"I love you, baby doll," I whispered.

Then I ran until I was pushing through the doors and into the lab where Dr. Vieira was softly crying as he slipped a slide under his microscope.

I went over to him and yanked him to me. "I don't blame you." He needed to hear those words from me, and I needed to hold on to someone.

A loud sigh escaped him. "You don't know how relieved that makes me feel."

I anchored my hip to the lab bench. "Everything has happened at the speed of light."

He picked up a glass beaker that had blood in it and took a sip. "There's more of this in the fridge. You look like you can use some."

Doc liked his blood warm, and he usually drank it in a mug, but I guessed a beaker was all he had.

I went over to the fridge and had stuck my head in when two things happened. Doors groaned open followed by glass shattering.

I pivoted to find Doc with his eyebrows pushed up into his hairline, looking at the entrance to the new wing.

I couldn't see what had him as white as a ghost. As I stepped into Doc's line of sight, a woman with a sheet wrapped around her was walking down the center aisle between the lab benches. She stopped across from Doc, then shot her electric-blue gaze toward me.

I stumbled back into the fridge. "Layla?"

**26**

---

# LAYLA

The harsh fluorescent lights overhead shone down on me like an intrusive spotlight, blinding and burning. The noises in the lab clamored in my ears like a cacophony of an unpracticed orchestra, extremely loud and earsplitting, and the sensation of the cold tile under my feet felt oddly ticklish.

Unease snaked through me like a rushing river after a torrential rain. Something wasn't right, but I couldn't put my finger on it. The fact that both Doc and Sam were pale, with their jaws on the floor, told me I shouldn't be standing there.

My brain wasn't firing on all cylinders until the tangy, metallic scent of blood wafted in the air. Suddenly, my gums throbbed violently, my throat burned, and as if in slow motion, I could feel my eyeteeth growing from my gums, painful and jarring. As the soft click of them locking into place resonated, I ran my tongue along one canine, then the other, sharp and pointy.

The color in Sam's face brightened even further to a blazing white. Dr. Vieira's did as well.

I scrambled to understand how I was now a vampire or… I felt extremely ill all of a sudden. Was I a monster like Rianne?

I touched my right ear—the one that Rianne had mangled. It seemed to be in perfect condition. I felt along my face. No wounds. I examined my arms. No deep gouges.

"Holy fuck. What am I? Do I look like Rianne? Or am I a vampire?" My voice was barely audible.

I wanted to be by Sam's side for eternity, but I could never achieve a transformation without succumbing to a serum like Rianne had. Yet, if I had turned into a lab-born creature, there was still no such thing as eternal life. But if I was a true vampire, then maybe.

Oh, the irony of my life. A vampire hunter turned into a bloodsucker would have every Aberdeen in my family—dead or alive—rolling over in their graves or burning me over their infamous firepit if I had become a full-fledged vampire.

Doc and Sam still hadn't broken from their traumatized zombie states.

The groan of the doors opening pierced my eardrums, sounding almost like a sonic boom.

Dane staggered in when he saw me, then blessed himself. "What the fuck?" He sniffed the air. I doubted he had to smell me since my fangs were sparkling from my gums. "She's a bloodsucker? How? That doesn't happen in your world." I'd never heard Dane's voice rise so high.

Sam finally rushed over to me. "You died." His hands were trembling as he studied me, not sure if I was real or not. "You've been dead for over twelve hours." He ran a finger over the tip of my canine. "Holy fuck." He gently stroked my face. "Is it really you, baby doll?"

I could hear his pulse soaring off the charts as though my ear was pressed to his chest. "Of course. Who else would I be?"

"A demon," Dane mumbled as he came over to us. "My

grandmother believes that demons inhabit some people. Or will you turn into your sister Rianne?"

Sam squeezed me to him with such force I couldn't breathe. "I can't believe this. You're in my arms. You're alive."

"Layla, what's the last thing you remember?" Dr. Vieira asked.

I eased out of Sam's embrace. "Rianne attacking me."

Sam was feeling my arms, neck, my carotid artery. "How is Layla alive, let alone a vampire?"

"Did Rianne turn me?" That was the only explanation I could wrap my mind around. "Will I be a monster like her?" My stomach lurched.

"Rianne killed you," Doc bit out.

Sam lifted my lips, touching my canines. "You were beautiful before you had fangs, baby doll, but man, I like seeing you with these babies."

"Don't rejoice just yet," I said. "Doc, am I like Rianne? Tell me, please."

"Her eyes are yellow," Dane stated, staying as far away from me as possible. "Not red like Rianne's."

"That's because I'm a witch," I said. "Wait? I don't have red eyes. Is that a sign I'm not a monster?" I was feeling dizzy.

Doc circled the lab bench. "Dane, there's a lab coat in my office. Can you grab it for Layla? Sam, get Layla a bottle of blood." Doc studied me as if he was examining a slide under his microscope, standing with one arm folded under the other while he placed his fingers on his mouth. "I don't know what you are just yet."

Great. Not the answer I wanted to hear.

Sam returned with an open bottle of blood.

I drank a mouthful and almost spat it out. "That's disgusting."

He chuckled. "It's processed with a hint of red pepper. My favorite of the bunch."

"You're probably used to Sam's blood," Doc said. "Is your bloodlust any stronger than when you were craving it during your pregnancy?"

"Not really. The only difference is I have a stronger sense of smell."

"You're not famished for blood?" Doc asked again.

"I'm not going to suck anyone dry, if that's what you mean," I said.

Awe and disbelief were stamped in Sam's expression. "I can't believe you're alive. Nobody will."

Jordyn? "Where's my sister?" From where I stood, I could see that her room was empty.

"She's at Jo's house," Sam said.

"She's going to faint," I mumbled after taking another sip from the bottle. The second taste seemed to be better.

"As is everyone else," Dane said as he returned with Doc's lab coat.

Sam held up the sheet to block me while I put on the over-sized piece of clothing that smelled like Doc, spicy and medicinal.

"How are our children?" I asked, buttoning the coat.

Sam closed his arms around me. "My dad is with them." He sighed. "It feels so fucking good to hold you again. I don't care if you returned to the living as an elf. You're here. My heart is mending as we speak."

I could actually hear how fast his pulse was racing and felt the elation soaring through him. But he shouldn't get his hopes up until we knew for sure what I was.

"I need to run tests. Lots of tests," Doc said with equal parts excitement and trepidation. "I'll be right back." He scurried in the direction of his office.

Dane leaned against the opposite lab bench. "I sure as fuck hope that a creature like Rianne, who was made in a lab, can't turn humans. If so, we're more fucked than we thought. Think zombie apocalypse."

I felt my forehead. It wasn't protruding like Rianne's. I glanced at my nails. No claws in sight. Just fangs.

"I don't see any inhuman resemblance to Rianne, Noah, or Carly," Sam said.

"Maybe not," I countered. "But it might take time for me to develop claws and all the other transformation features."

Doc returned with a folder, placed it on the bench next to Sam and me, and opened it. He sifted through the sheets of paper, fast and furious. "I highly doubt that Rianne's bite turned you, since her saliva is highly toxic."

"But doesn't her saliva have the serum in it?" Sam asked.

"I want all of you to take a step back for a second," Doc said sternly. "We can't rush to a conclusion. I think I know how this happened. Layla, remember the day in the birthing suite when you told me you drank a vial of blood that had Sam's name on it? But the tray of vials had been labeled wrong by the nurses. As it turned out, the blood you drank was Orion's." Doc found the paper he was looking for.

"Are you saying Orion's blood turned her?" Sam asked, beating me to the punch.

"That would certainly be better than Rianne's," Dane mumbled.

I was more concerned about me growing hair and claws or even going feral.

Then a light bulb came on. "If that's true, then could he be our child who's tied to the prophecy of turning witches?"

Dr. Vieira began to pace. "Again, don't jump to conclusions. I need to think. The babies gave you powers while they were in your womb. You craved blood while you were pregnant. Even after you gave birth, you still have that hunger for blood. Maybe the quadruplets are responsible for your change. Then Rianne's venom killed you, but your system fought off the poison, thus restarting your heart."

Sam pressed the heels of his palms into the counter. "Kind of like the process of natural-born vampires. We essentially die as our internal organs go through the change, right? Someone who's taken the serum doesn't die."

Doc was frantically pacing in the aisle between the two benches. "There is a window of time that the heart of a natural-born vampire stops in the process during the change, yes."

I set the bottle on the shiny black worktop. "If I'm hearing you correctly, I would've eventually turned into a vampire?"

"I will hold my answer until I run tests," Doc said. "Until I know more and can explain the science behind your change, I prefer we keep this to ourselves, except we'll have to tell Steven. After all, he's our leader."

"Not even my sister?" I asked.

Doc stopped abruptly. "I know Jordyn is suffering. But I would like to be sure of my findings that Rianne didn't turn you. The last thing we need is people panicking." He eyed Dane, wagging his finger. "You can't even tell Dr. Hammond."

Dane raised his large hands. "She probably wouldn't believe me. She would think the surgery to remove my chip screwed with my brain."

I'd completely forgotten that Dane had been brought in as a wolf and hadn't been able to shift.

Nevertheless, if Rianne was responsible, that also meant the genetic-altering experiments would truly involve a monster-type virus, and humanity wouldn't survive. Maybe a child of mine wouldn't upset the balance of the world. Maybe my mom's message was wrong.

My rebirth would certainly erase any chance of peace

between vampires and humans if Adam's program created monsters who had a supernatural virus.

The severity in Dr. Vieira's expression made me recoil. "I need to start testing. The sooner I can find the answer, the more we can relax. I need about twelve hours. I also need to postpone my meeting with Isadora Blackman, the witch scientist with the Midnight Raiders. She's due in tomorrow night."

"We should also cancel Zoey Thornton's trip as well," I said. "I might need time to grow into my supernatural skin." Or maybe the powers that be would lock me in a prison cell until they knew I wouldn't be a threat.

As if Doc knew what I was thinking, he said, "Layla, you'll need to stay in the infirmary until I have answers."

I nodded in agreement. As much as I wanted to see my children, I couldn't risk hurting them if in fact I was truly a monster.

"I'll alert my dad," Sam said.

"This has been fun," Dane piped in. "I'm heading home. I have a mess to help clean up. Sam, we'll be in touch. Layla, don't die again." He nodded at Sam. "You about killed your husband."

After we said goodbye to Dane, I went into a room on doctor's orders with Sam on my heels.

"How are you feeling about all this?" I asked.

He whisked a hand through his hair before wrapping his arms around me. "I'm so fucking relieved that you're alive. I've been a nutcase." He felt my face and arms, then examined me from head to toe. "My mind is blown." He kissed everywhere, sighing heavily.

I could only imagine what he'd been through. I knew if the roles were reversed, I would've been jumping off a bridge or curled up in a corner for years.

"I'm sorry, Sam," I said, holding on to him for dear life. "I should've run from Rianne. I thought I could use my mind control, but she was wicked fast, and before I could do anything, I was fighting her off me."

He cupped my face. "It's not your fault."

"I'm just praying that I don't turn feral."

If fate had a way of fucking us, it would be with something like that. I had to agree with Dane. If my sister was my maker, then the zombie apocalypse would commence.

**27**

---

# LAYLA

It was approaching noon the following day, and I'd risen from the dead only fourteen hours prior. I was flabbergasted that I was a vampire. I wondered if my change was fate's way of punishing me or rewarding me. After all, I'd killed bloodsuckers for years.

Were the vampire gods trying to give me a taste of my own medicine by me becoming an immortal to experience how it felt to be hunted? Or was it my destiny to spend eternity with Sam? Or maybe my transformation was all part of the plan to help humanity.

I was leaning toward the reward option and trying to stay positive that I wouldn't become a monster. If not, that meant I wouldn't grow old while Sam and my children lived on.

I was sitting on a barstool across from Dr. Vieira as he typed data into his computer. "You don't think my children will be in danger from me as a new vampire?"

Dr. Vieira had barred all doors from anyone entering after Sam had returned with clothes for me last night. Since then, I'd kept Dr. Vieira company as he ran lab tests, asked him questions about being a vampire, and paced like a madwoman. He'd almost given me a sedative because I'd made him nervous. But as the night went on, my adrenaline started to dissipate.

He kept his attention on his task. "Do you feel the need to attack me?"

"No. You smell normal," I said.

He chuckled. "Your children are vampire witches. They're not human, which means you'll be fine around them."

"Jordyn and Agnes will be another story," I mumbled.

"For sure." He stopped banging on keys and opened a drawer on his side of the lab bench. "These should help control your bloodthirst when you need to." He handed me a bag of candy.

"Fang Fizzlers." I giggled. "Funny name."

"A friend of mine developed those candies about two years ago," Dr. Vieira said proudly. "They're quite good. The insides are filled with blood. You can carry them in your purse or pocket for emergencies."

I opened the bag, unwrapped the hard candy, and popped one in my mouth. I jolted in surprise at how delicious the raspberry treat tasted. I crunched until it broke, and the gooey filling inside slid down my throat, cooling that mild burn that came with hunger.

"Huh, they're tasty."

He rubbed his temples and tossed a Fang Fizzler into his mouth. "I go through a bag quickly." Then he sighed. "Are you ready for the results?"

I looked at him like he was nuts as I wiped my sweaty hands on my yoga pants. "Of course." My heart was pounding as fast as I was chewing the candy to pieces.

I still hadn't shown any signs of red eyes, claws, or facial disfiguration. Dr. Vieira was almost certain I wouldn't become Rianne.

"Well, I can say for sure that Rianne's bite isn't the cause of your change."

"I won't turn feral, then?" I asked, just to be sure I was hearing him correctly.

"You are a hundred percent a vampire," he said with excitement in his voice.

I cried and laughed at the same time. "That's great news." Relief flooded my veins. "How?"

"Before I go into detail, I'll call Steven and ask him to join us along with Sam. That way I'll only need to explain things once."

"Can Jordyn be here too?" I really didn't want her suffering anymore. Although I was afraid of how I would react to my sister.

"I don't see why not, and Jordyn will be a test to see how you fare with her," he said as he dialed Steven. "But I suspect that since you've been drinking blood for months now, you can control your bloodlust around humans."

He had a lot of confidence in me that I wouldn't have until I could know for sure. "Ask Sam to bring our children too." I also had to know and be absolutely sure I would be okay around them. I would stab myself if I was even tempted to sink my fangs into my babies.

After Dr. Vieira called Steven, I drank two bottles of blood in preparation to meet my sister and Agnes, as well as my children, as a brand-new vampire. To say I was nervous was an understatement. I felt as though I was meeting everyone for the first time, and I wanted them to like me. After all, in my mind I was still Layla, but I was now a predator. If my dad was watching over me from his grave, he was probably cussing left and right.

Yet I was also jumping up and down that I wouldn't grow hair or claws. Fate was on my side this time.

I was biting my nails and pacing between the lab benches when someone knocked on the double doors an hour later.

Dr. Vieira hurried over and unlocked it.

My husband waltzed in, freshly showered—damp hair hung to his shoulders, his face was clean-shaven, and he was wearing his military uniform as he pushed the stroller with our son in it.

I rushed up to Sam and Orion and squatted down. "Hey, baby boy." My heart swelled as I sniffed the air. Aside from Orion's baby scent, nothing about him caused my fangs to drop or my bloodthirst to surface. "Where are the girls?"

"They're at Jo's house," Sam said, placing a hand on my back. "We decided to just bring Orion to test things out."

I smoothed a hand over Orion's thick black hair. His green eyes were bright as he watched me while sucking on his pacifier. I couldn't even begin to describe the love I had for him. Or the happiness I had that I had no desire to drink his blood.

I squeezed his tiny foot. He was dressed in a onesie, showing his chubby legs. His feet were covered in socks, and he had a bib around his neck. Then I leaned in and kissed him on the forehead. "I love you so much."

I stood to my full height and threw myself at my husband, who smelled amazing with his woodsy scent doing things to my body that weren't appropriate in front of Orion. "I'm a vampire."

"I heard." Sam laughed. "How are you?"

"Aside from wanting a hot shower and to sleep," I said, "I'm fantastic. It's like I'm seeing the world in a whole new light. I can hear sounds from faraway. My sense of smell is strong, and I feel invincible, almost."

He moved strands of blood-caked hair behind my ear. "All the benefits of being a vampire." He leaned into my ear. "When we're alone, you'll feel things like never before," he whispered. "If you get my drift."

Heat rose to pinch my cheeks as I understood his meaning. He'd always said he could smell my lust. If he could, then Doc could as well. So I picked up Orion. "Dr. Vieira, when will my children's fangs grow in?" I had to change the subject and shake off thoughts of Sam and me naked.

"Considering I don't have any experience with inhuman babies, I can't give you a firm answer," he said. "It might be when they start teething or when they lose their baby teeth."

Either way, it would be a challenge to deal with four children and their bloodlust. But I didn't care. I was alive. I was immortal. And I had my family for an eternity.

I carried Orion as Sam and I ambled over to the stool I'd been sitting in. "You were right, Dr. Vieira. I'm fine around Orion."

The doors groaned open, and Steven, Jordyn, and Agnes sauntered in.

My gaze rounded on Jordyn first.

She had her mouth hanging open. "Is that really you, Layla?" Jordyn's brown eyes were wide with amazement.

"It's me, sis," I said as Sam grabbed Orion from me.

"I can't decide if I'm more stunned that you're alive or a vampire," Jordyn said.

"Join the club," I volleyed in return, sniffing the air. A sugary mixture of vanilla and fruit wafted into my nostrils, and I couldn't stop my canines from dropping. Humans did smell totally different from vamps, even discounting colognes, perfumes, and scented soaps. Sam, Doc, Steven, and Orion had neutral odors.

*Holy shit!*

Agnes flinched. Jordyn didn't. Instead, my sister, brave as ever, padded over to me, chin held high, curiosity steeped in her brown eyes. "You're glowing. Every scratch that Rianne inflicted is gone. Your ear is attached again."

I closed my lips tightly until my fangs retracted despite that scratchy burn in the back of my throat. While I was pregnant, I had the same feeling when I needed blood. The difference now was that I had canines and my sense of smell had increased a hundredfold.

A crazed laugh broke out in my head. *I'm an animal. A predator. Hunters like my Aberdeen family would track me down and burn me over their firepit.*

I would be lying if I said I wasn't embarrassed and hurt. I wanted to act normal around Jordyn, even Agnes. I was failing miserably.

"You're not afraid of me, are you?" I asked Jordyn.

"Not at all," Jordyn replied. "One, you're not Rianne. Two, you would never hurt me."

Steven, who was already beside me as if ready to intervene if I attacked Jordyn or Agnes, gave me a kiss on the cheek. "The transformation suits you, Layla."

I had no idea what that meant, and I didn't have a chance to find out either.

"It broke my heart when I heard you died." Agnes finally spoke as she went over to stand on the other side of the lab bench next to Dr. Vieira. "Vampire or not, I'm beyond happy you're here. That means you have a purpose to fulfill." My grandmother was scrutinizing me, her brown eyes flickering from brown to orange. "I can feel your magic. You're still a witch."

"A vampire witch like my children," I said, rolling that around in my head.

"It seems the Mason family is now more powerful than ever," Steven said.

Considering five vampire witches were now part of the Mason clan, I would agree.

"Now that the introductions are out of the way," Doc said, "let's get started."

Sam placed Orion in his stroller and stood beside me as I sat on the stool while Steven flanked my right, and then Jordyn stood on the other side of him.

Dr. Vieira opened his folder and pulled out a sheet of paper. "The data is quite eye-opening. What I've discovered is a genetic phenomenon that is one for the history books." He pushed up the sleeves of his lab coat. "I ran test after test every which way and even reran them. In a nutshell, Orion is the key to your transformation."

Agnes gasped. "He's the prophecy?"

Sam and I exchanged worried looks.

Steven held up his hand. "Don't jump the gun yet. The last thing we need is witches banging on our gates."

Dr. Vieira gently touched Agnes's arm. "It is the prophecy, yet it isn't. The explanation lies in the difference between Orion's blood type and Layla's. To begin, Layla is Vel negative. Sam is AF negative. In humans, when two parents are Rh negative, the child will also be Rh negative. That isn't always the case in vampires."

"Orion is Rh positive," Steven said as if he were the doctor.

Dr. Vieira bobbed his head. "That's correct. In the case of the quadruplets, the girls are Vel-F negative. The F is the allele or gene passed down to them from Sam. Orion, on the other hand, is Vel-F positive, and because you're Vel negative, Layla, this is where genetics start to change." He glanced at the paper near his laptop. "Normally, when Vel-negative blood types such as yourself are exposed to the Vel-positive blood group that includes Vel-F—either from drinking, transfusion, or pregnancy—the Vel-negative individuals can become sensitized, thus producing an anti-Vel antibody, which in Layla's case happened."

Genetics weren't my thing, but I knew that antibody meant a defense mechanism. "You're saying that when I was pregnant, my body produced this antibody to fight off Orion's blood?"

"Exactly," Dr. Vieira said. "An antigen is the medical term.

Now, if you're exposed a second time to, say, Orion's blood, for example, then the antigen can bind to the Vel-positive red blood cells. As a result, the reaction reordered or modified your DNA mapping sequence, thus turning you into a vampire."

"And I drank Orion's blood in the birthing suite that day," Layla said. "That's what you mean by second time?"

Doc nodded. "Yes. That vial with Sam's name on it was in fact Orion's, since the tray of blood had been mislabeled. If you hadn't drunk it, you wouldn't be a vampire."

Steven cleared his throat. "Layla was exposed to Orion's blood a second time. What if she didn't die? How long before she would've turned?"

Dr. Vieira closed the folder. "Hard to say. But her death sped up the process."

Agnes gave Doc a sidelong glance. "I followed everything you explained. But can another witch turn like Layla?"

Dr. Vieira's Adam's apple moved up and down. "If every witch with Vel-negative blood was exposed to Orion's blood not once but twice, either by drinking it or a transfusion of it, then yes. That's why I said the change is related to the prophecy, yet it isn't. I don't see witches lining up for Orion's blood so they can become vampires."

"You make a good point," Agnes said, sounding like a weight had been lifted off her shoulders. "Yet, the Monroe seer had a vision of her entire coven being turned into vampires by an inhuman child born to a Monroe witch who had quadruplets."

"Agnes," Steven said, "that prediction was two hundred years ago. We both know that a seer only visualizes a flash of something and doesn't have the whole picture. Not only that, events change over time. For example, you have no coven anymore. All your ancestors are dead. Is that correct?"

"Yes," Agnes said. "Except for Layla, Abbey, and me. Jordyn's a Monroe, but she has yet to unlock her powers."

"I'm not going to either," Jordyn piped in. "I'm staying just the way I am."

"I hate to even bring this up." Dr. Vieira's tone was hesitant. "While this prophecy might not be relevant at this juncture, it could very well still be in play when Orion is older. Abbey has one tied to her."

Sam growled. "That doesn't make me feel good, Doc."

My mind was spinning with what I'd learned from Agnes and her father-in-law, Everett. "I'm confused about something. Everett told Sam and me that, according to you, Agnes, witches could lose their powers if they turned. Is that true?"

Agnes shook her head. "Technically, no. Over the years my kind *speculated* that could happen. Not that it would. That was another fear-driven assumption."

I hated that we were running scared from a simple vision of someone who wasn't even alive.

"The bottom line is this," Dr. Vieira said. "*Any witch* with Vel-negative blood could turn with Orion's blood, as I explained earlier. Outside of that, we need to make sure that witches far and wide know they have nothing to fear."

"He is the prophecy," Jordyn said. "But the loophole is that a witch would have to drink Orion's blood not once but twice. And this prophecy could come to light if Orion wanted a vampire witch coven of his own."

Sam and I whipped our heads toward her.

She shrugged. "What? Think about it. He could have his own harem of witches."

I snarled at my sister lovingly. Regardless, I couldn't help but recall something else my mom had said. *One of your children is prophesied to change the course of humankind, which will have a ripple effect that upsets the balance of the world.* Maybe Orion would do just that when he was older. For now, I had to focus on the here and now and take comfort that a witch could only change through genetic altering and not from a simple bite. I doubted they would be lining up to become creatures of the night.

"Damon, you'll need to present your findings to Captain Greer of the Midnight Raiders. They're the best source to spread the word through the witch community," Steven said.

"I emailed Isadora Blackman, their scientist, early this morning to cancel her trip here. She and I have been trading messages. I told her I would give her a call when I have a moment and explain everything," Dr. Vieira said.

Steven looked at his watch. "In light of Layla's change, Jo has called Zoey Thornton and postponed her trip here as well. I've informed Jack and Tabitha Aberdeen that we had to also reschedule their trip to see their son Noah. In the meantime, Layla, as my liaison, you can work behind the scenes. We'll talk more about that later. Plus, until we can deal with our enemies, we don't need any other distractions."

Zoey didn't have to fly here anyway. We could talk via phone or a video chat about the Mystic. As far as my uncle Jack and aunt Tabitha, it was best I didn't face them—at least not until I was comfortable in my new skin, so to speak.

For now, I needed a hot shower and sleep.

# 28

## LAYLA

I left the infirmary about an hour ago and asked if Jordyn and Agnes could watch Orion and his sisters. Sam had a strategy meeting to attend to, and I had to take a catnap. That way I would be in better shape to spend time with my children, sister, and grandmother.

The sun's rays pouring in through the wall of windows in our apartment was warm as I waved my hand through the beam of light. Natural-born vampires weren't affected by the sun, but my transformation wasn't natural like Sam's had been. After all, he carried the vampire gene.

I was giddy when the heat of the rays sent sparks of electricity along my arms and down my legs as if the hot ball of plasma was infusing me with energy rather than burning me to a crisp.

Sam came up behind me, clutching my shoulders and kissing my neck. "See, you didn't burn."

"You never know," I said, turning into his arms. "I still can't wrap my head around the fact that I'm a vampire."

"Join the club. I thought you were dead. I didn't know how I was going to tell our kids their mother died."

"Again, I'm so sorry."

He placed a finger on my lips. "Shh. You're here, and that's all that matters."

"And I'm immortal. That means we get to spend eternity together."

His face brightened. "Best fucking news ever. We should celebrate. I have two hours before the meeting." He waggled his eyebrows. "Do you want to experience sex as a vampire?"

I gave him a flirty smirk. "Do birds fly? But I have to take a shower first."

He scooped me up into his arms, carried me into the bedroom, set me down on the bed, then locked our bedroom door. "Just in case anyone comes in."

I stripped, then wiggled my bare butt in front of him as I went into our en suite. But before I did anything, I wanted to see what I looked like with fangs.

I stood over the sink and sucked in air. What the hell did Steven mean by the transformation suited me? I resembled something out of a horror show. Mainly because blood-caked hair and fangs weren't the most pleasing things to see.

Sam swaggered in naked, his cock growing as he wrapped his arms around me.

I smiled broadly, examining my canines. They weren't thick like Rianne's had been, nor did they resemble a wolf's. They also seemed shorter in length than Sam's fangs.

"How do you control whether they come out or not?" I asked.

He laughed, eyeing me in the mirror. "Like any physical action, you practice until it becomes natural. It's about mind and body control. Sometimes, though, you might not have a choice."

"You mean when I'm hungry?"

He nibbled on my ear. "Exactly. You know what I just thought of? You sinking your fangs into *me*. Fuck, I'm dying for you to properly taste me." He cupped my breasts and pinched my nipples, his canines sliding down. "You remind me of a sleek, beautiful tiger with those yellow eyes. I think my new pet name for you is tigress."

I laughed even though I didn't agree with what he said about my appearance. "I'll purr for you."

He chuckled, deep and husky, the sound feathering over my skin until goose bumps blanketed my body and my lady parts were pulsating.

"Come on." He ushered me into our walk-in shower and turned it on. While we waited for the water to heat, he examined my ear and the rest of my body.

"I can't believe my wounds are nonexistent," I said.

"You can't beat vampire physiology." He stepped under the spray and closed his eyes.

My hands trembled as I joined him, feeling a new rush of desire for every inch of his body. The skin over his abs felt like the finest silk beneath my fingers as I explored every dip and valley until I found my way to that pronounced V, trailing my fingers against the soft hair and down to his impressive erection. Every movement sent waves of pleasure radiating deep within me.

"Everything feels different. I have a heightened awareness. It's almost like I was in the dark as a human. I can't exactly explain it." I dragged the tips of my fingers over his velvety shaft.

He moaned in approval, shoving his hands through his wet hair. "Do you want to see how my cock feels inside you?"

I rolled my eyes. "I'm dying to, but I need to clean the grime off me."

He traded his spot for mine. Once under the water, he proceeded to lather me up with soap, taking his time around my tits, ass, then pussy while I washed my hair. By the time we were done and toweled off, I was ready to sleep. The weight of the last several hours, waiting for the test results, was starting to take its toll on me.

As if Sam knew how I was feeling, he lifted me up and carried me to the bed. "Why don't you sleep? We can resume later tonight."

"Just stay with me for a bit," I said on a yawn.

He curled up next to me so we were facing each other.

I slid my leg between his while he rubbed his hand over my hip and grabbed my ass, pulling me to him.

"I can't believe we're finally in our own bed," I said, exploring his upper torso with my hands. "It feels wonderful to be here." I rolled him onto his back with ease. My new vampire strength was exhilarating. "Maybe we can have a quickie before I fall asleep." I crawled on top of him.

He chuckled. "I'm here to please you."

My breath raced as I guided him inside me, my skin blazing with anticipation and desire. A whimper rippled up the back of my throat at the tightness, the wetness, and the fullness, sending waves of pleasure through me.

I anchored my hands on his chest and slowly lifted up and then down on him. The friction was explosive—fire and ice lighting up every nerve ending in my body.

His eyes held mine so singularly as he watched me watch him. As we moved like a well-practiced orchestra, my tits bounced—heavy and needy.

He shot up and sucked one nipple, then the other, making my flesh tremble.

I yanked on his hair, pushing my tit into him. "Suck harder," I squeaked out.

He did, giving each breast equal attention. But it wasn't enough. I needed to feel more pleasurable pain. I wanted his tongue, his lips, his fangs, and his dick all over me at the same time.

He flipped us over and pressed his hands into the mattress on either side of my head. "Are you doing okay?"

"I need something more, Sam. It's like I can't get enough of the sensations lighting up my entire being."

He fucked me like a vampire possessed.

"Yes. Harder." It was my turn to flip us.

He laughed. "I like that newfound strength you have now."

We fucked hard and fast, flipping and rolling, sweating and moaning. I think I died again and went to heaven this time.

On the last roll, I was on the bottom when he said, "Legs over my shoulders."

I obeyed, drunk on lust and him and the music we were creating.

He rammed into me, pulled out, and flipped us into a sixty-nine position.

I swallowed him as he fucked my mouth, my incisors abrading his shaft.

He growled. "Dig those fangs into my cock."

I was so far gone that I didn't even think.

Once my fangs punctured his dick, he roared. "I need to be inside your wet pussy."

I let go, and in a flash he was pounding into me.

"I don't want this to end, but I'm right at the edge," I said through heavy breaths.

"Let it go, baby doll. Feel the release pour through you. Savor it."

I grabbed his hair, jolted up, and bit into his neck. The first mouthful of blood was warm and salty. I took long pulls, and the more I drank from him, the more I felt as though I was flying, soaring over the planet with not a care in the world. He tasted like heaven and home. Sugar and spice. My skin felt tingly. My insides felt like a million bat wings partying hard.

My orgasm blindsided me. Wisps of pleasure blurred into a single cresting wave.

He thrust one last time, and when he did, he threw his head back, groaning his release before he propelled forward and drove his fangs into the swell of one breast.

I hardly felt the pinch as I arched my back, giving him room to take all he needed.

Eternity with Sam would be an amazing ride, and I had the feeling sex would be on the agenda every night. Because I was suddenly more addicted to and in love with him than I thought possible.

**29**

---

# SAM

I was riding a huge wave as I kissed my sleeping wife on the head before I left for my meeting. After we had what in my book was one of the best rounds of sex, I'd showered again. By the time I got out, Layla was snuggled under the blankets and softly snoring.

Eternity with her was going to be off the charts. I swore that I couldn't be any happier than I was at that moment, although I likely could when we finally ended the war with Adam Emery.

As I headed to the war room, I was processing the last twenty hours since Layla's rebirth, the way she'd changed genetically, the fact that our son had been the key to her waking up from the dead, and the list went on. Fate was one fucking roller-coaster ride. I was also relieved that Orion wouldn't be targeted by witches. However, I wasn't cool that the prophecy was tied to my son or that he could potentially upset the balance of humanity years from now. But I had time to ensure that didn't happen, if it did at all.

Reporter Tim Cox's voice was echoing in the spacious theater-style room when I entered.

Webb, Tripp, and my father were sitting at a table, watching a news segment on our new seventy-two-inch monitor rather than the old movie screen we'd had. A sea of people crowded the streets behind Tim Cox.

My gaze drifted from the screen to the familiar-looking box on the table. "Is that another head?"

Webb regarded me over his shoulder. "Yep. It's Tucker Whyte's. It was delivered an hour ago to the front gate."

I cleared the stairs at the bottom, and just like that, any sense of happiness vanished. "Rebekah's brother."

Tucker had gone missing around the time Layla had gotten lost in the West Virginia mountains not long after she'd been kidnapped by Roman. He had his men transporting her to Intech's facility in that state. After a car accident, she'd wandered the dangerous terrain until she ended up at a cabin where she met the wolf shifter—an Army Special Forces medic. Rebekah had been looking for her brother, who'd been at the Whyte's family cabin not long before the she-wolf had shown up.

Tripp pressed a key on his laptop, and the sound muted, then he and Webb were on their feet.

Webb gave me a tight bro hug. "I'm shocked Layla is a vampire but happy as fuck that she is. I've been gutted over her death."

It was Tripp's turn to embrace me. "So fucking happy for you, man. I'm blown away at Layla's transformation, which you can tell me all about later. We have a video call with Conrad in a few minutes."

Fine by me. I didn't need to relive my wife's death. Fuck, Layla had officially died four times now. That in and of itself made me dizzy. Yet knowing it would be harder for her to die again cleared the fog from my head.

"I hope Conrad has good news for us. I'm ready to end Adam Emery," I said. "Before long, it might just be one of our heads in a box. By the way, I hope that after we capture him, we're not keeping him alive to appease the federal government." Dane and I had plans for Adam's death.

I'd learned yesterday morning before the incident with Rianne that Conrad was following leads of sightings of Adam in Chicago. He'd also been talking to a retired Navy SEAL by the name of Grant Vega, who had sent a letter to us after the TV interview my dad, Eugene, and I had done recently. Supposedly, Grant had been keeping tabs on Adam after his news conference months ago.

"I don't think they'll balk at whatever we do," my dad said, lowering his phone to his lap. "In their minds, Adam is a terrorist who needs to be stopped at all costs. Actually, they're hoping a civilian takes him out."

I stabbed a finger at the box. "Where's the note?"

Webb retrieved the letter from beside his notepad and handed it to me.

I read it as I dropped into a chair beside Tripp while he and Webb resumed their seats side by side.

*Steven,*

*This is your final warning to meet my demand to free my brother, Fred, now! Otherwise, it won't be just one head but several that will be delivered to your doorstep now that I have intel from Tucker Whyte on shifter packs up and down the East Coast. If that doesn't light a fire under your ass, I'll find any person who matters to you and those around you and chop off their heads. And I won't stop until Fred is released.*

"Steven, maybe we should reconsider releasing the asshole," Tripp said.

At the head of the table, my father bared his fangs as his nostrils flared. "If we let Fred go, he'll give Adam the thumb drive with my brother's genetic files. If that happens, not only are we right back to square one, but we can't afford for those files to leak to anyone else. It's bad enough Draven Murphy is involved."

He jammed a finger at the monitor where people were crowding the streets, protesting with signs that read Murder Adam Emery or Adam Emery is the worst monster of all. "This country is about to riot, and I'm sure there are many humans out there who want to eradicate us as well."

"If we can show the public we've stopped Adam, then maybe that will sway them to our side," Webb said.

Not that long ago, humans were picketing with signs that read Free Layla all because some humans thought I was a monster. Thanks to Rianne, who had been at Adam's news conference and announced to the nation that Layla was being held by a bloodsucking vampire against her will.

How the tides had shifted in such a short time. Instead of the cameras being on us, they were on Adam. He was his own worst enemy. He'd started this fucking shit show when he'd gone on TV and announced that vampires were real, even going so far as having Matthew Costner prove to the nation we existed. But the spotlight could revert to us once again.

Still, I couldn't totally blame Adam. After all, I'd been the one whose vampire face went viral even before Adam's news conference.

"What do you think Adam's going to do next, Steven?" Webb asked.

My dad's green eyes swirled to a steely silver. "Probably come for his brother. That's what I would do."

"We've recently had all the gates reinforced, so it will be diffi-cult to plow through them with a vehicle like Carly did," Tripp said. "Nevertheless, we'll increase patrols on land and water."

If someone was desperate to penetrate our fortress, they would find a way, and Mount Hope Bay that bordered one side of our perimeter was probably the best way to attack us. We had boat patrols and guards stationed at key points along the water, but a group of divers could probably sneak by our troops.

"As soon as we conclude here, I want our scouts scouring the area outside of the naval base," my father said. "That includes neighborhoods, the downtown area, and the abandoned textile mills in Fall River. Everywhere and anywhere close by, just in case."

Tripp tapped a key on his laptop. "I definitely agree with searching the local area, but according to this news segment, there have been sightings of Emery in Chicago. And Conrad will have an update for us in a minute."

Tim Cox's brown hair was disheveled, and his tie was blowing around in the wind. "The crowds are growing larger here outside Intech's corporate headquarters. People are angry and up in arms with owner and CEO, Adam Emery, for his prototype program's failed attempts at using humans to genetically alter their DNA to build an army of super soldiers. There have been sightings of Adam in the city, indicating that he's returned to this building you see behind me."

Adam didn't strike me as someone who would be stupid enough to rekindle his program at the same building that we and the Feds had raided.

"It's time to bring up Conrad." Tripp punched several keys on his laptop.

Within seconds, Conrad, the vampire scout with black hair and hazel eyes, came on-screen.

"Conrad," Tripp said. "Can you hear me and see us?"

He was sitting in his SUV. "Yes."

"Good," Tripp replied. "Bring us up to speed."

"I met with Grant Vega this morning," Conrad started. "The retired Navy SEAL is now a building inspector for Chicago. He's found some activity in the industrial district, which is located several blocks from the property supposedly owned by Fred Emery. There are intermodal rail yards here, which might support the train you heard when you spoke to Adam by phone.

Also, last night, I spotted Draven Murphy and Adam entering a guarded warehouse that Grant had pinpointed as one possible location. I'll send you the address. I'm also checking the other spots Grant has given me."

"Conrad, follow their routine. I want to know every place they go," my dad said. "Webb, call Joan Chambers, our head of state for Illinois. She can set us up with a command center in Chicago."

"Pops, did you ever speak to Draven's old man?" In our last meeting, he'd mentioned he would call Baxter Murphy to see if he could knock some sense into Draven's head.

My dad leaned back in his chair. "Unfortunately, Baxter told me to fuck off. He's upset that humans know we exist. I'm not surprised at his response. He's just as much a dickhead as his son. He also claims he doesn't know jack shit about Draven working with Emery. I think he's lying, and I wouldn't be surprised if Baxter is the one ordering his son to do his bidding."

A phone dinged, but it wasn't mine.

My father picked up his phone off his lap. A few taps later, he said, "Adam sent me a video."

Tripp, Webb, and I gathered around my dad as he hit Play.

Adam Emery's ugly mug brightened the screen. "I'm sure you got my latest package by now, Steven." Adam looked as if he hadn't showered or shaved in days. His brown hair was oily, and he'd grown a beard since I'd seen him in the basement of the farmhouse. "If you've read my letter, then you know what's at stake." The video panned around an empty room until Adam zoomed in on a man with reddish hair and blue-gray eyes tied to a chair.

"Is that Jack Aberdeen?" I asked, knowing it was him.

Webb and Tripp said in unison, "Yep."

They'd fucked Jack up good. His face was bloody, he had a

gag in his mouth, and behind him was Draven Murphy, bald and deadly, holding a machete to Jack's throat.

Adam returned to the camera. "Jack Aberdeen is my next victim. You have seventy-two hours. If I don't hear from you by then, Jack's head is next." Then the video ended.

I checked my watch. "Four p.m. We have three days."

My father was about to throw his cell across the room when the side door opened.

Layla ran in, her blue eyes shifting to yellow and her fangs sparkling. "My aunt Tabitha is on the phone. My uncle was kidnapped by bloodsuckers. Tell Steven what happened, Aunt Tab." She placed the phone on the table in front of my dad.

Webb and Tripp hadn't seen Layla since she turned. Both were studying her, although Webb had yet to see her eyes turn yellow.

Tripp regarded me. "Turning vampire suits her."

Webb nodded in agreement.

Jordyn had mentioned that Layla was glowing. I had to agree. I was digging her canines, especially.

"Jack and I had just pulled into Big Timber, Montana." Tabitha's voice snapped my attention away from my gorgeous huntress. "We took our younger kids to stay with my mother. Thank God they weren't with us. Anyway, I ran into the grocery store while Jack stayed in the car. I was about to leave the store when I saw two men shoving Jack into a black SUV. I know they were bloodsuckers because one was baring his fangs at my husband. What's going on?"

"How long ago was this?" my dad asked, trying to keep his composure.

Layla walked into my arms, her eyes sleepy.

"Yesterday," Tabitha said in a high-pitched tone. "I would've called then, but I lost my phone. I'm actually using a friend's, who I've been staying with. I'm afraid to go home."

"Send Layla the address where you're staying," my dad said. "I'll have a member of my team who's not far from you pick you up. Layla will give you the name once I confirm who it will be."

"You haven't told me where my husband is," Tabitha said.

My dad pushed to his feet. "Unfortunately, I don't know yet. What I can tell you is Adam Emery is behind this."

Tabitha grunted. "I really want that man to die. Honestly, if my brother-in-law, Ray, wasn't dead or my mother-in-law, Harriet, I would've personally done the deed myself. My son, Noah, is an animal because of Ray and Harriet."

She wasn't wrong. Ray had made the deal with Fred Emery to capture me for a boatload of money. Ray had included Noah and Rianne in his dealings, as well as Harriet.

"Aunt Tab," Layla said. "I'll call you later. Okay?"

"Don't take long," Tabitha replied. "I have a feeling someone is watching me."

"Aunt Tab, do you have your weapons with you? Jack's flamethrower would be a good one to have. You said you're staying with a friend. Is this person prepared to fight?"

"Yes, yes, Layla," she said. "I'm fully prepared."

Once the call disconnected, Layla regarded my dad. "We have to help her. I know you're sending someone to pick her up, but can we fly her here? My aunt has been through hell. I know all of us have. But she doesn't stand a chance against our kind." Layla jerked slightly. "It's weird that I now can include myself in 'our kind.'"

Tripp chuckled.

Webb didn't. My brother-in-law was laser focused on the issue at hand. "Conrad, you have twenty-four hours to confirm without a doubt that Adam has set up shop at that warehouse. In the meantime, Tripp, prepare the team. I want boots on the ground in Chicago the moment we hear from Conrad. We end this fucker before the seventy-two-hour window is up."

"Copy that," Conrad said.

I had to call Dane. If he wanted in, which I knew he would, then he needed to get his ass down here ASAP.

"I'm coming with you guys," Layla said, her gaze bouncing around to everyone, me in particular. "And before any of you protest, this is my fight too. They have my uncle, and I'm more well equipped to help now that I'm a vampire witch. Agnes will help me practice my magic."

I had no problem with her fighting with us. I was much less concerned about her dying than ever before.

"I think we need Layla," Webb said.

Layla's mouth dropped open. "You do?"

Layla thought Webb wasn't a fan of hers. In the beginning, he wasn't, and I couldn't fault him. After all, the Aberdeens had been our enemy. But my wife had proven herself, and no one on the team now had any reason to distrust her or be concerned about her safety since she was no longer human. That didn't mean I wouldn't worry about her, however.

Webb nodded at her, and his brown hair fell forward over his forehead. "If you can wield magic, you'll be an asset. But you follow orders like any other of our soldiers. Is that clear?"

Her eyes lit up. "I'll start practicing with Agnes right away."

"Our success in this mission," Tripp said, "is the element of surprise. We don't have much time to prepare."

"Then let's get to work," my father said, with excitement in his voice.

Fuck yeah. I felt as though I could see the light at the end of a hellacious tunnel. With Adam out of the picture, all of us might be able to finally unwind and enjoy life. And maybe I would be able to give Layla that happily ever after I'd been promising her.

# 30

## LAYLA

After my aunt had woken me and I interrupted Steven's meeting yesterday, Agnes had been teaching me the ins and outs of spells and how to control my powers. But I was ready for a break, and I'd promised my aunt I would make a point to see her son Noah.

Tripp gave the approval, and Sam was with our children while Jordyn accompanied me to the prison building. She had something to say to Carly that she'd been itching to get off her chest. I wouldn't mind visiting our cousin-in-law for the simple fact that I wanted to see what she looked like. I could also give her a piece of my mind, but it wouldn't change anything for me.

Regardless, I also wanted to spend alone time with Jordyn before I left for Chicago with the team that evening. Conrad had confirmed Adam's new headquarters.

Jordyn and I hadn't had a chance to really talk since I'd become a vampire, and I wanted to be sure she was doing okay.

"Are your witch powers ready?" she asked as we climbed down the stairs from my apartment.

"My mind control works great," I tossed over my shoulder.

"Can I snap someone's neck with a flick of a wrist or send them flying like Abbey? We'll see."

Sam had graciously offered to be my guinea pig, but breaking my husband's bones wasn't something I wanted to do to him. Apparently, Patricia had knocked him out by snapping his neck. I also knew how to stop bullets from hitting me.

But I had to put what I'd learned into play. The key with magic that my grandmother made very clear was not just knowing the spells but the four cornerstones of magic—belief, desire, will, and visualization. "Without one, the power inherent in you will weaken," she'd counseled. "Always stay focused, especially when you're attacked. You must be aware of your surroundings and act with the four cornerstones in mind. If so, you will do great."

It helped that Agnes believed in me, as did my sister and husband. As far as Webb and Steven went, I believed they were enthusiastically cautious of my supernatural abilities, which I understood. If I had more time, that might not be the case. Tripp had seen what I was capable of, so he was more confident of my skills than Webb and Steven were.

"What about you, sis? How are you feeling about me as a vampire?"

She snorted. "I don't know that the shock will wear off quickly, but I think it's cool. You were worried about growing old while Sam would not. Now you can snuggle up to your man forever. Not to mention, you'll be there every step of the way with my nieces and nephew. I'm really happy for you, Layla. I'm also pleasantly surprised you're not wanting to suck my blood."

I laughed, the sound echoing in the stairwell. "The Fang Fizzlers help a great deal. But Dr. Vieira believes that because I've been drinking blood since I'd gotten pregnant that I'm in more control than others might think."

"Fang Fizzlers," she said. "That's such a goofy name."

"Do you want to try one?" I teased.

"I think I'll pass," she said, tittering.

"So, how are you feeling?" I asked my sister. "You seem like you're doing okay from your injuries."

"My back is still bothering me, but it will take time," she said.

"Know that whatever you need, I'm here for you."

"I know. For now, I just want to relax and help with my nieces and nephew until I decide what I want to do long-term, if that's okay with you."

"God, sis. Of course. I love the help, but don't feel like you have to be their full-time nanny."

"I want to right now."

I wasn't about to argue with her. Frankly, Sam and I didn't have time to find anyone, and I would prefer Jordyn and Agnes to care for them. My grandmother was already helping greatly.

The late August sun's warmth washed over me the minute we stepped into the courtyard. The smell of fresh-cut grass hung in the air, reminding me of days when my dad would ride his John Deere lawn mower on our property in Montana.

Before long, winter would be here and the holidays too. I had yet to celebrate Thanksgiving and Christmas with Sam, so I was looking forward to decorating the apartment with a tree and all the trimmings.

Jordyn and I were halfway across the courtyard when she said, "Not to change the subject, but I really like Agnes. She and I have chatted quite a bit."

"I'm glad we're both getting to know her," I said.

"I really wish Mom was here." Sadness colored her tone. "She would've loved the quadruplets."

"I have no doubt Mom would've been a wonderful grand-mother. But I'm not sure she would be accepting of who I've become—or rather, what I've become."

My statement fell on deaf ears as we approached the prison guard. "Ladies, Petty Officer Peterson is waiting for you inside."

The second I walked in, a musty odor stung my nostrils, and I wrinkled my nose.

Petty Officer Peterson climbed down the stairs. The crooked-nosed vampire grinned. "Good to see that you are one of us now, Layla. I was gutted when Rianne killed you."

He'd been the guard who'd escorted Rianne to the infirmary. Regardless, icy fingers tiptoed down my spine. I wanted to erase any memory of the attack, but it was still too fresh, since it had only been two days.

"Carly and Noah are in cells in the basement," Petty Officer Peterson said. "Once the metal doors to their cells open, there's a two-foot-thick bulletproof glass separating you from the prisoners. Behind that glass are steel bars as an added layer of protection. You'll be completely safe."

I could hear Jordyn's pulse racing as if it were my own, so I threaded my fingers through hers.

Several minutes later, Jordyn and I were outside Carly's cell with Peterson nearby.

Déjà vu hit me as Carly rose from her bed, reminiscent of Rianne when I stood outside my sister's glass barricade at the sheriff's station in Maine. Now, I was the one whose pulse was ticking higher on the charts. Once I left here, I never wanted to see another prison cell again.

Carly came over and wrapped her fingers around the steel bars. "Layla. Jordyn. I never expected to see you again."

Steven told me that Carly was reacting to the serum at a slower rate than Noah and Rianne. The last time I'd seen Noah was when he'd dragged me through the mountains in West Virginia that stormy day after he and Rianne had captured me. My cousin had morphed into something I'd never seen before—

bright-red eyes, cheekbones protruding outward, canines, and nails curling around his fingertips.

Carly had those features along with her forehead jutting out and hair growing out of her face. But it wasn't as thick as Rianne's had been.

"What are you doing here?" Carly asked.

Jordyn's shoulder was touching my arm as though she wanted me to protect her. "I vowed that if I ever got the chance to see you that I would punch you for breaking Junior's heart," she said through gritted teeth. "You're a fucking evil bitch. How could you pick science over the man you married? He loved you, Carly. He died because of you. He would've burned down the world for you." She guffawed. "Here you are, killing innocent humans. You have no soul. I hope you rot in hell."

That was Jordyn—straight and to the point.

Carly frowned, her red eyes filling with tears. "I know you won't believe me when I say I loved Junior. I know I'm going to hell. But I also know in my heart that I truly wanted to find cures for diseases."

"That still doesn't justify the pile of shit you and Adam started," Jordyn snarled. "You think coming to the naval base to hand over files is your salvation? Do you even know that because of you, Junior's father could die as well?"

Carly's jaw dropped.

"That's right," Jordyn continued, her volume increasing. "My uncle has a machete to his neck right now, all because Adam wants his brother, who supposedly has a thumb drive with data from genetic experiments on it. Maybe we should hand you over to Adam."

Jordyn had rendered Carly speechless.

"Do you know where Fred's thumb drive is?" I asked, knowing she'd already told Sawyer she had no clue.

She darted her gaze at me. "I don't. You can hand me over to

Adam. I'm dead either way. And not that this makes a difference, but after I was injected with the serum, I took off to a lab I set up long before I'd met Adam. I wanted to experiment on myself and hopefully find a way either to reverse the process or block the change from happening. But I was starting to decline. One reason I came here was to share my work with Dr. Vieira. Maybe he'll be able to discover a solution."

It was clear she was seeking redemption, but it was far too late for that.

Petty Officer Peterson marched up from his spot about ten feet away. "Ladies, we have a shift change coming up. If you want to see Noah, now's the time." He twirled his finger at the camera, then got on his radio. "Close up cell three and open up four."

"I truly am sorry," Carly said as her door began to shut.

"Do you feel better?" I asked Jordyn as we followed Peterson to the next room.

"I do," she said. "I've been carrying around this weight of the accident that Junior and I were in. And if I'm being honest, I'm happy she's gotten a taste of the crap she created."

I smiled, then was taken aback when I laid eyes on Noah.

Jordyn did a double take.

Noah was lying on his bed curled into a fetal position, not moving but looking directly at Jordyn and me.

Our handsome cousin, who'd had the ability to turn girls' heads in high school with his dark hair that had curled around his ears, the smattering of freckles around his nose, and his big dark eyes framed by long lashes, was now unrecognizable. He was now all animal—hairy, sunken red eyes, talons that had to be three inches in length, and he was bony as if he hadn't eaten in months.

My heart sank to the floor. I was glad his mom wasn't here. Tabitha would break in two if she saw him. He and I had hardly gotten along, but I was about to cry. I could see why his father Jack had collapsed after seeing his son.

Jordyn was frozen next to me.

"Noah." Emotion sliced my tone in half. "Your mom loves you. She wanted to be here."

His red eyes shifted back and forth as if he understood me.

"Your dad loves you too," Jordyn said. "I do as well, cousin." She started to cry.

"And your brothers and sister," I added. Noah was the second oldest behind Junior. "They wanted me to tell you that you were their favorite big brother."

He climbed off his bed and swayed as he came over to the steel bars and tilted his head.

"He can't speak anymore," Petty Officer Peterson said behind us.

The best thing we could do was to end his suffering. I was at a loss for any more words, and I needed air. But one thing was certain—seeing my cousin only served to fuel that spark of rage I needed for the battle ahead. Granted, Noah was his own worst enemy, but we had to remove the head of the snake, and his name was Adam Emery.

## 31

### SAM

The clock was ticking down. We had fifteen hours before Adam Emery followed through on his threat to whack off Jack Aberdeen's head. Layla was as nervous as a drug addict who needed a fix. I wasn't a fan of his, but he didn't deserve to die.

The good news was we finally had confirmation on Adam's new headquarters—a warehouse in the industrial district, the same one where Conrad had first spotted Draven Murphy and Adam. The bad news was that Adam hadn't been seen there since we'd arrived in Chicago twenty-five hours ago. We were ninety-five percent sure Jack Aberdeen was being held at the warehouse, but we were hoping to kill two birds with one stone and take out Adam as we rescued Jack.

Layla bounced her knee in between Dane and me as we waited in the briefing room for Webb and my father to come in. Webb had called us down about ten minutes ago. The only other person in the room was Tripp, two seats over, and he was absorbed on his laptop as usual.

Olivia, Ben, and Kraft, the Vampire Navy SEALs on this mission with us, were keeping an eye on the building Fred Emery

256

owned, which was located several blocks from the warehouse. But so far they hadn't seen any signs of Adam nor had they found anything or anyone inside. Then we had two of Joan's men joining us tonight. The same two who'd been sitting in a van, keeping an eye on our target.

Layla bit her nails. "I hope this meeting is to tell us Adam is at the warehouse. Time is running down, and I'm sick with worry that my uncle will die because of us. I also want this over with so we can go home and get on with our lives."

Dane was dozing with his legs kicked out and crossed at the ankles. "Nothing would make me happier."

I moved a wispy strand of hair off Layla's face. "If Adam doesn't show himself by four a.m., then we're going in regardless." Our missions were always better between midnight and four. There were fewer people around, and the darkness provided the best cover.

"That's three hours from now," she said. "By then, I'll have chewed every one of my fingernails off."

We knew the fucker was in Chicago. Joan's men had tailed Draven picking up Adam at his apartment in the city and followed them to a restaurant. At the same time, Sawyer and his team were monitoring commercial and private flights to be sure Adam hadn't flown to our city by the bay in Massachusetts.

I draped an arm around my wife and leaned close to her ear. "Maybe you can practice your mind control on Dane."

"Hell no," Dane fired at me like a heat-seeking missile.

"I'm good on that," Layla said. "I'm going to call Jordyn. I want to make sure everything is okay with the babies." She motioned to stand.

"I'm pretty sure your sister is asleep. It's one in the morning, baby doll."

She puffed out her cheeks. "Oh. I've had no sense of time since we've been holed up in this place."

We were staying in a three-story brick structure that the vampire government owned in Chicago. It was mainly for storage, but Joan Chambers used the place on occasion for secret meetings with her scouts and guardians. The top floor had rooms with bunk beds or twin beds, just like military barracks.

Webb and my father finally strode in. Both appeared wiped out but dressed for battle like the rest of us—black uniforms with weapons attached and bulletproof vests.

Dane straightened in his seat, and Tripp closed his computer.

"It's a go," Webb said too excitedly. "Joan's team trailed Adam and Draven from the restaurant they were at tonight to a house in Joliet where they picked up a gray-haired man named Rudolph Parsons. The background check we have on Mr. Parsons reveals that he's a genetic scientist who was working for Lyle Biotech up until last month. The three men pulled into the warehouse about thirty minutes ago."

Dane and I swapped an enthusiastic look. He and I were positively vibrating, almost unable to contain the primal urge to finally have the opportunity for vengeance against Adam Emery.

Everyone was on their feet, ready to get the show on the road.

Webb held up his hands. "Before we depart, a few last-minute reminders. As we've been studying and discussing for the last two days, this facility has several areas where they could be harboring Jack Aberdeen. The container yard is one of them. This will be our biggest challenge. There are a shitload of shipping containers stacked two to three high. Also, confiscate any hard drives, and if at all possible, we want the scientist alive. Outside of that, take no prisoners. If there aren't any questions, then stay safe."

"I'm assuming that you alerted Ben, Kraft, Olivia, and Conrad?" Tripp asked Webb.

"Conrad won't be joining us," my dad said. "He's on his way to Europe to do some investigating on Draven's father for me."

"Tripp, to answer your question," Webb said, "Ben, Kraft, and Olivia are heading to ground zero."

"Any sign of Roman in the area?" Layla asked.

We hadn't seen or heard anything from Roman. Then again, if he truly had escaped the farmhouse fire and was the naked blond man walking on the road behind the farm, he would need a blood bank and a few months to recover.

My father slipped his phone into the pocket of his bulletproof vest. "Negative. Nor have our scouts in North Dakota seen anyone fitting Roman's description."

"While all of us would love to capture Roman," Webb bit out, his muscles tensing, "our mission is your uncle's rescue and taking out Adam and Draven."

Dane raised his hand. "I would like to add that this military operation is great, and I thank you for including me, but if anyone captures Adam, he's mine to kill." He narrowed his reddish-brown eyes at my father. "Steven, you owe me that much."

"I have no problem with that," my dad said in a firm tone. "However, whoever finds Adam has orders to shoot to kill. We don't have time to fuck around." Then he wagged his finger between Dane and me. "Whatever torture tactics you two were planning, nix them. Is that clear?"

I was sure my father and everyone else on the planet had heard Dane and me talking about ways to fuck Adam up.

As much as I wanted to hang that bastard off his Intech skyscraper, I said, "Crystal clear."

A muscle jumped in Dane's jaw. "Then I better find him first."

"Move out," Webb ordered. "We'll check in and synchronize our watches when we're in position."

Layla rose up on her toes and ghosted her lips over mine. "Be safe, husband." She gave me one of her ball-squeezing smiles as she flashed her fangs.

My pulse raced at the sight of her as my eyes ran over her luscious curves in her skintight black leggings, military boots, and formfitting sleeveless black shirt. Her back was adorned with two daggers, while two more were in sheaths strapped to her legs, and she wore a gun on her hip.

I leaned into her ear and whispered, "You look fucking badass, especially with your fangs." I was still more dumbfounded that she was a vampire than I was that she was a witch.

The smell of lust filtered into my nose, but she said, "Mission first, husband."

I chuckled. "Are you ready to snap necks?"

"More than prepared," she said excitedly. "My newfound supernatural abilities are weird, but I will do my best." She puffed out her chest and quickly kissed me. "I'll see you on the other side."

She was teamed up with my dad and Webb. They were going in through the front, and Olivia, Ben, and Kraft through the rear. Tripp, Dane, and I were in the container yard with Joan's two men. From our intel, there were eight guards stationed outside. We didn't have eyes inside, but we suspected at least six guards.

I followed her out and into the parking lot. This was her first fight as a vampire but not as a witch. But Agnes wasn't here to give her each spell word for word like she had on the farm. Tonight, Layla was on her own when it came to witchcraft.

"Baby doll, just remember what your grandmother taught you about the four cornerstones of magic. Belief, desire, will, and visualization. You're going to kick ass."

She blew me a kiss, then darted over to Webb and my dad's vehicle while I hopped into the back seat of the rental SUV Tripp was driving.

"She'll be fine," Tripp said from behind the wheel.

"I know. It's just that she hasn't put her spells into actual practice. I offered myself as a practice target, but she refused, not wanting to hurt me."

"Wise woman," Dane replied from the passenger seat in front of me. "She could've knocked you out for days, then you wouldn't be here."

"Aw, and you would miss me," I teased.

He threw me the finger. "Just remember, bloodsucker, Adam is mine to kill."

"I promised you that if I got to Adam before you I would hand him over," I said.

I was bursting with excitement that this was our chance to put a permanent end to Adam and his attempts to fabricate humans into supernatural creatures once and for all.

## 32

## LAYLA

Fat rain drops splattered to the ground and kicked up those first scents of wet, decaying earth as Steven, Webb, and I exited the vehicle a block from the warehouse.

"Over here." Steven ducked under the metal portico of Acme Plastics.

Webb and I crowded beside him just as a harsh wind pushed errant trash along the sidewalk gutters. A soda can rolled by—the *ting, ting, ting* sound competing with the pelting rain on the roof over us along with my pulse that was racing like a damn greyhound around a track.

*Get your shit together, girl. You've hunted and killed before.* But not with the Vampire Navy SEALs. I wanted to show them that I could kick ass. I was worried my vampire strength would fail me or that my magic wouldn't work. After all, I'd only listened to Agnes explain how to snap necks. I hadn't practiced on anyone.

Webb checked his watch, then pressed on his earpiece. "Team leads, report when you're in position."

As I watched Mother Nature unleash her wrath, I prayed we

could do the same tonight. I prayed the mission would be a success and that my uncle Jack wasn't dead.

We still had almost fourteen hours left before Adam's deadline, but I didn't trust that bastard. I knew battles and wars weren't without setbacks or casualties, but we had to win. We had to end Adam once and for all. More importantly, I had to keep my promise to my aunt Tab.

Lightning flashed, thunder boomed, and a fishy aroma carried on the wind from Lake Michigan, which bordered along the backside of the warehouse beyond the container yard.

"We're in position," Tripp said into our comms. "But Joan's men haven't shown up yet. I can't reach them on their radio either."

"Fuck. They might've been compromised." Anger threaded through Steven's words.

I hoped we weren't about to abort. If so, my uncle was sure as hell dead.

"We're ready," Olivia reported in.

"We go on my command," Webb said as Steven called Sawyer.

The last piece of the puzzle before our attack was the techie's role in shutting down the security cameras around the warehouse.

I huffed out a breath, relieved that we wouldn't abandon my uncle. Then I tugged my bulletproof vest down and felt for my gun on my hip and the daggers in sheaths on my lower back, then the two around my legs.

My stomach was a freaking ginormous ball of knotted nerves. Would I freeze? Would my witch powers fail me? *Mind control is your strongest power*, my inner voice supplied. *Remember: belief, desire, will, and visualization.*

Webb touched his comm. "It's go time. Eyes on the prizes, ladies and gents."

I took in several quick breaths and released them, then jogged behind Steven and Webb, wiping the rain from my face.

Webb held up a fist and stopped at the corner across from the warehouse. "I don't see any guards along the perimeter or gate."

We backtracked the way we came.

"Team, update," Webb ordered in his comm. "Any guards in the rear or in the container yard?"

"That's a negative," Olivia relayed. "No guards on our end."

"We don't see any in the yard," Tripp chimed in.

"They know we're here," I said as my stomach pitched and rolled.

If I was right, what did that mean for my uncle?

Steven nodded. "I believe you're right, Layla."

"We've come this far. There's no turning back," Webb said into his comm.

Thank fuck. I couldn't bear to see my aunt Tab freak out. She'd already lost two sons—one to a car accident and one to the genetic-altering serum.

We kicked our legs into gear, running through the rain, and cautiously approached the gate that stood open as if Adam was inviting us in. He probably was.

Steven led the way and banked right under one of four decorative trees inside the fence.

The rain was coming down in sheets, pelting off the roofs of the cars in the parking lot before us, sounding as though we were in the front row of a concert hall.

A light spilled out from a corner window at the right end of the warehouse, and the glow from another bulb sprayed out from the building outside the front entrance as well.

"Whether they know we're here or not," Steven said, "stay low. Move quickly to that car there." He pointed at a white SUV.

Webb led the way.

I sniffed, listened, and scanned the area as I ran.

When we reached the SUV, the three of us huddled behind it.

"I smell dead bodies," I said low. Amazing that I could detect the slightest of odors even beneath the rain that I was sure was masking scents.

"That's the aroma of fabricated humans." Webb peered around the SUV.

"You mean like Rianne?" I asked.

"Yep," he said. "Their scent is a cross between wet dog and dead dog."

I guffawed at the disgust in his tone, although my nerves were making me want to laugh and scream at the same time. I was a vampire because of Rianne. My sister's final act had killed me, as Abbey had predicted the very day I'd driven onto the naval base with Rianne. Abbey had never seen how Rianne would take my life, but the little seer had been right. On top of that, I'd seen myself dead in a coffin with a mangled ear. Although the coffin part hadn't come true, Rianne had disfigured my ear.

Shivers of terror careened down my spine, turning into ice when a voice blared through a bullhorn.

"Steven Mason." Adam's voice pierced through the sounds of Mother Nature. "I hope you brought my brother."

Steven walked out into an open area, faced Webb and me, then looked up toward the roof.

I peeked in that direction. Adam was standing on top of the building, bullhorn in hand and a bald dude beside him. The same guy in Adam's video who had a machete to my uncle's throat—Draven Murphy.

"Where's Jack Aberdeen?" Steven asked, his arms at his sides and slightly behind him.

I knew what he was about to do. Right before Sam weaponized himself with one of the four elements, he always took on the same body posture and stance.

"Show me my brother first," Adam said.

"Can't do that," Steven tossed up at him. "And why are you up there? Come down here and face me like a man. No weapons. Just you and me. If you win, I'll hand over your brother."

Adam's laugh could probably be heard in the city from here. "No, you won't. Which is why you've left me no choice but to kill Jack Aberdeen."

My heart sank to the rough concrete. I popped up and joined Steven. "Hand him over, or I'll personally give you a taste of your own medicine."

Draven leaned in and said something to Adam, who in turn nodded.

Then Draven bent down and rose with a head dangling from his hand.

I was ready to puke. I couldn't quite see if Draven was holding my uncle's head or not.

Draven launched the dead man's head at us like he was throwing a football down the field.

The severed skull splashed into a puddle behind a car near us and rolled awkwardly toward us.

Steven muttered, "It's one of Joan's men."

Draven whistled, which was odd, but then Tripp's frantic voice rang in my comm. "We need help in the container yard. Monsters heading your way."

It took me a second to realize what was happening when twenty or more seeming clones of Rianne—men and women, short and tall, all with red eyes, long, thick canines, and talons— spilled in from around the right and left of the warehouse. Growls and howls rent the air as these creatures ran toward us.

"Try like hell not to get bitten!" Steven shouted. "Their saliva can be toxic. It won't kill us, but it sure as fuck will knock us out."

Dr. Vieira had an antidote for toxins. Unfortunately, not one for the specific poison he'd found in Rianne.

Steven began launching fireballs. Webb used his gun.

I dove into action, conjuring up what I'd learned from Agnes but hadn't practiced in the field.

I flicked my wrists at one female creature who reminded me of Rianne with her hairy face and red eyes. "Strecta!" I shouted.

But nothing happened. I tried again as the woman with claws sped toward me. I failed a second time. It must be my nerves overshadowing my belief. I had the desire and will. Maybe I wasn't visualizing.

Just as she reached me, I clutched the sides of her head and twisted, like Sam had done to Rianne. Thank fuck for vampire strength. She collapsed as a bolt of lightning cracked open the sky above. But I didn't have time to take a breath.

A male creature tackled me from the side and knocked me forcefully to the ground. The instant I fell on my shoulder, a loud crack echoed through my body as a bone snapped. Pain registered instantly. When I tried to catch my breath, he pounced, striking me across the face with his razor-sharp claws, leaving bloody lacerations in their wake. But before I could gasp for air or push him off me, he had an ironclad grip on my throat.

I couldn't move my left shoulder, but I reached for the dagger on my right leg, yanked it from the sheath, and drove it into his neck.

Blood spurted out and onto me, mixing with the rain pouring down.

He let out a guttural roar as he fell off me. Choking and gasping to fill my lungs with oxygen, I rolled over onto my left side despite the pain, then sliced the fucker's throat before I scrambled to my feet. I wiped blood and rain from my face as I scanned the area.

Burnt and dead creatures lay on the ground while Steven and Webb were fighting off what looked to be vampires now.

One man with stark black eyes trudged toward me.

"Come on, motherfucker," I said as I dug deep for that magic I was supposed to have.

*Belief, desire, will, and visualization.*

I could certainly see this asshole with a broken neck. I rolled my broken shoulder back. It clicked into place, and the pain disappeared. Got to love being a vampire.

*Okay, little witch inside me. Don't fail me again.*

Anger and determination had my arms loose, my wrists ready to do the damage I was born to do.

I met him head-on, igniting my magic to pinpoint sharpness. Baring my fangs, I flicked my wrists. "Strecta."

His neck snapped, and as he fell, I heard Adam's voice.

"We need to go," Adam said.

I looked up to the roof and caught sight of Adam leaving.

I ran past Steven, who was fighting off a vampire. "I'm going to find my uncle."

"Webb, go with Layla!" Steven shouted. "I got the rest of these assholes."

Webb tore off the head of a creature as I ran by him and to the front entrance.

I pulled on the handle, but the door was locked. No matter. I kicked the glass with all the vampire strength I had, and the door shattered. Once I was inside the lobby, that decaying and cloying dead-dog aroma made me wince.

Webb rushed up behind me, and I hurried through the lobby and into an enormous space filled with mostly empty cots and IV poles from one end to the other. Suddenly, a macabre thought slammed into me. What if Adam had injected my uncle Jack with the serum? I was about to run around the outer perimeter when Webb caught my arm.

"Not so fast," he said. "Listen first. What do you hear?"

I lowered my head, breathing through my panic, and sharpened my hearing. "Four heartbeats."

"Good," he said. "The way to tell a vampire from a human is by their heart rate. Given the odors in here, you won't always be able to distinguish one from the other. Our hearts beat much slower than a human's—anywhere from twenty and fewer beats per minute." He was looking around as he was talking to me.

I was stoked he was schooling me and also keeping me from acting before thinking.

"Listen, and tell me what species are in here," he said.

Inhaling, I zeroed in on the sounds. "There's a body on a bed, but the victim's pulse is over a hundred beats per minute." I suspected it was a creature. "There's one human and one vampire through that door in the distance directly ahead and one human in the last room on the right side."

"Excellent," he said, scanning the room while walking along the edges of the beds to our left with his gun at the ready. "First, we rule out the body on the bed. Adam might have used Jack as one of his subjects."

Bile crept into my throat at the thought as I followed his lead, my gaze roaming around the room, my magic teetering on the edge.

The female in the first bed had open blue eyes and no heart-beat. The young man next to her was still alive, and when Webb sidled up to the blond man, he sat up.

I jumped. Webb stabbed a dagger through the man's heart before I had a chance to blink.

Then we proceeded to the room in the corner to find Rudolph Parsons, as his name read on his lab coat, huddled in the corner by a supply cabinet, his dark eyes wide, his body trembling.

"Where's Adam?" Webb asked Rudolph.

"He took a syringe of the serum and left." The scientist's voice shook.

"Do you know where they're keeping a prisoner by the name of Jack Aberdeen?" I asked.

Rudolph hugged his knees to his chest. "All I know is he's in a freight container."

I rubbed my lips together. "You don't know which one?"

He shook his head furiously back and forth. "I don't."

It would be like finding a needle in a haystack. The aerial view I'd seen yesterday in our morning briefing showed too many containers to count. We needed to start looking. Tripp, Sam, and Dane had been assigned to do just that, but then the monsters had emerged.

"Stay put," Webb commanded Rudolph.

I left the lab first, making my way to the back door carved into the wall in the middle of the aisle between the rows of beds lining both sides of the room. We had to find my uncle. I was so consumed with worry that by the time I heard the grunt and looked up, the bald man jumped from the rafters.

He landed on his feet effortlessly, pointing a machete at me as he closed the distance between us. "I've heard so much about you, Layla." His shiny bald head glinted beneath the muted lights, as did the sharp blade of his weapon.

"You must be Draven," I said, glaring at him.

Out of my peripheral vision, I could see Webb stalking up, holding his gun out.

Slowly, I reached around to my back where I had two daggers tucked into sheaths in case my magic failed me. The blades wouldn't kill Draven, but they would stop him or at least slow him down.

"Draven Murphy," Webb said in a derisive tone. "Put down the machete."

With a steady arm, keeping the blade pointed at me, he replied, "Why would I do that?" Draven's voice was hoarse as if he'd smoked a pack of cigarettes. "The way I see this little tryst ending is with you dead while Layla comes with me. I could use a witch on my team."

That wasn't happening. The only one who would die among us three was Draven. I imagined him pressing his blade to his throat.

Suddenly, his arm began to shake as he turned the machete toward his neck. "What's happening?"

I lasered my focus on the asshole, picturing blood pouring out of Draven as he sliced through his own skin and bone.

He roared as he stumbled backward. His eyebrows were high on his forehead, his jagged fangs bloody. He gripped the blade with two hands and jammed it into himself, staggering, bleeding, and sweating.

He dropped the weapon and held his throat as I rushed over to him and confiscated the blade.

With his gun primed to fire at Draven, Webb sidled up to me.

Draven's hazel eyes were dilating as he gurgled and choked.

I gripped the bloody leather handle, prepared to finish what I started. Draven Murphy wasn't leaving here alive. That was for damn sure. But his wound was healing. Of course it was.

I inhaled deeply, stretched out my arms while tightening my grip on the handle, and swung hard and fast like a baseball player at home plate. The sharp-as-fuck blade sliced through Draven's neck effortlessly before his head fell to the red-stained floor followed by the rest of his body.

A celebratory silence stretched between Webb and me. Both of us had smiles on our faces.

I threw the machete at Draven's head. "Asshole. Now, we need to find my uncle."

Sam's and Dane's voices filtered from behind Webb and me as we started for the back exit once again.

"We checked every container in the yard," Sam said, jogging up to me.

Rudolph bravely came out of the lab. "The person you're looking for might be in a box on the train about a mile north of here."

"And Adam," Dane said. "Where is he?"

Rudolph shrugged.

"With all the creatures and vampires we'd been fighting, it is possible he slipped by us," Sam said. "Not only that, but it also wouldn't be hard. With all those containers around, Adam could've easily used them as his shields to make his escape."

"Any idea which container Jack would be in?" I asked Rudolph.

"As I said, I don't know."

I loved that Webb had taught me a couple of things about vampires and how to use that information in a battle, but I was in no mood to slink around my enemy. So I tore out of the building and through the container yard, running faster than I ever had in my previous life as a human. Rudolph had given Adam a syringe. He could be using it on himself, but Adam needed his wits about him if he wanted his prototype program to be a success.

Sam and Dane hurried beside me.

Facing the lake, I pointed to our left. "That's north."

The three of us took off in that direction as the rain continued pouring down with the wind whipping around and lightning illuminating our way.

I was soaked, chilled, and ready for a warm fire and a bottle of bourbon.

I wiped water from my face, blinking to orient my vision. When I had, I spotted a man limping and running along the water's edge.

"Is that Adam?" I asked. It was hard to see through the rain.

Regardless, at the mention of Adam's name, Dane lit a fire under his ass and sprinted.

When Sam and I finally reached Dane no more than a

minute later, he was in wolf form, growling and tackling a man to the ground.

"Get off me!" Adam yelled as he covered his face with his arms.

"Dane," I snapped. "Stop."

Dane swung his snout at me, baring his teeth as Adam rolled over and crawled into the water—or was trying to when Dane snagged his ankle. The alpha was itching to feast on our enemy, but he couldn't yet.

I stuck my hands on my hips. "Dane, you'll have him, but first, I need to know where my uncle is."

Dane dragged Adam from the water to a muddy area along the shore.

Adam rolled over, blood oozing out of his leg. He must've been shot or bitten.

The aroma of blood was weak within the scents of Mother Nature. Just the same, I was hungry to sink my fangs into him— more to tear out his carotid artery than taste his rancid blood that I could faintly smell.

Sam dug his booted foot into Adam's stomach. "You're not going anywhere."

I loomed over the asshole, lowering my fangs. "Where's Jack?"

Adam stuck out his bearded chin, trying to exude confidence he didn't have, and when his gaze landed on me, his eyes bulged out. "How are you a vampire?"

"Not from your fucking serum," I said through gritted teeth. "But it doesn't matter. Where is my uncle?" I paused on each word in that question.

"Why would I tell you?" Adam retorted. "You're going to kill me anyway."

He had a point. I glanced at the train just ahead, and as far as I could see under the cover of darkness and through the rain, the freight containers were stacked two high and went on forever. There certainly had to be more on that train than there had been in the yard. Jack would be dead by the time we found him.

Then a faint pounding noise filtered into my ears. "Sam, do you hear that?" I jogged toward the train, and the sound grew louder as I passed the first three stacks of boxes. "Uncle Jack!" I shouted.

*Bang. Bang. Bang.*

The banging grew louder and louder until I got to the fifteenth or twentieth stack of shipping containers. I slapped a hand on the bottom orange metal box. "Uncle Jack."

Whoever was inside answered me with another bang.

I frantically slipped between the green-and-orange boxes and opened the one I hoped my uncle was in.

When I saw my uncle, I flew inside. "Oh my God."

Jack had a swollen eye and cheeks, a cut on his forehead, blood on his neck, and tape over his mouth.

Relief settled my nerves, and I sighed heavily as I ripped the tape off his mouth. "Are you okay?"

He jerked as his jaw came unhinged. "You're a bloodsucker! How is that even possible?"

I helped him to his feet with ease, and the newness of my supernatural strength still wasn't registering. I imagined it would take a long time for me to get used to my preternatural powers. "It's a long scientific story that I will share with you on the plane ride home. But first we need to have you checked out by a doctor."

He touched the back of his head, then examined the blood on his hand. "I've been knocking my head against the wall." He stumbled toward the door. "Seriously, a vampire, Layla?"

I guided him outside, retracting my fangs as I ignored his comment. No one was more shocked than me that I was a blood-sucker. But I wasn't disgusted with myself like he was by me. If I could rewind the clock and change the outcome, I wouldn't. I believed that this was my destiny. I was fated to become a vampire witch.

Sam jogged toward us as I held on to Jack, and we met Sam halfway.

"Jack, good to see you're in one piece," Sam said.

My uncle grumbled. "I hope you killed that asshole, Adam."

Sam wiped battle grunge from his face. "Dane is feasting on him as we speak."

I could hear Dane growling and bones crunching.

By the time we reached the alpha wolf, Adam's head was dangling from his mouth.

I beamed at the wolf, whose white fur was covered in blood. "I'm happy you got your vengeance."

I was overly ecstatic that Adam wouldn't be a problem anymore. Nor would Draven Murphy. That vampire gave me the creeps.

Once we returned to the warehouse, the team was in cleanup mode, carrying bodies from outside and piling them inside where the beds were.

Steven rounded his attention on Dane. "I'm happy to see you got what you came for." Then he regarded Jack. "Come with me. I'll have one of my soldiers patch you up until you see a doctor."

"I'm fine." Jack brushed Steven off.

I rolled my eyes at my uncle. The grumpy Aberdeen wasn't even appreciative, but that didn't surprise me. I was glad I'd kept my promise to Tabitha, and Jack would return home in one piece.

Webb started to bark orders at Sam and me. "We need help. The faster we clean this mess up, the faster we can go home."

Home sounded like heaven.

"Layla, I understand that you have a spell that can set fire to a structure. Would you like to do the honors?" Steven asked.

Jack looked at me like he didn't know me. He didn't anymore. I was no longer Layla Aberdeen, vampire hunter. I was Layla Mason, vampire witch.

"I won't even ask," Jack said. "In fact, I think I might be dreaming."

A laugh barreled out of me, and boy did it feel wonderful. "I would love to light the match."

Once we had moved all the bodies into the warehouse, I stood just inside the doorway of the open bay with Sam by my side while the team waited for us in idling vehicles.

"Adam's head looks good on top of that mound," Sam said with a smile in his voice and a grin on his face.

As I stared at our dead enemies and the poor lifeless and innocent humans, I thought back to seeing my mom in the afterlife and the words she'd spoken.

*"You and Sam are instrumental in making sure humanity survives."*

*Confusion snaked through me. "You mean it's up to him and me to stop the genetic engineering?"*

*She tilted her head slightly, frowning. "Yes."*

I released a sigh as my muscles loosened, the adrenaline draining from me ounce by ounce, tears filling my eyes. "Can you believe we've made it to this point?"

"We've had a tough road, baby doll. But every hour, minute, and second since we met has been the best ride of my fucking life despite the challenges we've faced." His voice oozed with love and elation. "Eternity with you is the best happily ever after I could've asked for."

"You'll always be my happy ending, Sam Mason."

He crashed his mouth to mine in a quick, sloppy, tongue-tangoing kiss, then said, "Ready to burn this place down?"

I answered with a bow of my head, feeling the energy throbbing and vibrating through my limbs. "Fire purifies." I held out my arms. "Fire cleanses." A spark ignited on Adam's head. "It's by my hand that this warehouse doesn't stand," I chanted, envisioning fire everywhere. "This is my will. This is my way." Smoke billowed up from between a vampire and a monster at the bottom edge of the pile. "When I walk out, wash it away." As I lowered my arms, flames danced and spread.

Sam and I watched for several seconds, then he clutched my hand. "Let's go home, baby doll."

We walked through the lobby, our eyes locked in a fierce gaze brimming with an intense love that radiated between us. We'd overcome the impossible and emerged victorious, our hearts bursting with an uncontainable joy.

Our love for each other had defied all odds, transcended every obstacle, and was born from a fiery passion of human versus vampire, hunter against the hunted. But now, we were so much more. We were two souls, entwined in an unbreakable bond of love, forever bound by our four beautiful children and a future of an eternal life spent basking in pure and unadulterated bliss.

# 33

## SAM

Four months had passed since we'd finally ended Adam Emery's genetic-engineering reign. The public's outcry and demand for Adam's execution had ceased once word spread that Adam had perished in a fire at his new headquarters.

The shock and awe about vampires living among humans had died down, but tension still existed. We couldn't expect everyone to like us, and there would always be those who wanted to hunt us down. As far as humans turning into wolves, hardly anything had surfaced about a white wolf in Boston. We'd thought some rumor would propagate given that Dane's wolf had been spotted in Boston, but Cooper Gray and his team had hacked into most media outlets to delete any news or videos of Dane's wolf. Anything else related to videos of the white wolf were nothing but speculation that the animal had lost its way from the wild.

Regardless, with Layla as my dad's liaison, she was slowly making an impact on behalf of vampires by announcing key programs that could help those in need. Additionally, we'd also followed through on our promise to help the families impacted by

Adam's program by paying down mortgages and starting college funds, to name a few. Of course, that wouldn't erase the grief and suffering of losing a mother, father, husband, or child.

I sat at the kitchen island, surfing the net for beachfront properties as snow fluttered to the ground outside the wall of windows in our apartment and behind the seven-foot Christmas tree I'd cut down at a local tree farm.

"Jingle Bell Rock" played in the background as Layla danced with Ellie in her arms. Our little redhead with blue eyes was definitely a mini Layla.

"Papa, come dance with us," Layla said, in between singing to Ellie.

We were about to celebrate the holidays and every other milestone—our marriage, the birth of our children, rescuing Orion and Luna, and the battles we'd won. Not to mention, toasting to our future.

"I'm not a dancer, baby doll."

Watching my wife and daughter made my heart swell. I was happier than a pig in shit. I'd fallen into a routine of training new recruits for the Vampire Navy SEAL program, spending time with my family, and searching for property where Layla and I could build a life of our own. We loved Maine and the location where Jo and Webb had their beachfront property, but we wanted a warmer climate where it didn't snow in the wintertime. We hadn't found anything yet, but we weren't in a rush.

"You're a party pooper," Layla volleyed back. "Just this once. Come on. You're going to have to do things with the kids that you've never done before. So you might as well start now."

I rolled my eyes and padded over to where they were, near the Christmas tree. "Okay. I'm not a hip-swaying guy."

Layla handed me Ellie, then picked up Luna from the playpen. "Your turn."

That left Rorie in the playpen as she chewed on a squishy

teething toy. Our three little girls were outfitted in cute red-and-green dresses with bows in their hair. I melted every time I looked at them. My son was in the nursery with Agnes while she changed his diaper, but he had the same effect on me as his sisters did.

Raising four vampire witches was proving to be a challenge, and we wouldn't be able to do it without the help of Agnes and Jordyn. My sister-in-law insisted on doing as much to help as she could before she decided what her plans were for her future. Agnes, on the other hand, wasn't going anywhere. She was content to stay for as long as we would have her. In a way, we needed her. She was proving to be an invaluable asset as she taught Layla the basics of witchcraft. In turn, Layla could teach our children once they were old enough to understand.

Nevertheless, at close to six months old, they were developmentally ahead of human infants at the same age—crawling, making sounds, curious, and teething. We hadn't spotted any fangs on them yet, but according to Doc, their inhuman incisors might grow in after they lost their baby teeth.

I held Ellie and moved my feet, following Layla's lead as she danced around us. Ellie smiled, touching my face. I even tried singing the words, but I was horrible. Instead, I peppered kisses over my daughter's face, basking in the love swirling around us.

The song ended, and Layla pouted. "That was fun."

I chuckled as Layla placed Luna into the playpen, and I followed suit with Ellie.

Then I snagged my wife's arm and tugged her to me. "You're glowing."

My gorgeous huntress smoothed a hand down her tight-fitting black cocktail dress that hugged every curve on her body to perfection. "I'm happy, vampire."

"I want to show you something." I guided her to my laptop at the kitchen island.

She eyed the papers beside my computer. "Please tell me that's not another letter from Roman Brown. I really want to enjoy our party today without any bad news. It's been so nice these last several months. Adam is gone, no more genetic engineering, and our kids are safe. But Roman—"

I snaked an arm around her waist. "I don't want you to worry about him."

We weren't surprised that Roman was alive. However, it would be difficult for him to engage in any sort of genetic engineering. We'd destroyed all the data on Adam's cloud servers and hard drives. Plus, Rudolph Parsons, the scientist, wouldn't be an issue. We'd confiscated his notes but then offered him a job. He'd been working for Adam against his will, and he'd expressed his interest in helping us find a way to reverse the genetic-altering process or blocking it altogether in the event someone like Adam came on scene again.

She snorted. "My concern is more for Abbey. She's still having dreams about Roman, and that letter he sent you last month is just creepy as fuck."

He'd mailed the letter to me, but the note inside was addressed to my niece. "*Abbey, my dearest love. Roses are red, violets are blue, watch your back because I'm coming for you.*"

Webb had gone into a wild rage like I'd never seen before. I couldn't blame him. Jo had talked her husband down off a ledge —at least for now. Abbey, the young seer, had dreamt what her encounter with Roman would be when she was older. So we were operating as normal, with tight security, scouts on the hunt for Roman or any threats, and two bodyguards assigned to Abbey when she started at Sacred Flame Academy the following school year.

Webb and Jo knew they couldn't keep her locked up. Abbey needed room to grow, hang out with kids her age, and most importantly, she needed to learn how to control her witchcraft.

"Enough about Roman. I want to show you this property on the coast of Georgia." I handed her the sheets of paper with pictures of the house inside and out, the details of the sprawling four-thousand-square-foot home, and other information about the area.

She glanced over the document. "This looks beautiful. But the price, Sam."

I touched a finger to her lips. "Shh. I have a nice nest egg I've been saving up."

"Georgia sounds like a great spot," she said.

I traced a finger over the swell of Layla's tits and down her cleavage. "It's perfect, like you."

She blushed, goose bumps popping up on her chest and arms as she set the papers on the counter. "Then maybe we should take a trip down there to check out the home."

"I'll call the realtor next week," I said, pecking her on the lips.

She stroked her fingers through my close-trimmed beard. "I really like this look on you."

I chuckled. "You mean you like how my facial hair tickles your pussy."

She gave me a flirty yet seductive smile. "Okay."

Someone knocked on the door, shattering our sultry moment.

Two hours later, our party was in full swing. Guests chatted in small groups. Some doted on our children, others were gathered by the Christmas tree with drinks in hand, and I stood beside my wife as we listened to Zoey Thornton. Layla had been talking to her on and off for the last three months and learning about what it meant to be a Mystic. But Zoey had family in New England, so it only made sense for her to drop by.

"I have so much on my plate now, Zoey," Layla said.

The short witch with salt-and-pepper hair regarded Layla with her gray-blue eyes. "The Mystic is your destiny, Layla. You are the Monroe witch with quadruplets, and your yellow eyes also confirm the prophecy. Through my extensive research and delving into our archives, the last destined Mystic in the seventeenth century had yellow eyes as well."

I had a beer in one hand and placed the other on Layla's lower back. "If I'm hearing you correctly, Layla doesn't have a choice."

"We always have a choice," Zoey said, then addressed Layla. "But embracing your destiny will show our community that a Monroe witch shouldn't be feared. That alone will plant the seed of light and over time will extinguish the darkness we've been living in for so long." She sipped on her wine.

"The fact that I'm a vampire doesn't affect whether I become the Mystic?" Layla asked.

"Not at all," Zoey said. "Word has spread that witches can't be turned."

"Technically, they could," I said.

Zoey cocked an eyebrow. "You know what I mean. I can guarantee that witches will not be lining up to drink Orion's blood. The bottom line is this. This role is your destiny, Layla. You'll have the power of a coven, and with that power, you'll be able to heal the disharmony and bring together the witch community."

Layla smiled weakly. "Agnes has been saying the same thing. I have a meeting with Captain Greer of the Midnight Raiders after the holidays. She's introducing me to her Marine Special Forces group that has been preparing for the Mystic for years. Once I talk to them, I'll make my decision."

"They formed a second group within the Midnight Raiders for the Mystic for two reasons. One is to protect you. And the other is to make sure you don't abuse your powers," Zoey said. "If you want to chat after you meet with them, let me know."

My wife wouldn't even consider anything like dark magic,

which was the abuse of power that Zoey was referring to.

Layla acknowledged Zoey with a nod. "I will." Then she turned to me. "We should probably address the crowd before people start leaving."

The snow was falling quite steadily, and while most of us lived on base, some of our guests were heading out to spend the holidays with their families.

She and I went over to the stereo, and I cut the music. "Can I have everyone's attention?" I asked loudly.

Grinning, I swept my gaze over Jordyn holding Rorie, Agnes with Ellie, my dad with Orion, Dr. Vieira holding Luna in his arms, then Tripp, Webb, Jo, Abbey, Sawyer, his sister Harley, Alia Costner, Zoey, my SEAL team, Ben, Kraft, Olivia, Kodiak, and a few younger SEALs.

I raised my beer bottle. "Layla and I want to thank you for joining us, not only in celebrating the holidays but for your help and love in everything Layla and I have been through—our union, the birth of our children, fighting and winning the war on genetic engineering, and Layla's rebirth as a vampire witch."

Layla wrapped an arm around my waist. "Sam and I know that no matter what we face in the future, we are stronger, not only because of our bond with each other but also because of the family we have in you." She paused. "Steven, Jo, Webb, Tripp, and Dr. Vieira, I thank you for taking in Jordyn and me. For giving us a chance when you hated the Aberdeen family, and rightly so. Agnes, Jordyn, and I couldn't be happier that our paths have connected us with you. I wish we would've met years ago, but everything happens for a reason. You will always be welcome in our home."

"Let's raise our glasses in a toast to teamwork, friends, family, and a future filled with love and happiness," I said. "We love you."

Cheers erupted, glasses clinked, and tears spilled.

I finally felt at peace for the first time ever.

# EPILOGUE
## LAYLA

A million stars twinkled above, and the air tingled with magic as vampires and witches gathered on the sprawling manicured grounds of Alia Costner's estate.

The holidays had flown by, spring had come and gone, and life had moved on without incident. Sam and I were busier than we'd ever been, with hardly a moment to spare. When he and I weren't working, we were chasing around four littles. There was no question they were inhuman. They'd started walking at six months old, they were talking with a limited vocabulary with words like *Papa* and *Momma*, their fangs were growing in, and they healed just like vampires.

I stood under the portico of the mansion, looking out at the sea of people taking their seats. Magistras, witches who led their covens, had been invited to the ceremony to witness my induction into becoming their Mystic—a feat that hadn't happened since the seventeenth century.

I'd gotten letters from many witches around the world expressing their excitement and hope to end the wars and to stop living in the Dark Ages. I wanted the same thing, not just for them, but for humanity—and more importantly, my children. I wanted them to grow up in a better world, to have the opportunity to thrive, to be free to do as they pleased, to start their own families, to hang out with friends without looking over their shoulders, and the list went on.

Sam and I had talked for hours about the pros and cons of me becoming the Mystic. In the end, it didn't matter what obstacles I had to overcome. He and I agreed that this was a great opportunity to step up and embrace my destiny. To make an impact that we hoped would be beneficial for us, our children, and mankind.

I inhaled the scent of lavender, fresh-cut grass, and a myriad of other floral scents that wafted on the soft breeze as I listened to the conversations about the past, the future, and how witches were hopeful yet unsure of a witch having the power of a coven.

I'd learned from Zoey and Captain Greer of the Midnight Raiders that the team of military witches assigned to the Mystic would ensure I didn't abuse my power. Performing dark magic or bringing someone back from the dead wasn't something I would do. Still, I understood the trepidation that some witches had about the Mystic.

In the distance in a grassy area on the right, Zoey was at the podium, reading through her notecards. Sam and Agnes were seated near her with Ellie, Rorie, Luna, and Orion. The festivities were about to begin, and I was a nervous freaking wreck. I had been ever since I made my decision in January. After that, things seemed to have fallen into place.

Alia Costner had graciously offered to host the ceremony on her estate. She was still mourning the loss of her father and son. But she was also hopeful of her future and wanted to take part in helping in any way she could.

Zoey Thornton had been named by a collective group of Magistras to officiate the ceremony. Captain Greer and my personal tactical team of five witches of the Midnight Raiders, along with the Vampire Navy SEALs, were responsible for security around the estate. My father-in-law, Steven, had also assigned his vampire guardians to assist in securing the property. And with the help of Zoey's students, invitations had been sent out to key Magistras of each coven.

Her vanilla scent announced her before Jordyn called my name from behind me. "You look beautiful, sis," she said as she sashayed out of the mansion.

I was wearing a simple ankle-length white dress with a ballerina neckline and empire waist, a pair of comfy flats, and my hair was tied up in a messy bun.

"Thank you. I'm ready to puke," I said.

"Me, too, I think." She giggled. "These witches here kind of scare me more than vampires."

"Why?" I asked.

Jordyn twirled a leather bracelet she was wearing around her wrist. "They could snap their fingers and break my neck." She let out a nervous laugh.

I moved a stray brown strand of hair off my sister's face. "You could be a witch if you want."

"Nope. I'm leaving on my trip around the world next week. I'm going to find myself, relax, get laid if I can, and send you postcards from every location. I want nothing to do with magic or supernaturals for a while."

I entwined my fingers with hers. "I'm happy for you even though I'll miss you terribly. What about Sawyer? You've been pining for him."

Jordyn lifted a shoulder. "I need to fix me first before I jump into any relationship."

"That's probably a good idea."

Captain Greer, a tall woman in her midforties dressed all in black with her light-brown hair pulled tightly into a bun, marched up across the circular drive and stopped at the bottom of the stone steps. "It's time, Layla."

I gave her a nod. "I'll be right there."

"I better go help Agnes and Sam put my nieces and nephew into the magic circle." Jordyn pecked me on the cheek, then dashed off toward the crowd.

I sighed as I joined Captain Greer. "A vampire witch becomes the Mystic." My voice cracked.

"Never in our history has a witch become a vampire," Captain Greer said. "But I believe your dual status will serve you and us well."

Two witch guards snapped to attention when I approached the aisle that separated two sections of guests.

"You and the Midnight Raiders have a lot of faith in me. Why?" I asked Captain Greer as she escorted me to the front. I felt as though I was walking down the aisle to get married.

She nodded to people we passed. "Because, Layla, our seer has seen the good you'll do for us."

No pressure at all. I was tempted to ask what exactly her seer envisioned, but I didn't want to know. I did, however, want to throw up—until I laid eyes on my gorgeous husband, who was standing outside the magic circle to the left. His forest-green eyes glimmered amid the lighted torches flickering around the guests.

*You look absolutely stunning*, he said telepathically.

I flushed as I walked into the white magic circle etched into the grass. With my children in their strollers and strategically placed on their rightful symbols of air, earth, fire, and water stamped into the grass, I took my spot on the five-pointed star in the center before three witches closed us in. I didn't need a coven to perform the ritual since I was destined to be the Mystic.

Directly ahead of me, Zoey stood behind the podium, while Ellie was slightly up on my left and Luna on the right. Orion was behind me on the left side, and Rorie was across from Orion.

All four were sleeping. I didn't expect them to be awake at midnight, and they didn't need to be for this ceremony. They just had to be inside the circle with me and next to their respective symbols. The other requirement that Zoey had found in the witch's archives was that the ritual had to take place at midnight on the summer solstice.

Zoey adjusted the microphone, bowed her head to me, and began. "Tonight, we are gathered to witness something very special that hasn't happened since the seventeenth century. I am excited and honored to be standing here to officiate this ceremony and to help unlock Layla's true power as she leads all witches into a new age."

Whispers zipped around, the mood electric.

"Layla," Zoey said. "Are you ready?"

"I am." I dipped a shaky hand into the pocket of my dress and pulled out my note card with the Mystic's oath written on it.

Zoey grabbed the mic and stepped around the podium. "Then turn around and address the crowd." She swept her hand upward toward the sky. "Everyone, please stand."

I eyed Sam, who hadn't left his spot just outside the circle, as I pivoted on my heel and scanned the seats filled mostly with witches, who'd come from as far away as Australia to take part tonight.

Jordyn and Agnes were smiling at me from the front row where they were sitting along with Steven, Jo, Abbey, Webb, Tripp, and Dr. Vieira. I'd invited my uncle Jack and aunt Tab, but they declined. This wasn't their scene, and my uncle still hadn't come to terms with the reality that I was a vampire witch. Regardless, after my aunt had finally flown out to see her son Noah, she didn't want anything more to do with vampires. Sadly, Noah and Carly had both taken their last breaths in early November of last year.

I glanced at my note card, dug deep for confidence, rolled my shoulders back, then started. "I stand before you on this beautiful night as a Monroe witch, a vampire, a mother, a wife, and a person with a hopeful spirit who wants the same thing as you do—peace. We all strive for the absence of conflict and the presence of harmony, and despite our differences, we want the ability to coexist with one another no matter our species." I took a breath as I scanned the crowd. "As I accept the role as your Mystic, I cannot do it alone. It will require effort and commitment from all of us."

Agnes rose, holding a chalice of my children's blood mixed with mine, walked up, and handed it to me before returning to her seat.

With both hands on the silver cup, I raised it high. "Fire brings passion, a kindling flame." I dipped my fingers into the cup, then painted a small triangle on Rorie's forehead, careful not to break the element of fire stamped into the grass beside her stroller. "Air brings focus, a windfall change." I smeared blood in the shape of a triangle with a line through it on Ellie's forehead before glancing at her element beside her. "Earth brings grounding, a solid base." Orion was next as I drew an upside-down triangle with a line through it on him. "Water brings flow, a cleansing grace." I dipped my fingers into the chalice and painted an upside-down triangle on Luna's forehead.

My grandmother Agnes, a powerful witch in her own right, had once told Abbey in a vision that my kids were special but also feared because together they were the perfect storm.

Alia Costner, who'd taught Jo and Sam so many things, including how to craft spells using number theory, had argued otherwise. She'd explained that in some schools of thought, the number four was feared, but in others, the number four was also revered.

From years of studying the philosophy of Pythagoras, Alia believed that my children were the metaphysical symbol or the

Tetracyts, a triangular figure consisting of ten points arranged in four rows that was sometimes called the Mystic Tetrad. This symbol represented unity, power, harmony, and the Kosmos along with the four elements—air, fire, water, and earth as well as other mystical meanings, such as the four parts of the soul.

In Alia's opinion, my quadruplets were the metaphysical symbol binding me to the role of the Mystic. Their blood would give me the power I needed to bring unity and harmony, not bloodshed or wars.

Whatever was meant by the perfect storm, I believed Alia was right, and even Captain Greer's seer had seen a bright future for witches with me at the helm.

Once again, I held up the chalice. "Belief is the seed, desire the spark. Will is the fuel that illuminates the dark. With visualization as our guide, the cornerstones of magic join side by side." I brought the cup to my mouth and drank.

Instantly, a surge of electricity traveled through me as a strong breeze picked up, rustling the trees dotting the property. My body tingled, throbbed, and vibrated as the magic flooded my veins.

"Ladies and gentlemen," Zoey said. "As the four elements and the four cornerstones of magic join as one, we embrace a new beginning and new era."

The witches in the audience bowed, as did Jordyn, Agnes, and my vampire family.

Sam closed the distance between us, stepped in front of me, took my hand, and got down on one knee. "I am proud, humbled, and honored to call you the Mystic." He lowered his head.

Overcome with a multitude of emotions, I fought off tears. I wanted to project strength and show my fellow witches that I was their true Mystic. That I could snuff out the darkness that had plagued them for centuries. That I could lead them toward a brighter and more hopeful future. And while I would do my best to show them I could, my husband was making it hard for me to reel in my feelings.

Sam Mason, my handsome, sexy, powerful, arrogant, devoted husband and the father of my children was the brightest star in my world, and I couldn't do any of this without him.

As everyone began to chant my name, I suddenly felt emboldened as well as hopeful, not only for my family or witches or any supernaturals—but also for mankind.

The end.

———

Turn the page and read a short bonus scene of where Sam and Layla are two years later.

# BONUS SCENE

## LAYLA

The humid breeze off the ocean felt amazing as it blew through the open doors of our new beachfront house on Kiawah Island, South Carolina. Sam and I had been searching for the last two years for the perfect house on the ocean. The Georgia property we'd looked at didn't wow us like this one had. Still, after our big showdown with Adam Emery, so many good things had happened, and purchasing a nine-thousand-square-foot home was definitely something I'd never thought possible.

I waded in the shallow end of the pool, playing with Luna while Agnes relaxed on a lounge chair under the umbrella, reading. Sam was teaching Rorie how to swim while Orion looked on in his floatie, and Ellie was napping beside Agnes.

At the age of two, the quadruplets were well beyond human years. Their vocabulary multiplied seemingly by the day. They could each carry on a conversation like a three- or even four-year-old. They were growing faster than we expected.

"Orion," Sam said in a stern voice. "Stop splashing Rorie."

"It's my turn," Orion whined with a frown on his face.

Our son was turning out to be quite impatient and always

trying to garner Sam's attention. He didn't like when Daddy doted on his sisters.

"Momma, can I have some fruit?" Luna asked, her violet eyes dancing in the sunlight.

"Of course," I said. "It's lunchtime anyway."

She climbed the steps of the pool and walked over to Agnes. "Nana, can we make cookies after lunch?"

Agnes set her book on her lap and put her reading glasses on top of her head. "What kind would you like?"

My grandmother adored her great-grandchildren and loved taking care of them. With Jordyn in Europe, I'd planned to hire another nanny, but Agnes insisted she could take care of them when Sam and I were working. It also helped that we had four bodyguards around our children at all times. So if Agnes needed a hand, one of the guards jumped in.

Luna took Agnes's hand. "Cranberry."

I grabbed a towel off a chair near the pool just as Petty Officer Ryan Hawk came out from the house with a tense look on his face. Hawk had been assigned lead guard on the quadruplets' team.

"Sir," Hawk said, standing at the pool's edge and dressed in his casual attire. We'd asked the guards to dress down while at the beach house. While our neighbors were a mile away on each side of us, we didn't want to call attention to ourselves. "The reporter Tim Cox has arrived. Would you like me to show him to his room?"

Sam and I had developed a friendship with Tim over the past couple of years. We'd given him the exclusive that we'd promised, sharing a little more about Sam and me, something the public was dying for, especially since Sam and I were well-liked by the nation. Regardless, Tim was in town for our charity event later this week, and we'd invited him to stay with us.

Sam lowered his sunglasses, his green eyes sparkling. "Have

him get settled, and let him know we're having lunch in about thirty minutes."

"Sure thing, sir," Hawk said before he left.

Sam picked up Rorie and handed her to me. "Are we all set for Friday night?"

I toweled Rorie off. "I have some last-minute preparations to do with the caterers at the hotel, but we'll be ready." Our event was to raise money for a local college scholarship foundation.

I kissed Rorie on the cheek. "Why don't you go inside and find Nana?" She and Luna had already disappeared.

"Momma," Rorie said. "When is Auntie Jordyn coming home? She said she would bring me a gift from London."

I curled her wet red locks around her ear. "I'm not sure. We'll call her tonight."

My sister was having the time of her life, traveling around the world. Well, the first year she'd been gone, she'd spent most of her time in Spain and Portugal. Currently, she was in London, and she'd found a job working for a tour company. Now that her trips were paid for, I doubted we would see much of her, which made me sad since I didn't see her that much anymore. I was overly envious but extremely happy that she was doing something fun and building her life without fighting vampires or worrying about me.

Rorie pecked me on the cheek. "I can't wait to talk to her." Then she ran into the house.

"Slow down," Sam said with a raised voice at Rorie as he and Orion got out of the pool. Before either Sam or I could dry off Orion, he dashed behind Rorie.

"Maybe I can wipe you down." I waggled my eyebrows at my husband, whose tanned and muscled body was heating up my lady parts.

He placed his sunglasses on his head, sizing me up as his green eyes melted to silver. "I can think of something better you can do." He closed the distance between us. "Have I told you how hot you look in this turquoise bikini?"

"Not enough." I giggled.

"Dad," Orion called from behind me. "Grandpa is on the phone for you."

Sam pressed his forehead to mine. "Never a dull moment."

Understatement, especially when Ellie woke up and called out for me.

I wrapped a towel around my body and went over to my daughter. "Hey, what's wrong?"

Sam hesitated as he regarded our little redhead.

I waved him off. "Go talk to your dad. I got this."

Ellie had tears in her blue eyes. "I had a bad dream about Auntie Jordyn."

I stiffened as I sat next to Ellie on the chair. "About what?"

"Someone was chasing her," Ellie said. "I couldn't see who it was, but Auntie was frightened. I think we need to help her."

Sam and I believed Ellie would be a seer like her cousin Abbey. As of late, Ellie had been waking up with nightmares. She didn't remember details, but most of them involved a wolf.

"Did you see a wolf in your dream?" I asked, hugging her to my side.

"Not this time," she said.

"We'll talk to Auntie tonight. I'm sure she's okay." I infused confidence into my tone despite my stomach knotting. I hadn't had any visions or dreams that showed me the future, not since I'd dreamed that I was dead. That had been two years ago. "Come on. It's time for lunch."

Later that afternoon, Sam and I were in our spacious family room while the kids were down for their naps. Lunch had been very animated, with the kids chatting up a storm about swimming, seashells, and building sandcastles. All of them loved the beach. Orion especially liked the sand crabs, and he talked Tim's ear off about them as well.

Sam wrapped his arms around me from behind as we both looked out at the calm Atlantic. "I never thought I would see us in our own place with this view."

I leaned into him, rubbing his hands that were on my stomach. "Our life turned out better than I imagined."

We were a tight-knit family, the kids were thriving, and Sam and I were more in love than ever. Our busy lives kept us on our toes, but I wouldn't have it any other way.

"How's the school in New Hampshire coming?" Sam asked, dragging his lips over my ear.

"Mystic Academy will be ready for the fall semester next year." I had a dedicated witch council that was formed not long after I'd become the Mystic. The group was made up of lead Magistras who'd been voted in by their peers. One of the first orders of business was to build a school. Sacred Flame Academy was the only one that supported all witches far and wide and could only take in so many students.

Silence glued us together as we listened to the waves slide along the shore. I loved Jo and Webb's house in Maine, but I was more in love with ours on Kiawah Island. There were so many more amenities here—a private boardwalk from our house to the beach, enough bedrooms for guests and family when they visited, a pool, and Sam and I had our own private Jacuzzi outside our bedroom that we used frequently after the kids went to bed.

I heard Tim and Hawk talking before they entered. Even though I had been a vampire for a couple of years now, it still shocked me that my senses were so sharp.

Sam and I sighed before we found seats on one of two couches as Tim came in carrying a notebook and his cell.

Tim glanced past us. "Beautiful view. You and Sam have done great for yourselves with this property." He pocketed his phone in his tan shorts as he skirted the oversized chair, then sat in it.

"At lunch, you mentioned you had some news for us," Sam said to Tim.

Tim frowned. "I've heard from a reliable source that Adam's brother, Fred Emery, is being released from prison next month on good behavior."

Sam and I exchanged surprised looks.

"Does my father know this?" Sam asked. "If he does, he didn't mention it to me when I spoke to him right before lunch."

Tim shrugged. "Not sure. But we know Fred still has that thumb drive with data from genetic experiments on it, even though he denied having it during his trial."

In our agreement with the human government, we'd agreed to release Fred to them. They wanted him to stand trial just like any human, and the state's attorney for Massachusetts had pressed charges against him for his role in genetic engineering. He'd been found guilty of being an accessory after the fact and was given a three-year sentence. I'd been hoping he would spend life in prison. After all, he'd murdered my father, but we had no proof other than our word against his.

Then Ellie's dream sharpened to a pinpoint before me. I wondered if Fred was that someone who was chasing Jordyn. Fred Emery had a thing for my sister. He'd come on to her once, and he'd also tried to snag her when I'd been kidnapped by Roman Brown and his men at a local hospital in Fall River, Massachusetts, when I'd been pregnant with the quadruplets.

My stomach roiled with nerves that Fred would pursue Jordyn.

"We cannot let Fred pick up where Adam left off," Sam said through clenched teeth.

I certainly didn't want another war on our hands. However, the threat that some power-hungry asshole could start another genetic engineering program was real, particularly since humans knew about vampires. If they didn't want to study us, they would probably want to clone us.

"I'll keep my ear to the ground," Tim said. "I thought you should know."

The news put a damper on our day, but I wasn't about to dwell on it. There was nothing we could do yet, and we had time to devise a plan before Fred's release next month. Still, Jordyn wouldn't be thrilled to hear about Fred's release.

After a long day of sun, fun, and chatting with Tim about the charity event, Rorie was curled up beside me on the couch, while Sam and Tim were talking out by the firepit, and Agnes was putting Orion, Ellie, and Luna to bed.

I'd promised Rorie that she could talk to Auntie Jordyn, but my daughter was fading fast. It was nine p.m., an hour past her bedtime, but she had to ask Jordyn about her gift.

Jordyn's beautiful face was on the TV over the fireplace. My sister looked well-rested with her brown hair tied up in a messy bun. Her brown eyes danced with happiness, and she seemed to be glowing.

"I'm sorry this was the only time we could talk," Jordyn said. "I'm driving to Paris in a few minutes."

The five-hour difference between East Coast and London time did have my sister up before the crack of dawn.

"When are you coming home?" Rorie asked.

"Soon," Jordyn said. "And don't worry, I have many gifts for everyone."

Rorie clapped. "Tell me what you got me."

Jordyn giggled. "I want it to be a surprise, but I know you don't like them. So I found a magic wand that you'll like."

Rorie beamed up at me, then at Jordyn. "Is it a Harry Potter one?"

Jordyn nodded. "It is."

Rorie's mahogany eyes filled with joy. "I can't wait. I'm going to tell Daddy." She hopped off the couch and out the patio doors.

"Well, sis," I said. "You made her day. What's in Paris? Work or pleasure?" I'd decided before she called that I wouldn't mention Fred Emery's release. Sam and I had discussed finding out more details about Fred before we spilled the bad news to anyone. Plus, Fred wasn't being released for another month. So I would definitely alert Jordyn before then.

Jordyn looked off to the side and raised her finger. "I'll be right there."

"Who's with you? A guy?" My voice hitched.

"Maybe," she said, blushing. "I have to go. Just wanted to see your beautiful face and tell you I love you. Kiss everyone for me."

"Jordyn, wait. You're not going to share even a small detail about him?"

She shook her head. "Just know that he makes me happy. I'll fill you in when I return." She blew me a kiss. "Hugs and love." Then the screen went blank.

I sat there, frustrated and curious but smiling about the fact that Jordyn had found someone who made her glow and she could maybe settle down with.

Now I was like Rorie, excited and eager, but not about a gift though. I wasn't sure I could wait until Jordyn and I spoke again.

Sam's laughter tickled my sensitive vampire hearing. "A Harry Potter wand. That is awesome," Sam gushed to Rorie.

"Yep," she said. "I'm going to use it for my spells."

I giggled as I wound my way out to the patio.

Rorie had her tiny hand on Sam's face. "Daddy, I love you."

My heart swelled as happy tears stung my eyes.

Sam kissed Rorie on the forehead. "I love you, too, baby girl." He sounded choked up.

The joy that our children brought into our lives was beyond anything I could've ever  imagined. Our home was bathed in love, and I was flying high that I was immortal and could spend eternity with my powerful vampire husband, who had my heart and soul, and four beautiful vampire witches, who made me the happiest mother on earth.

# ABOUT THE AUTHOR

Bestselling author **S.B. Alexander** is an independent author with over 30 titles to date. She writes paranormal, new adult, and sweet romances that feature hot heroes stealing hearts.

S.B. or Susan as she likes to be called is a navy veteran, former high school teacher, and former corporate sales executive. She's a lover of sports, especially baseball, although nowadays you can find her on the golf course, swinging for that hole-in-one.

Her motto: "Life is too short to waste. So live every moment like it's your last."

**You can connect with S.B. Alexander in the following ways:**
Reader Group: http://sbalexander.com/sbareaderroom
Author Website: https://sbalexander.com
Newsletter: https://sbalexander.com/newsletter
Email: susan@sbalexander.com

facebook.com/sbalexander.authorpage

twitter.com/sbalex_author

instagram.com/sbalexanderauthor

amazon.com/author/sbalexander

bookbub.com/authors/s-b-alexander

tiktok.com/@susanbalexander

# GLOSSARY OF TERMS

**Natural-born vampire**: A human born with the vampire gene that, when activated, will turn them into a vampire.

**Activation process**: Those who carry the vampire gene can only turn by drinking the blood of their vampire father at the age of sixteen years or older.

**Council of Elders** – A group of five vampires who set the laws.

**Genetic engineering**: Turning humans into vampires through a process of restructuring their DNA.

**Cobalt** – A vampire's kryptonite. The metal will kill a vampire if staked through the heart. It will also burn a vampire's skin if they come in contact with it.

**Reproduction**: A natural-born vampire is born by a male vampire and a human female with a rare blood type of Vel negative.

**Council of Eternal Affairs**: The legal department of the vampire government.

**Vampire characteristics**: Sunlight doesn't burn them. Their hearts beat at <5 bpm. Skin temperature is ten degrees cooler than a human. Eye color changes to black except for a few chosen ones.

**Steven Mason**: Vampire and father to twins Jo and Sam Mason. He's dubbed the most powerful of all vampires because of his many powers, including his mind-reading abilities. He can only read minds when touching someone except when it comes to his children. His normal eye color is green. His vampire eye color is silver.

**Jo Mason**: Turned at sixteen. Powers include seeing the future through her dreams, mind-reading without touching a person, telekinesis, and she's an elemental with the ability to manipulate water, air, earth, and fire. Her normal eye color is silver. Her vampire eye color is violet.

**Sam Mason**: Turned at sixteen. Powers include feeling what others feel (Empath), telekinesis, and he can compel a person using a series of numbers woven into a magical spell. He's also an elemental with the ability to manipulate water, air, earth, and fire. His normal eye color is green. His vampire eye color is silver.

**Guardians**: Vampires who are equivalent to the human police.